A Predator's Threat
Kit McKenna

McKenna Publishing, LLC

Other Books By Kit McKenna

THE OKLAHOMA SKIES SERIES

All Sorrows Are Less

https://mybook.to/AllSorrowsKitMcKenna

Paint the Earth Red

https://mybook.to/PaintEarthKitMcKenna

The Heart That Returns

https://mybook.to/HeartReturnsKitMcKenna

Perfect As You Are

https://mybook.to/PerfectKitMcKenna

The Art of Passion

https://mybook.to/ArtPassionKitMcKenna

A Matter of Trust

https://mybook.to/MatterTrustKitMcKenna

Get a FREE copy of the Valentine Short Mr. Wrong door

https://dl.bookfunnel.com/myptwbvjh0

THE BELLADONNA SOCIETY SERIES

A Pointed End

https://mybook.to/PointedKitMcKenna

A Murderous Intent

https://mybook.to/MurderousKitMcKenna

A Secret Revealed

https://mybook.to/RevealedKitMcKenna

A Devil's Snare

https://mybook.to/SnareKitMcKenna

A Predator's Threat

https://mybook.to/ThreatKitMcKenna

THE MORRIGAN MAFIA SERIES

Crossed

https://mybook.to/CrossedMcKenna

Coup

https://mybook.to/CoupKitMcKenna

Crashed

https://mybook.to/CrashedKitMcKenna

Trigger Warning

This book contains an instance of assault
which may be triggering for some readers.

Prologue

Serena

Eight years ago

"The jury's ready," the bailiff says through the partially open door.

"Thank you, Randy," I reply.

Once he closes the door behind him, I take a deep breath, steeling my spine. Regardless of how the verdict goes, someone is going to be angry. That's usually the fact, but this case has the entire city on pins and needles.

In so many ways, it's a powder keg waiting for a match. High-profile cases always are.

As soon as I step through the door, Randy's voice calls out, "All rise."

I take my seat behind the bench and wait for everyone in the courtroom to be seated. Once everyone has resettled, I turn to the jury. "Madam forewoman, has the jury reached a verdict?"

She stands and answers, "Yes, your Honor, we have." Randy steps over and takes a piece of paper from her and hands it to me. I open it and read the verdict, then hand it back to Randy, who returns it to the forewoman.

This is going to be a clusterfuck, as my daddy used to say. The match is about to be struck and the city is going to explode. I fully expect there to be riots and I can't say that I blame them.

"How do you find?" I ask, taking my gavel in hand, ready to silence the uproar I know is coming.

She reads the verdict, her voice quavering slightly, "We the jury find the defendant not guilty on the charge of first-degree murder..." She goes on, reading off each charge, and the verdict is the same on all counts.

Not guilty.

And it pisses me off.

The courtroom erupts in a cacophony of voices, some shouting vitriol while others shout victory. I bang my gavel, trying to regain order, but there's so much chaos as people rise from their seats that the bailiffs have to step in when a fight almost breaks out. My eyes are fixed on the woman who crumples at the verdict as her husband attempts to keep her from falling to the floor.

Based on the presentation in the courtroom, I can't say I'm surprised at the ruling of the jury. The defendant is from a prominent local family that has wealth enough to hire the best of the best for representation. The prosecution was a green attorney still wet behind the ears because apparently that's all a poor young African American girl deserves from the district attorney's office.

I return to my chambers, disgusted with the outcome, but my hands are tied. In a fit of pique, I lift the paperweight from my desk and throw it against the wall. It just bounces off undamaged and settles on the plush carpet on the floor.

With a sigh of discontent, I go over to pick it up and place it back on my desk.

Two months later

My career choice was driven by a deep and abiding love of the law. After working my ass off in the trenches, I decided I wanted to become a judge, envisioning myself as the lovechild of Clarence Thomas and RGB. That goal was accomplished, and I became one of the youngest judges to sit on the bench in Georgia.

That was no minor fete for an apparent black woman in the south. I say apparent because I'm actually more white than I am black with my mama being white and my daddy being half black and half Choctaw. However, my medium brown skin and textured hair lead people to make an assumption about my ethnicity and they usually land on me being African American.

Lately, my love for the rule of law has waned as I see so many injustices carried out when criminals walk free and victim's families experience the heartbreak all over again. As an attorney, I worked hard and rarely saw defeat. As a judge, I feel like so much of the process is out of my control.

Today has been another challenging day that has me wondering if this bone-deep frustration is my new normal. It's Friday, so I think it's going to be a two-glass night. I'm thinking of a nice red to go with the microwave lasagna.

As soon as I step inside the foyer of my townhouse in southwest Buckhead, I know I am not alone. There's something in the air that makes the hair on my forearms stand up and an itch burn at the back of my neck. Rather than drop my umbrella in the stand by the front door, I keep it in hand as a potential weapon.

When I turn, I see only a silhouette, a dark smudge revealed by the ambient light provided from the glow of streetlamps through the living room window. I expected a much larger form, but the shape is diminutive. She steps forward and the light glints off the gun in her hand.

Headlights from a car passing on the street wash over her grief ravaged face. "Mrs. Jackson," I say. "What brings you here tonight?"

The gun is hanging heavy at her side, so she's not hellbent on doing me harm. Not yet, anyway. Her lips move, but the sound is so faint, I can't make out her words.

She rolls her shoulders and swallows. "They're all gone and I'm all alone," she says.

I frown. "Mrs. Jackson, can I call your husband to come get you?"

Her bark of laughter is full of grief and venom. "I told you," she says angrily, "they're all gone. You let that boy get off for killing my Jasmine." Just as quickly as the anger flashed, it's gone, replaced with pure grief. "My poor Hank couldn't handle losing our little girl. He had a heart attack last week and died. Now they're together and they've left me here all alone."

Oh, dear, God. I had no idea. There must be a way to help her calm down long enough for me to get that weapon from her before she hurts someone.

"Mrs. Jackson, I'm so sorry." I take a slow step closer to her. "Please, let me fix us some tea and we can talk about it."

Her hand goes to her forehead, rubbing as if she has a headache. I can imagine she probably does.

One more slow step closer.

Her head snaps up, and the gun rises. "Stop!"

I extend my hands, palms out in a conciliatory gesture, the umbrella dropped to the floor. "Please, let me help you..."

She barks out another strangled laugh. "You can't help me. No one can help me. I just miss them so much..."

Before I can think of a response, her hand swings up, puts the barrel of the handgun into her mouth, and she pulls the trigger.

Chapter 1

Serena

I'm not too proud to admit that when I took this job eight years ago and moved almost a thousand miles away from the life I'd so meticulously built, I was running away. You'd think I would have gone home to Louisiana, but there was still too much of my father's ghost lingering there, along with the two brothers who wanted nothing to do with me.

Instead, when I heard an older, close to retirement colleague talking about a teaching position he'd applied for at a university in Oklahoma, I did everything in my power to get the job. If that makes me a bitch, I'll gladly shoulder that burden.

He was looking for a cushy, low demand job in which to wile away his golden years. Me, I needed this job.

Needed it.

My entire world tilted on its axis after Mrs. Jackson splattered her brain matter all over my front hallway. Although I've never experienced that kind of heartache, I have known that feeling of emptiness. At the moment she pulled the trigger, I felt the black hole where my heart had been.

So much so that I was afraid I might follow her path if something didn't change. And change it did. At first, I just needed a place to land, but through teaching, I've found my love for the law again. I've also reconnected with my half-brother, the only person in my family besides my mama I ever felt truly close to.

I love seeing students' faces light up when they suddenly gain an understanding of a concept. It's very rewarding when I read a student's paper and discover they've gone deeper than the surface, diving into doing the research to support their claims.

"That's all for today," I say, and on cue, the students begin to rise from their seats and file out of the room. "Miss Flores, I'd like to see you for a moment."

The young woman pauses like a doe that's suddenly had a spotlight shone on her. Magdalena's entire body sighs, but she gathers her things and comes down the steps to my desk. When she stops in front of me, her eyes are on the floor.

This is the second course she's taken with me and during the last course and the first half of this one, I found her to be an exemplary student. She's bright and able to grasp complex legal content easily. I also enjoy the way she's able to look at a problem to find multiple solutions.

However, since the mid-term exams, she often shows up late and has missed several classes. Her work is shoddy and thrown together of late and if she can't remedy it, she's in danger of having to repeat this course. The semester is almost over, so an excellent score on her final exams may be the only thing that carries her through.

Now that I see her up close, it's worse than I thought. The evidence that something is going on in her life is written all over her. Her normally well-kept appearance is disheveled, her hair looking as if it hasn't been washed recently and her clothing is rumpled and stained.

"Miss Flores, I'm a little concerned about you. Until a few weeks ago, you were an excellent student, but now your focus seems to be elsewhere."

She shuffles her feet. "Yeah, I just have some personal stuff going on."

"I understand that sometimes life presents us with obstacles that make it difficult to do the things we'd like. If there is anything I can help with, even if it's just an ear to listen, I hope you know I'm here."

"Thank you, but I'm not quite sure what I'm dealing with yet. Anyway, I'd better get to my next class."

"Go on, but remember what I said."

"I will," she calls out over her shoulder as she darts up the steps to the door.

I watch her as she goes, even more concerned than I was when class started. She's an adult and I've offered to help, so there's not much more I can do right now. Hopefully, she'll be willing to accept my offer before things get any worse for her.

Putting it out of my mind, I gather my things and clear out of the room to make way for the next class. In my office, the visage of Magdalena Flores comes to mind again, and I can't dispel it. What on earth could have her making such a startling about face?

Based upon her appearance, perhaps there is some instability in her access to shelter. I wonder if she lives in an apartment or with her family. That's something I can check into.

My mind is so distracted that I'm not going to be able to give appropriate attention to the papers I need to review. There has to be some way I can find out more information about her situation without broadcasting that there's a problem. It might be a temporary situation and I could be ringing a bell that can't be unrung. That could make things worse for her.

When I look her up in the system, it's as I expected; there is only the barest of information. My first call is to the registrar's office, but they can't give me anything beyond what I already have without a good reason. With a thank you, I disconnect the call.

I thought that perhaps I could get her address and... What? Do a drive by like some crazy stalker?

No, I'll just have to trust that my offer of help sank in and that she'll take me up on it if she truly does need aid. Even then, my ability to help will be predicated on whatever the problem is. It could be that all I can do is lend an ear and pray it's enough.

Professors getting involved in a student's personal life could be a whole can of worms that shouldn't have been opened. There have been teachers that have lost their jobs because they got over involved. However, I can't just sit around and watch a brilliant student go down in flames.

It might get me fired, but I'm not willing to sit passively on the sidelines if there's something I can do.

Chapter 2

Vance

The man across the desk from me is huge. A far sight bigger than me, and that's saying something because I'm no shrinking violet. When he stood and shook my hand, he was at least three inches taller and I stand at six-two.

"Jack Carver," he'd said as he gripped my hand.

He's one of the brothers that owns the company. I did my research, so I know there are two of them, but they're smart and kept their photos off the website. When dealing in all facets of security, it doesn't do to be overly recognizable.

However, this dude would be impossible not to recognize after meeting him once. He's all kinds of distinctive.

"Vance Douglas," I reply and take my seat.

He holds up a piece of paper and sets it aside. It looks an awful lot like my resume. "You've had an impressive career," he says, and plants the tip of one blunt finger on the page. "Tell me what's not on there."

I shrug. "Not much, really. I'm a pretty simple guy. Married my high school sweetheart and went from high school into the army because it would provide a stable income and get me the GI bill for college after service. Figured I'd do the two years active, then do two in the reserves while I went to school. I liked it better than I thought I would and after two years applied to Ranger School. Spent six years as a Ranger and left with an honorable discharge. Got a job as a beat cop and went to school. Got a degree and a detective shield soon after."

"Why leave Atlanta for Oklahoma City?"

He's direct. I appreciate that in a person. I've never been one to beat around the bush and don't like it when others do.

"My ex-wife and I divorced several years ago, my kids are in college, and I was ready for a change from Atlanta. My mother moved up here to Del City a few years ago to live with her sister. Neither one of them is getting any younger, and they need someone to look out for them."

"Why security?"

"Seems like it would be a bit more forgiving than the constant demand policing can be. I'd also like to get my PI license to add a layer that puts my detective skills to work."

We talk a while longer, mostly casual, with a little interrogation mixed in. He quizzes me about security systems and approaches to protection. When he rises from the chair, it squeaks under his bulk.

I get the feeling he's the muscle of the business. Based on the way he moves, as he shows me around the facility, I'd say he probably spent some time in special forces himself.

We pause by a mat with a ring on it where two men are sparring as another man watches on. The watcher has the same coloring as my tour guide, but looks to be slightly older and slightly smaller. Probably the other brother. Yeah, my powers of observation are impeccable.

The brother stops the two sparring and gives tips to each man, then tells them to go again. They punch and dodge and eventually end up on the ground grappling. When he calls for the opponents to stop again, he comes over to where I stand with Jack.

With an extended hand, he says, "Hi, I'm Jerald Carver."

Yep, the brother.

I introduce myself.

"Ah," he says, "the Ranger. Jack here was a SEAL for several years. We could use some more of his level of training. We train everyone in hand-to-hand, but as I'm sure you know, some people pick it up faster than others. It's almost easier to train someone on the technical stuff than to train a technician in self-defense. Some excel in one or the other, but we're trying to build up our team members who can do both."

"Makes sense," I answer.

Jack lifts his chin toward the mats. "Want to give it a go?"

With a shrug, I say, "I can. I was planning on a trip to the gym after I was through here. My bag's in the car so I can change and let you test me to see if I really am who I say I am."

"That's not..." Jerald begins.

"Excellent," Jack interjects.

He shows me where the locker room is, and after a quick dash out to my car, I get changed. This place is pretty nice. They have an excellent set of quality weights and equipment for just about any kind of workout you'd want.

The locker room is well kept, clean and free of stink, which can be a challenge with a bunch of men involved. It's also set up to be able to keep things here for potential overnight shifts.

At a place like this, I would be able to keep my soldiering skills honed while keeping up my detective's eye once I get my PI license. I step onto the mats in shorts and a tee, choosing to leave my feet bare. When I meet Jack there, he's dressed much the same.

"You want gear?" he asks, and I discern he means protective gear.

I shake my head. "Nah. If we're both who we say we are, we should have enough control of our moves that we shouldn't need it."

That gets me a grin. "Excellent."

With that, he claps, officially beginning our match. We circle each other and begin the dance of warriors. It truly is a dance, and it's a thing of beauty.

Jack Carver and I are evenly matched. He's a little stronger, but I'm a little faster. It's been ages since I sparred with someone who could push me to be better. The last time was with my Ranger brothers.

Maybe this is a place where I can find a new brotherhood to be part of. When Jerald finally calls the match, Jack and I are both breathing heavily. Seems I was able to challenge him, too.

As we suck down water from the cooler on one side of the room, Jack holds out his hand to me. "Thanks. It's been a long time since I've had someone who was able to push me."

I shake his hand. "Same."

"I like him," he says, looking over my shoulder.

"I can tell," his brother answers, stepping into our space. "Why don't you come with me? We'll talk about all the stuff that Jack probably failed to mention."

By the time I walk out of Jerald's office, I'm hoping they offer me the job. It seems like a solid company and I like both of the brothers. I had it right when I thought Jack was the muscle and Jerald was the management. Between the two of them, they seem to be a well-balanced set of leaders.

It seems like the kind of place I think I'd like to settle in at.

Chapter 3

Serena

My concern for Maggie Flores grows when, two days later, she doesn't show up for class. I called her phone, one of the few tidbits of information I have access to, after I finished teaching and left a message. It was a low-key, just checking on you, message, but my concern is anything but casual.

Perhaps I'm overreacting, but something about it won't let me go. If I don't hear from her soon, I'll find some other way to track down her information. She might not appreciate me showing up on her doorstep, but at least I'll have more information to gauge her level of safety.

"Hello ladies," I say as I take a seat for dinner at the Belladonna Society. "What's new and exciting?"

After I first joined, I wasn't sure I'd made a good decision, but last year, I started showing up more often. I've been pleasantly surprised by the budding friendships.

At almost forty, three of the women in our orientation cohort, or quint, as we call ourselves, were several years younger than I and one, Caitlyn Foster, was a few years older. However, this diverse group of women has grown on me.

Gabriella Masters, Demeter Lawson, and Alicia Pham are all mature for their ages, having been seasoned by the difficulties life has thrown at them. When I first met Gabriella, she was single, but married Morgan Masters this past Christmas in a small, but beautifully intimate ceremony. Demi, as Demeter prefers to be called, is now engaged to Morgan's youngest brother, Kellen.

Alicia is in an orthopedic surgical residency program and is not present for dinner this evening. Just a little over a month ago, life threw her another curveball when her young cousin, of whom she was guardian, was tragically killed.

"Serena!" Cait says, "So glad you could make it. Ford has finally agreed to take some time off so we can go on vacation. That's about as exciting as it gets for me."

That gets a laugh from the group. She's been trying to talk her partner into taking a vacation for months, but as an OKCPD Homicide Detective, he hasn't been able to pull himself away from work long enough for them to go anywhere.

"As for me, it's all wedding planning, all the time," Demi says. "Who would have thought that eight months wasn't enough time to plan a small wedding?"

"The bulk of my excitement is changing diapers and nursing. At least I'll get to go to a wedding where I'm not pregnant," Gabriella teases.

"Well, I think you set the precedence for Masters Brothers' weddings," Demi says cryptically.

Then it sinks in and I grin. "You're pregnant?"

Demi's cheeks turn pink as she nods. "Yes. Just barely, but we got confirmation from the blood work on Monday. Henry is ecstatic about being a big brother."

Congratulations echo around the table.

"What about you, Serena?" Cait asks. "What's new and exciting in your life?"

"The semester is almost over and summer break is just around the corner," I reply with a chuckle.

Gabriella queries, "How's Diondre?"

That brings a smile to my face. Diondre Wallace is a man I've been dating for several months and so far, it's looking very promising. "He is well. We're spending so much time at each other's homes that I'm thinking we'll be transitioning to co-habitating soon."

In reality, he spends a lot of time at my home, but I only rarely spent time at his in the beginning and I haven't been there at all for a while. He says it's because my place is more comfortable, but sometimes I wonder.

"I'm a big fan of living together," Demi says. She and her fiancé, Kellen, have been living together for almost six months.

"I've mentioned it as a possibility, but part of me wonders if maybe we're too independent. There are times when I love being at home alone and don't have to answer to anyone about anything."

"It is a compromise," Gabriella adds.

"Because of what was going on with Benjamin, Ford and I were practically living together from day one because he wanted to keep me safe," Cait says.

Benjamin was Cait's husband. She was trying to find a way to divorce him when he attacked her and she killed him in self-defense.

Cait's presence reminds me that, through the police department, Ford might have access to a lot more information than I do. As we eat our meal, I weigh the choice to ask her if Ford might be willing to look up Maggie's information for me.

We're finished eating and winding down when Gabriella and Demi take their leave. Cait is gathering her things, and I decide to test the waters.

"Cait, I have a question." I tell her about the situation with Maggie. "Through the school, all I have access to is her phone number. She missed class today, so I left a message. I'm not overly alarmed yet, but something about her demeanor is making me anxious on her behalf."

"Perhaps you have some sort of intuition going on," Cait says.

"Perhaps," I agree. "I was wondering if it might be possible for Ford to look up her information and maybe get an address. Like I said, I'm concerned, not alarmed yet, but if I don't hear from her soon, maybe he could have someone do a drive by or wellness check or something. Or, if he feels comfortable, he could give me the information and I can go knock on her door."

She nods. "That might be a possibility. Let me know if you don't hear from her by the weekend and I'll talk to Ford about it. I'm with you. If she's changed that much in such a short time, something is going on."

"Thank you," I tell her, putting a hand on her arm.

"Certainly," she says.

We walk out together and say our goodbyes on the sidewalk. Knowing I might have a potential ally in Ford who might be able to help, I feel much better. Although I doubt I will, as I make my way home, I wonder if I'll have a handsome man there waiting for me.

On the nights that I go to the Society, we usually sleep apart because I get home late after having dinner with my friends. A sister can hope, though.

Chapter 4

Serena

B y the end of classes on Friday, I still haven't heard from Magdalena Flores, so I call and leave another message. Cait suggested giving it a couple of days. Although I'm her professor, I'm not someone she'd have contact with on a daily basis, so I don't know if she's really in trouble.

I'm rescued from stewing in my concerns when my phone dings with a text that brings a smile to my face.

Diondre: *Missed u this week. All done for the day?*

Me: *Missed you, too. Just leaving. Will I see you tonight?*

Diondre: *Yeah but might be late.*

Me: *Work keeping you busy?*

Diondre: *Client dinner.*

Me: *Okay.*

The smile is gone now. We've been seeing each other for almost nine months and when we first met, we were together all the time and couldn't get enough. He swept me off my feet in the best way.

However, over time, all that heat has tapered off. More and more, it's seeming like we only see each other when it's convenient for him. When I'd said at dinner last night that I'd talked to him about moving in, that did happen, but it was months ago.

I guess with all of them finding the kind of love in their lives that it seems few do, I did a little propping up of my own love life. The truth is that even though I'm in a relationship, I spend a lot of time feeling lonely and that isn't right.

Instead of going home to my empty house, it's early, so I drive right past the turnoff to my house and continue on to the City to go to the Society to work out and have dinner. At least at the Society, if you're sitting at a table alone, unless you're reading a book or doing something that signals you don't want company, you won't be alone long.

I'm joined by three other women as I eat dinner. The conversation is light, friendly getting to know you stuff, but it's exactly what I needed tonight. When I finally do head home, I'm in a much better frame of mind.

I've been home long enough to shower, change, and pour a glass of wine when Diondre comes through the unlocked door. He's moving strangely, and when he draws near, I understand why as the aroma of whiskey and cigars envelops me, so strong I have to stifle a cough.

"You smell like you've been having fun," I say as he turns me and pulls me into his arms.

"'Bout to have a lot more fun," he mumbles as he nuzzles my neck.

Part of me wants to push him away and tell him to leave, but a bigger part of me craves being touched by someone. His kisses are sloppy and uncoordinated and I wonder if he got a rideshare here. Hopefully, he wasn't driving.

Quit being the law. You've got your man here, so focus on him.

Reaching a hand between us, I stroke him through his pants but he's very slow to rise. He must have really had a lot to drink. There have been a few times when he's indulged to excess like this, so it's not surprising, but it is concerning because the last time was just a couple of weeks ago.

His dick doesn't even reach half-mast and the way he's slobbering all over my mouth and mauling my breasts isn't doing anything for me. My first instinct to push him away was the right one. With a sigh, I back away from him.

"Whaswrong?" he asks, swaying on his feet.

"Honey, I think maybe you've had a little too much to drink tonight," I say, trying to be as delicate as I can.

"Naw," he replies, putting a hand on the counter to steady himself. "I'm fine. Come on, baby..."

He reaches for me again.

"Maybe if we wait a little while, you'll be able to..." I wave a hand toward the region of his flaccid penis.

He scowls and steps back. "What the fuck are you talking about?" Unzipping his pants, he takes the organ in question into his hand and strokes it. "I am so DTF...down...to...fuck."

His mouth is telling me all about his sexual prowess, but he doesn't have any better luck at getting his dick hard than I did. Angry now, he stuffs his limp dick back into his pants and zips them up. "Knew I shoulda just went home."

Turning on his heel, he heads for the door. "Diondre!" I call after him. "You're drunk, you shouldn't be driving!"

I go after him and try to take his keys, but he's bigger and stronger and easily pushes me away. An "oof!" blasts out of me when my back slams into the wall and I'm struggling to catch my breath. By the time I straighten up, he's in his car.

For a moment, I think I should call the police before he has a chance to kill someone, but he doesn't back out. I wait for a couple of minutes, then go out to look at him through the window. He's passed out.

He wasn't even sober enough to get the car started. I open the car door and go through his pockets until I find his key fob. He's too big for me to wrangle into the house, so he's just going to have to sleep in his car.

Rather than taking them into the house with me, I put the fob onto a small table by my front door, where I often put seasonal decorations. If he's sober enough to find them there, he should be sober enough to drive, and it saves being awakened in the wee hours of the morning by him pounding on the door.

I'm kind of glad I never gave him a key. So much for wanting to move in together. After tonight, I'm not even sure I want to see him again.

I go into the house, turning off lights on my way to my bedroom, only pausing for a moment in the kitchen to pour my glass of wine down the drain.

Wow…tonight did not go the way I thought it would.

Chapter 5

Serena

When I wake up the next morning, Diondre is gone. A glance at my phone tells me he hasn't messaged or phoned, but someone else has. Maggie Flores has sent me a text.

Professor, sorry I've been out of touch. There are some family issues I'm dealing with right now. Thank you for your concern, but I'm all right. I should be back in class next week.

Thank goodness. Although I'm still concerned because it would appear the family issues she's dealing with are affecting her on a level that is creating problems with school, she's an adult. Sometimes you have to put family before all else.

The sun is barely climbing over the horizon, so I decide to go out and work in my flowerbeds before it gets too hot. Hours later, I'm sweaty and tired but pleased with how beautiful my beds look.

There's still no word from Diondre. There's a temptation to be pissy about him showing up so drunk last night, but because I'm an adult and a little worried about him, I break down and send a text.

Me: *Just want to make sure you made it home safe.*

The afternoon is spent grading papers and my evening takes me to one of those wine and paint classes with two of my fellow professors from the university. When someone posted the flyer, I thought it would be fun. However, when I saw there were only three of us signed up, I started to back out.

I'm great mingling in large groups where there are plenty of other people and you can just float through without having to get too deep with any one person. In small groups, there are greater expectations of how much you share, and that's where I falter.

Opening up to others is not something that comes easily for me. It's also something that makes it difficult for me to make new friends, which is why it's taken me so long to warm up to the women in my quint at the Society.

Growing up, my father was a big believer that children were to be seen and not heard, especially me, his only daughter. My mother was a debutant in the south from old money and traditional values. She was taught to be smiling and submissive to her husband and taught me the same.

Further reinforcing my ingrained and natural reticence was my career of choice. Talking about work was usually boring for other people and, as a judge, became something that couldn't be allowed. The only parts of my job I could talk about then were the ones that were already well known to the public and plastered all over the news.

"I think yours turned out great," I tell Willa Leggett honestly. "But mine is going to be tossed in the bin as soon as I get home."

"No! It's not that bad!"

I chuckle at her response.

"It's okay. I know it's not great. Creative pursuits have never been my forte, but I'm glad I came because this has been fun."

Frances Gunn says, "Me, too. I didn't know what to expect, but we should do this again sometime."

"Agreed," I say, raising my glass to them. "Here's to good wine and bad painting." They clink their glasses with mine and we all laugh.

It's late when I get home so I set my alarm for a later than usual time. Normally on Sundays, I go to the early church service because I'm usually awake early in the day, but I think I'll be inclined to sleep in a little in the morning.

My thinking was correct because I'm wakened by the blaring of my phone, which is a rarity. I can't remember the last time I didn't wake up to turn the alarm off before it sounded. Once I turn it off, I get out of bed to start my day.

The music is excellent this morning. I've only been coming to this church for a few weeks. My previous location changed pastors, and I didn't care for the new preacher's hellfire and brimstone approach. The God I believe in is one of love, not of the kind of hate the new man was spewing.

As the praise and worship music fades to the background, one pastor takes the stage. "Good morning, brothers and sisters. We have a very special ceremony happening today. This is something we do twice a year as new blessings are added to the members of our congregation. If you have a recent addition to your family or are new and have children who have never been blessed, please come up to the platform with your little one and family. We'll say a prayer over and bless each one."

A dozen or so families make their way up to the front with small children and babies bundled in blankets. I freeze in my seat when I see someone I know.

Once everyone is gathered, the pastor makes his way down the line. He introduces each family and their baby or child and prays a blessing over each one. It's mostly the same brief prayer over and over, but he adds tidbits for those he must know personally.

Then his hand falls onto the shoulder of the man I know. "This man, I've known for over twenty years. We went to high school together and man, did we get up to some mischief, but don't worry Brother Diondre, I won't tell any of your secrets if you won't tell any of mine."

The entire congregation is laughing, and it's then that Diondre looks over the crowd and his eyes meet mine. He stops laughing. The pastor introduces Diondre's wife, Ernestine, and their daughter Jamila, who has blessed them with a four-month-old grandson.

Thoughts crowd my brain and I don't hear anything else as I sit there frozen in my seat. When Diondre and I first met, he told me he was separated and his divorce was close to being finalized.

He would mention it from time to time in those first few weeks we were together, making it seem as if they were still working out the details. But it would appear that they'd reconciled and that asshole never bothered to tell me.

How could he do that? No wonder he's deflected any time I've asked about his kids or talked about moving in together. I thought we were looking toward a future together, but apparently I was just some woman he was fucking and don't really mean anything at all to him.

Round and round my mind spins, the thoughts growing darker and darker. I hate liars. Hate being lied to. Hate being made a fool of.

Although I'm not sure who is the bigger fool, me or his wife. Regardless, my days of being fooled by him are over. I can't say that his wife's are. Who knows if I'm even the only woman he was messing with?

The service ends and I try to make an escape out the door, but the people at both ends of my row are caught up in conversations. Because I'm in a church, I draw on my patience, but that doesn't last long. I've got to get out of here.

Standing, I move to the end of the row, choosing the side without the elderly woman, who looks like she's melded with the pew. "Excuse me," I say to the large man standing in the row.

He looks around, surprised. After some shuffling around, they make enough room for me to pass through their group to freedom on the other side. At the exit, the pastor who went to high school with Diondre is standing, talking with people as they leave. He has spoken to me a few times, but I prefer not to speak to him today, especially since this is the last time he'll be seeing me.

I step to the side of a small family exiting at the same time, putting them between me and the pastor. Just when I think I'm going to make it through the door without being stopped again, "Sister Serena!"

Closing my eyes for a breath before I turn, I steel my spine and plaster a smile on my face. It freezes there as I see Diondre standing just beyond with his wife, daughter, and grandson.

"Pastor Fulton, so good to see you again."

"I was concerned when I didn't see you at the first service, but I'm glad you made it to this one."

He holds out his hand and I put mine in it just as he covers the back with his other hand. My father used to do this kind of double-handed shake and I hate it, but that's my issue, not the pastor's.

"Yes, I had a little bit of a late night yesterday and decided to sleep in this morning."

"Well, I'm glad you made it." He turns, still holding my hand with both of his. "Have you met the Wallaces?"

"I'm sorry, pastor, I really have to go," I say, pulling my hand from his.

The look of puzzlement on Diondre's wife and daughter's faces is clear. I know I'm being rude and my mother would be scolding me if she could, but I simply cannot grin and glad-hand Diondre and his family like I haven't been taking the man to my bed for months.

Internally, I berate myself for being the foolish, hopeful girl I used to be. The woman I am today should know better.

Chapter 6

Serena

Sitting bolt upright in bed, I try to figure out what startled me. As I hold my breath, my ears strain for the slightest noise, but I don't hear anything out of the ordinary. Then I do.

Someone is knocking on the front door. My first thought is that it must be Diondre coming to say his piece about this morning at church, but he'd be pounding the door down or standing on the doorbell, not knocking quietly.

I take my robe from the end of the bed and pull it on as I make my way to the front door. Apprehension ripples through me as memories of another darkened entry with an unexpected visitor swim to the surface. The person on the other side of the peephole is definitely not who I expected it to be, and definitely not a ghost.

"Miss Flores?" I ask when I open the door.

"I'm so sorry, but we didn't have anywhere else to go."

"We?"

A girl who looks to be twelve or thirteen steps into view, her arms wrapped around herself in a hug. "My cousin, Isabel and me. Please, if we could just come in, I'll explain everything."

Fear from the old memories is the devil on my shoulder telling me to send them away and lock the door. However, the concern I've been feeling for her wins me over and I step back and open the door wider. "Come in."

The girls hurry inside, and I close the door behind them, locking us in and setting the alarm. I lead them through the dark to the kitchen and finally turn some lights on. While I run some water into a kettle and put it on to warm, I talk.

"Do you want something to drink? Water, tea, milk?"

"A glass of milk would be nice, thank you," the girl says.

Her voice is quiet, and she doesn't make eye contact. She keeps touching the cuffs of the heavy hoodie she's wearing. It's far too warm for the weather and I'm surprised she's not sweating.

I pour her a glass of milk and place it in front of her. "Maggie? Anything for you?"

"No, thank you. I'm fine."

"All right, why don't you tell me what's going on? You said you were dealing with some family issues?"

Magdalena slides her eyes over to her cousin, some unspoken communication passing between them until Isabel gives the barest of nods.

"The reason I've been missing classes is because of Isabel. She contacted me and asked me to help her, but the only thing she told me was that she couldn't stay at her mom's anymore. We've always been thick as thieves, me and her, because we're a lot alike. She was a happy-go-lucky straight-A student until two years ago."

While Maggie talks, I'm watching Isabel out of the corner of my eye and she is clearly agitated. That starts me wondering if she needs to be on some sort of medication.

"She won't tell me the entire story, only that something bad was happening. For a few weeks, I managed to keep her with me. Then a couple of cops caught up to us and took her back home. From there, she went somewhere else, but I don't know where because the next thing I know, I'm getting a call from her mom, my aunt, that Isabel's in the hospital because she tried to commit suicide."

My eyes snap to the girl, but Maggie keeps talking.

"The cops came back to the hospital to check on her, but they didn't stay. While they were gone, my aunt wrote out a note that she was having some problems and gave permission for Isabel to stay with me. It was witnessed by the doctor. When we were leaving, the cops were outside waiting, but we gave them the slip and have been moving around constantly since yesterday. We can't go to her house, or where I've been staying, because they'd know to look for us there."

"When is the last time you ate?"

Maggie shrugs. "It's been a while."

Turning back to the fridge, I begin pulling out food, lunch meat, cheese, condiments, and bring a loaf of bread to the kitchen island. I encourage the girls to make sandwiches for themselves while I pour water from the kettle over a bag of chamomile tea.

Once they're well on their way through their first sandwich, I ask the question that needs to be asked, "Isabel, I know you don't know me, but you can trust me. I believe your cousin trusts me or she wouldn't have brought you here. Can you tell me what has happened to you?"

The girl looks at Maggie, who nods in return.

Her voice is so quiet when she speaks that I have to lean in to hear her.

"There are some bad men who have been doing bad things to me."

That's all she gives us before she goes back to eating her sandwich. It doesn't take a genius to figure out what kinds of bad things they're probably doing that would drive her to commit suicide to make it stop.

"I'm so sorry that happened to you. It's late, so I want you to stay the night here. You can shower, get a good night's rest and some food in your bellies and we'll talk everything over tomorrow to come up with a plan. How does that sound?"

Maggie visibly relaxes. "Thank you, professor. I don't know how I'll ever repay you."

I wave a hand as if it's no big thing.

"Once you're finished eating, I want you to move your car into the garage next to mine. That way, it's not sitting on the street where one of my neighbors is likely to call it in."

We get the car put away and I give the girls some of my clothes to wear to sleep in while we wash theirs. Almost as soon as her head hits the pillow, Isabel falls asleep in my guest room. Maggie and I talk further, keeping quiet to avoid bothering Isabel.

Maggie tells me I know just as much as she does at this point, so we'll have to wait until the morning to see if we can get more of the story from her cousin. However, if she's traumatized, that may be a difficult endeavor.

Chapter 7

Serena

"I don't have classes today," I tell the girls over breakfast, "but I would like to go to the grocery store to get some things. If you'll make a list of your sizes, I can also pick up some clothes and other things for you since it's not safe for you to go home. You know, underwear, toothbrushes, toothpaste, and the like."

"You don't have to," Maggie starts.

"I know I don't have to, but I'd like to. When I get back, I'd like to talk more about what's going on and come up with a plan."

Maggie's eyes grow misty. "Thank you, professor. I didn't know what I was going to do if you told us to leave."

"Please, call me Serena. I'm going to get dressed and get moving because I have a couple of other errands to run while I'm out. While I'm gone, I think it's best if you stay away from the windows. I doubt anyone will come by, but don't answer the door."

She nods.

At the store, I go a little overboard. The girls have nothing but the clothes on their backs, so I get everything we talked about as well as a couple of backpacks so they can easily carry everything. I also get plenty of food, including snacks I wouldn't normally allow into the house because I'd end up eating all of them.

My phone pings to let me know I have a message. I quickly pull into the next available parking lot to see if perhaps it's Maggie. It's not her; it's Diondre.

Diondre: *Can we talk?*

That is a simple question to answer.

Me: *No.*

I'm tempted to turn my phone off, but don't in case Maggie needs me. Instead, I just drop it back into my bag. After a few more stops, I head back home. Closing myself into the garage, I gather up bags and heft them into the house.

No sooner have I set them onto the kitchen island with the girls chattering about all the bags when there is a knock on the front door. With a jerk of my chin and a wave of my hand, I shoo the girls out of the kitchen. They race to the spare bedroom to close themselves inside.

When I step into the entry, I see a silhouette of a man. His hands are cupped around his face, which is pressed up against one of the windows on the side of the front door, peering inside. His uniform is blurry, but discernable through the decoratively frosted glass.

He doesn't even have the decency to step away when he sees me coming. When I open the door, I only leave about a six-inch gap, keeping my shoulder and hip braced against it.

"May I ask why you're peeping in my windows?" I ask, with an edge to my voice.

"Are you the homeowner, ma'am?" asks the haughty officer.

"I am."

"Might we come inside to speak with you?"

"About what, Officer Draper?" I ask, pointedly looking at his name bar. Draper is medium-height and has a wiry build and sparse wiry hair that he's coiffed into a ghastly comb over.

The way he's smiling makes it seem as if he's supposed to be the good cop, but the smile is a lie. It's a shark's smile and behind his eyes, something dark lurks. I've seen eyes like that on men I sentenced to prison. This is the kind of man that will smile to your face while he drives the knife into your gut.

The second officer comes to stand beside him, and I see his name bar reads Pierce. I file those names in the back of my mind. Officer Pierce is barrel-chested and burly, with a gut that's starting to creep over his belt. The redness in his cheeks and nose make me think he's more drunkard than jolly old elf.

"Ma'am, we're looking for a missing child," Draper says, saccharine in his tone.

I frown. "Missing child? Why would you be coming here to look for a missing child?"

"If you'll just let us in, we can tell you everything."

Pierce puts his hand on the door. "Let us in or we'll come in. We're the law; we can do that."

I raise an eyebrow and let my southern roots come out in my tone. "Y'all should do some research before you go knockin' on someone's front door."

The look that crosses Draper's face is almost comical. However, Pierce's face grows dark. Before he can push open the door, I figure I'll let him know who he's dealing with.

"First of all, Officer Pierce, you should be careful what you say because these newfangled camera doorbells record everything." His hand drops from the door.

"Second, I am licensed by the local bar. I've been an attorney on both sides of the table, was a sitting judge for over ten years, and now teach law. Don't come up in here with that shady flim-flam kind of law enforcement because it's not going to fly. Tell me what you want, and tell me now, before I call in and report your behavior to your superiors."

Pierce's face darkens even more, his face turning a shade of crimson that would make the university proud. I can read it all over him how much he'd love to shove open this door and show me who's boss.

"My apologies, ma'am," Draper says. "My partner meant no disrespect."

I snort in response to that blatant lie. Draper looks over his shoulder at Pierce, who steps back and off the porch. Officer Draper extends his hands in a conciliatory manner.

"As I said, we're looking for a missing child."

"There is no missing child here. When did this child go missing? I haven't received any Amber alerts on my phone. Nor have I seen anything on the news about a missing child."

"It's a recent development in an ongoing investigation. We were given your name by a relative as someone who might know the child's whereabouts."

"Well, someone lied to you. Although some of my students are young, they're all adults and I don't know their families. The only children I know, which are few, are exactly where they're supposed to be with their parents or guardians. Unless you have a warrant, you're not coming into my home and you have exactly zero probable cause to do so."

I hold out my hand. "Now, if you don't mind, gentlemen, I have groceries to put away, but if you have a card, I'd be happy to take it and report back if I come across any unattended children."

Unsurprisingly, they don't give me a card. "I'm sorry, ma'am, we're fresh out of cards, gave our last one away a few houses back. We'll be in touch."

With a shrug, I swing the door closed and turn the lock on the knob as well as the deadbolt. Knowing that the big man, Pierce, is probably watching me through the window, I set the alarm then return to the kitchen and make as if I'm putting groceries away. Once I step out of sight from the front door, I go down the hall to the room the girls are using.

Sticking my head in, I say, "Stay put and quiet for a bit longer. I want to make sure they have plenty of time to leave. I'll come get you when they're gone."

The girls are huddled together at the head of the bed, but they both nod. When the sound of the mail person's vehicle catches my attention, I go out front to meet her, not only to get my mail, but to take a look around. The cruiser and officers are nowhere to be seen, so after we chat for a few seconds, I take my mail from her and go back inside.

Back inside the house, I tell the girls it's safe and they join me in the kitchen. They help carry in the rest of the bags and review their haul. I'm sure some things will have to be returned, but they'll at least have more than one set of clothes to wear.

The doorbell rings and both of them freeze, ready to race back to the bedroom to hide. However, it's about the right time for my invited guest to arrive, so I tell them to stay put. When I open the door, Demi is standing there smiling.

"I like your house," she says.

"Thank you and thank you so much for coming. Please come in."

Chapter 8

Isabel

When the lady comes back, there's another woman with her and I start to get scared. She doesn't look mean, but after the past few years, I've learned not to trust anyone. Well, except maybe Magdalena. I still trust her.

"Magdalena and Isabel, this is my friend Demi. Isabel, I know you've been through something horribly traumatic. She's a therapist, so I thought it might be helpful for her to be here as we talk about what has been happening to you."

"Thank you, Serena. That was very thoughtful of you," Maggie says as she takes my hand in hers. I'm not sure if she's trying to reassure me or herself.

"Let's go to the den," Serena says. "We can be more comfortable in there."

Maggie curls up on a big comfortable couch with me, still holding my hand while the two women sit in chairs across from us. I know I need to tell them, but I'm scared. The last time I tried to tell, terrible things happened.

Maggie squeezes my hand. "You can trust Serena and if Serena trusts her, I do, too."

I pull my hand out of hers and cross my arms over my chest. That isn't enough, so I grab the pillow next to me and hug it close.

"It started two years ago..."

When I was a little kid, my mom had some problems. That's how my grandma put it...problems. I don't have a lot of memories of my grandma because I was just a little kid, but I remember her saying that about Mom. Really, she was a drug addict, but I guess that's a problem, isn't it?

She was so bad that I lived with my grandma for a while. But then Mom got clean and got a great job and was able to take me back to live with her. Mom met a super nice man, David, and they had a daughter together, my little sister Sophie. Life was wonderful for a few years.

We had a house with a yard. There was food on the table every day and we spent a lot of time laughing and hanging out together. Mom was happy, and I was happy, too. I think that was the last time I was.

But then David got hurt at work and got hooked on the pain pills the doctors gave him. Two years ago, he got busted buying drugs. That's when Mr. King came into the picture.

I can still remember the day he first walked into our house. He looked like he was disgusted by it, but he sat there in a chair in our dining room talking about David's case, and I remember thinking he must be a lawyer or something.

Despite all his big talk, he didn't keep David out of jail. A few days later, he came back to our house and told Mom that she could be in trouble, too. From there, everything went downhill.

Mom started using again, and I think Mr. King is the one who gave the drugs to her. She couldn't afford to pay the legal bill, because, of course, when she started using, she lost her job, but he was willing to take something else in payment.

I can still hear my mom's pleas. She was messed up and just kept saying, "Please baby, just do this for mama. It's the only way. You don't want me to go to jail, do you?" Grandma had died, so there was nowhere to go and Mom wasn't going to take no for an answer.

Maggie is squeezing my hand so tight that I think she might break my fingers. When she spits out a string of swear words in Spanish, I can't stop the laugh that ripples out of me.

"A few weeks ago, I managed to sneak out of the house where Mr. King kept me and went to the police. Just walked right into a station and made a report. They called Mom to come get me. Two days later, a cop car came to the house with two officers. They said they needed to take me to the station to ask me some questions. Mom didn't even try to go with me because she was in bed, stoned out of her mind."

Miss Serena makes a noise somewhere between a growl and a huff. She sounds a lot like those she-lions I saw on the Discovery Channel once.

"They didn't take me to the police station. They took me to Mr. King's house. He rewarded them for it."

I press my face into the pillow, shamed by the admission.

"After they left, I decided I'd rather be dead than go through anything like that again. Because I'd lost so much blood by the time he found me, he had no choice but to take me to the hospital."

Thankfully, Mom was a little less high than usual when Mr. King had her go to the hospital for me and she called Maggie. Before Mr. King could get back to stop it, Mom had written the note about giving temporary guardianship to Maggie and the doctor, who had been all kinds of concerned, witnessed it and helped us get out of the hospital.

Maggie and I have been moving around ever since.

Getting all of it out has left me exhausted. The past two years have been hell on earth and right now, all I want to do is sleep. However, there's one more thing I need to say.

"Now that I'm gone, I'm worried about Sophie. I was ten when he started with me and she's only eight, but I don't think that will stop him, or his best friend. At first it was just the two of them, but later, there were others. I don't want her to have to go through that."

I can't look at anyone because I'm scared of what I'll see on their faces. They might think I'm as ugly and dirty as I feel.

"Isabel," the new woman says. I can't remember her name, but I lift my eyes to hers. They're a blue so light that they look icy. But they're not cold, they're filled with care and warmth. "This is not your fault. Men like Mr. King prey on vulnerable women like your mother so they can take advantage and do horrible things."

I look back down. Part of me wants to believe her, but I'm not quite sure I can.

"So, what do we do now?" Maggie asks.

"Well, we need to get Isabel somewhere safe," Miss Serena says. "I have a friend with DHS and will talk to her about pulling Sofie out of the home. Perhaps we can get your mom to do the same thing with Sophie as she did with you, Isabel. The granting of temporary guardianship to a family member is much easier than getting it for, say, me, or someone else non-familial."

"Where could we go, so she's safe?" Maggie asks. "There's no one in our family we can stay with. We can't stay here, either. You have class tomorrow and if we're here alone, those cops will probably come back and break down the door to get to us."

Everyone is quiet for a few moments. I don't know how long that lasts because I'm startled out of a doze when the blond woman with the blue eyes says, "I have an idea."

She says she knows someone who owns a security company and part of what they do is keep people safe. Then she asks me, not Maggie, not Miss Serena, me, "Would you be okay with me calling him?"

I look at Maggie, and in her eyes I can see the hope. When we came here to Miss Serena's last night, it was a last-ditch effort to at least get a peaceful night's rest. If she had turned us away, we would have had nowhere else to go.

Maggie trusts Miss Serena, and I do, too. Miss Serena trusts the blond woman and if the blond woman trusts these other people, I'm willing to give it a try. Just about anything is preferable to staying on the run or, worse, going back to mom's.

Chapter 9

Vance

I'm about to head out the door at the end of my first day on the job when a gorgeous woman comes through the door. She's tall and curvy, with a riot of dark curls down past her shoulders. Jack calls out, "Hey baby, what are you doing here?"

I school the lustful look off my face.

She crosses the room and presses her body to his while tip-toeing up to kiss him. "Demi has someone she needs to keep safe. She asked me if Carver Security might be able to help."

"Depends on the situation," Jack says, wrapping his arms around his woman.

"That's what I said." She looks over at me with a grin. "Hi, I'm Sarah, Jack's girlfriend."

Normally, I'd hold out a hand in greeting, but considering her hands are pressed to my boss's backside, I refrain, and just smile over at her. "Hi, I'm Vance, the new guy."

"Oh, Jack told me all about you. Welcome aboard."

"Why don't you come with us?" Jack asks me. "I'd like to get your take on the situation."

"Sure, I'm good with that."

Jerald comes out and greets Sarah, then Jack tells him where we're going. The three of us pile into a Carver Security SUV and Sarah plugs the address into the GPS while Jack drives.

The neighborhood we arrive at fifteen minutes later is upper-middle class on the south side of Moore, north side of Norman. Could be either.

There's a Mercedes SUV parked in the driveway. As we pull in and park next to the SUV, Jack asks the same question on my mind. "Do we know whose house this is?"

"No, just that it's a friend of Demi's from that fancy women's club she belongs to. That's Demi's car, so we're in the right place."

While we walk to the door, I look around the neighborhood, wondering if the danger is here or somewhere else. A lot of people would see the higher-end homes and immediately discount that anything bad could be happening here, but sometimes money only makes things worse.

A tiny blond woman opens the door, and a grin spreads across her face when she sees Sarah. "I figured you'd be coming, too."

"You know me, curious as ever."

They hug, then Jack hugs the woman. He turns and motions to me.

"Dr. Demeter Lawson, this is Vance Douglas, a new hire brought on specifically for personal security. He's former military and law enforcement, so I asked him to come to give his take."

She stretches out a hand to me. "I'm pleased to meet you, Mr. Douglas. Please call me Demi. Your expertise might come in handy, as we've a bit of a legal issue going on."

I can almost see the mantle of authority dropping over her shoulders as her demeanor changes when she speaks again.

"The person in question is a girl who has been severely traumatized, so, although I know it will be difficult for two big guys like you, I'm going to ask you to be as non-threatening as possible and tread lightly with her."

"Yes, ma'am," Jack says in a halfway teasing tone. When she looks at me, I give her a nod. I have two children and understand how emotionally fragile children can be.

She leads us inside, and we follow her, single file, toward the back of the house. My eyes take in the people in the room we enter, a girl and a young woman, both of whom appear to be mixed race, but with a healthy dose of Latin blood, and another woman whom I haven't seen for a very long time.

"Serena?"

"Vance?"

She looks as shocked as I feel. The last time I saw Serena Chilton, she was a judge in Atlanta. We'd become acquainted through the court system and were friendly.

My wife and I had separated for a time in Serena's early days on the bench, and we had gone out on one date. I'd been admiring her from afar, so to speak, and was excited to go out with her.

It was a great date, but soon after, my estranged wife cajoled me into a reconciliation for the sake of our children. Other than occasionally passing Serena in the halls of the courthouse, we didn't see each other again.

She looks exactly the same except her face has a few more lines. Otherwise, she still has the same hourglass figure with curves that makes a man want to put his hands on her. However, the chin-up, regal bearing of her entire body dares him to try.

The poise she learned as a southern debutante still informs her every move, but those eyes of hers still give her away. I didn't miss the fiery flash as recognition sank in. She covered it quickly, though.

"Sorry," she says. "It's good to see you again, Vance, but we'll have to catch up some other time. Right now, we're here to talk about these two."

She indicates the two girls huddled together on the sofa, then does a quick introduction of everyone.

"Magdalena is one of my students and the other young lady is her cousin Isabel. I won't go into specifics, but Isabel was put into a dangerous and abusive situation by her mother. In a lucid moment, her mother assigned guardianship of Isabel to Magdalena. They escaped and now her abusers are looking for her. We need to come up with a plan to keep them safe and possibly her younger sister, too, if we can legally extricate her from the situation."

"How do you intend to do that?" Jack asks.

"It's my hope that we can convince the mother to voluntarily give temporary custody to Maggie as well. If necessary, I'll contact some people I know at DHS to have the girl removed from the home," Serena answers.

"You're not finished with classes yet, so they can't stay here," Demi says.

"I know," Serena replies. "Maggie also needs to finish her classes. They've been on the run for several days, but they can't go back to doing that. There are members of law enforcement involved and they could easily put out a BOLO on Maggie's car, pull them over, and while Maggie's in jail, they could return Isabel to her abusers."

I'm listening and watching the girls. When Serena mentions Maggie going to jail, she shivers, but the look of panic that crosses Isabel's face at just the mention of being returned to her abusers tells a prolific story.

"Is there somewhere we could stash Isabel while Maggie and Serena finish up classes?" I ask. "Then the focus could be on liberating the younger sister and stashing her in the same place while Serena and I dig up enough proof to take to the higher ups at the department?"

Serena's eyes snap to mine. "Don't look so surprised," I tell her. "I know you intend to dig up evidence and you'll need help doing that. Just in case you forgot, I used to do that sort of thing for a living."

She scowls at me, and I grin back. Out of the corner of my eye, I've also noticed an unspoken communication going on between Sarah and Demi. "What were you two thinking?" I ask them.

"Serena," Sarah says, "do you remember Felicia's sister, Roni?"

Her eyes light up. "Yes, do you think she'd be willing?"

"Ah, that's kind of brilliant, baby," Jack says with a grin.

"Who are Felicia and Roni?" asks Maggie, entering the conversation. I'm glad she asked because if she hadn't, I was going to.

"My brother Dale is married to a woman named Felicia," she answers, "who has a sister named Roni, short for Veronica. She and her husband own a horse ranch about a little over an hour southeast of here."

"I'll call her," Sarah says. "Roni's like a sister to me, too, because my sister is married to their cousin and lives on the same mile section of land. Dale and my brother-in-law are both former military. Another sister, Heather, also lives about a mile away and is tribal law enforcement. Her partner is a former OSBI agent."

"Wow. Sounds like an almost ideal situation," I reply.

"Unless someone knew all the connections among these three, it would be a tough location to ferret out. It's about as safe as a safe house could get," Jack says as Sarah walks out of the room with her cell phone in hand, followed by Demi. "They have security out the wazoo, thanks to Jerald. There are guard dogs and trusted ranch hands who live on the property. It would be damn near impossible for someone to sneak into the compound."

It sounds like I've stepped into the middle of more than just two brothers running a security company. They appear to have connections with connections with connections. I like how they're willing to mobilize to help someone who needs it with only tenuous reason to do so.

I love it when people do the right thing just because it's the right thing to do.

Chapter 10

Serena

While Sarah's out of the room and the two men are talking, I sit on the sofa next to Isabel. She's clinging to Maggie's side and I'm sure she's probably scared to death to have all these adults making decisions for her.

"How are you doing, Isabel?"

She shrugs. Yes, she's completely overwhelmed and frightened.

"I know it's probably scary having everyone talk and make decisions about you without asking what you want, isn't it? Especially when some of them are people you've never met before."

She looks over at me and nods, eyes wide.

"I thought so. Now, I know you don't know me as well as Maggie does, but do you trust me?"

After a glance at Maggie, she turns back to me and nods.

"Is there anything you'd like to say or questions you'd like to ask?"

She swallows. "You said your brother lives there?"

I smile. "Yes. His name is Dale, and he lives in the nearby town. He owns a construction company with Sarah's brother."

"So you know the people they want me to stay with?"

"I do. They are very nice and have a daughter that's just a little younger than you. If we take you down there and you don't want to stay, we won't force you, okay? We'll just have to figure out something else."

"Really?" she asks.

"Yes, really. I promise."

She seems to think that over for a moment, as if she's not sure she can believe me. After the life she's had, I completely understand why that would be. Maggie has been the only person who has stepped up to care for her while everyone else close to her has used and abused her.

"They have a little girl like me?" she finally asks.

"They do. If I remember right, she's about eleven and her name is Emme. They also have a son and another little girl. Like Jack said, they live on a ranch in the country where they take care of and train horses. So, what do you think? Would you like to go take a look?"

She looks at Maggie again, but Maggie doesn't respond, leaving the decision up to Isabel.

"Will I have to stay there forever?"

"No, not at all. It would probably be best if you stay there while Maggie and I finish out school over the next few weeks, but then we can revisit the subject and talk about what happens next. Does that sound okay?"

Clearly relieved, she nods.

"However, if anything happens and you don't like it there, you can call Maggie and we'll come get you and figure out something else."

She relaxes even more.

Sarah comes back into the room. "Roni and Takoda are good. They said we can bring her down tonight if you want since y'all have to be at the university tomorrow."

"All right. Thank you, Sarah," I say. "Now, Isabel, this is going to feel a little scary and there will be a lot of new people and names, but believe me when I say there is nothing to be afraid of there. Are you ready?"

"Can I take my backpack?"

"Of course."

Isabel pops up off the sofa and races back to the room she and Maggie stayed in last night. I'm unsurprised when she comes back quickly, as if her bag was already packed. Traumatized children often stay in a state of hyper-preparedness, ready to run at a moment's notice.

Demi comes to Isabel and puts her hands on her shoulders. With a warm smile, she says, "Isabel, it was wonderful to meet you and your cousin Magdalena today. I think you're going to have enough people going with you, but I want you to know that where you're going is a wonderful place and the people there are very nice. They'll take good care of you while you're there. If you need me, or just want someone to talk to, this is my card, and it has my cell number on it. Call at anytime."

"Any time?"

"Yes," she says with a smile and a nod. "If you need me, I'll be there."

We load into two vehicles, Maggie, Isabel, and me in mine and Vance, Sarah, and Jack in the Carver Security SUV. Jack tells me to take the lead so that he can make sure we're not followed. I hadn't even thought of someone following us. That's probably why he's a security expert and I'm not.

Isabel and Maggie talk most of the way there, primarily in Spanish. I pick up words here and there, but let them have their private conversation. Letting their voices fade into the background, my mind turns to Vance.

The fact that he's here is astounding. What are the odds that two people who knew each other so many years ago and went out on one date almost a thousand miles away would randomly run into each other again? I can't even begin to calculate that.

The date we had was lovely and the goodnight kiss we shared at the end of it was even more than lovely. It was toe-curling. Unfortunately, shortly after, he went back to his wife for the sake of their children.

He'd been up front with me from the beginning, so it was not a surprise. I had a feeling it would happen because that's the kind of stand-up guy he is, or was. Seems like he probably still is based on his declaration that he wanted to help me dig for evidence against the people who hurt Isabel.

I was shocked to see him, but the younger, more idealistic woman I used to be who still lurks inside my heart, thrilled at the sight. She'd had high hopes after that date all those years ago. There are so many questions I want to ask when we have a moment alone.

How did he end up here in Oklahoma? Is he still married? How are his kids doing? He talked about those children a lot on our date. They should be just about grown now, maybe college age. Is he still married? Oh, wait, I already thought of that one.

We're just outside Ada when Jack passes me to take the lead. He knows where he's going. I do not, other than knowing how to get to my brother's house. As we pass through town, the girls stop talking and stare out the windows.

"This town is called Ada," I tell them. "It's the closest town to where we're going. From what Sarah said, we're almost there. About ten more minutes just outside of town."

"It didn't take long to get here," Maggie observes.

"No, it's not far at all. My brother lives just a few blocks over in that direction," I say, pointing toward Dale and Felicia's house.

When we pull up to the ranch's gate, Jack punches in a code and waves for me to follow him through. The house is lit up like Christmas, and there are several cars parked outside.

With a glance in the rearview mirror, I can see that Isabel has moved close to Maggie again. For her sake, I hope this works out the way we all hope it does.

Chapter 11

Serena

I put on my brightest smile and look at them in the mirror. "All right ladies, let's go say hello. Remember Isabel, if you don't want to stay, you don't have to."

Once we're out of the car, Isabel slings her backpack onto one shoulder and positions herself between her cousin and me. She's gripping Maggie's hand tight, but I'm surprised when she puts her other hand in mine. I squeeze her back, trying to be as reassuring as I can.

A girl about Isabel's age comes racing out of the house and heads straight for Jack. "Uncle G!" she squeals as she launches herself at him.

He catches her mid-air, laughing at her antics. "Hey squirt." After a hug, he sets her on her feet and she loops her arm with Sarah's.

When they join us on the way to the house, Emme eyes Isabel and for a moment, I wonder if the girls will get along.

"Hi!" Emme says. "I'm Emmeline, but everyone calls me Emme." Two dogs come trotting up from the direction of the large barn. "That's Daisy and Jett. They're our guard dogs, but they won't bother you, just strangers and animals that try to hurt the horses. Daisy, she's the big white one. My mom says she's part horse and part floof. I'm not sure what a floof is, but it seems to fit."

We step up onto the porch and through the door Emme left open. Inside, if I didn't know better, I'd think the entire family has gathered, but I do know better. There are a lot of people, but it's only a small fraction of the enormous family.

Veronica is one of four sisters, then there's their cousin Luke and his wife's family. Although they aren't all related by blood, I've never known a more closely knit group of people.

My brother is in the kitchen with his wife Felicia, who is also Roni's sister. Roni's husband Takoda is there, too, along with Beth, who helps with the cooking and cleaning in the ranch house.

Ignoring my urge to go wrap my arms around my brother and say hello, I stick close to Isabel and Maggie, leading them into the kitchen where Roni and Takoda are patiently waiting. As soon as Roni sees the girls, she's coming toward us, a warm smile on her face.

"Hi," she says to Isabel. "I'm Roni, and you must be Isabel and Magdalena. Are you thirsty or hungry?"

"They're probably hungry," I say. "Things moved pretty quickly this afternoon."

"Why don't we have something to eat while we get to know each other a little better?"

From the refrigerator, Beth takes out the makings for sandwiches and puts them on the enormous kitchen island along with chips and side dishes. Jack, Vance, Sarah, Dale, and Felicia fade into the background so as not to interfere. The girls take a seat at the island and before I can sit next to Isabel, Emme slips onto the stool beside her.

Emme chatters to Isabel while Roni talks to Maggie, asking her about school. Since they're doing all right, I move to where my brother and the others are gathered in a room just off the kitchen.

"Hey sis," Dale says, pulling me into a hug.

Although we only share a father but came from different mothers, Dale has always been more of a sibling to me than the two brothers I'd known since birth. They were too much like our father, and it seems Dale and I took after our respective mothers.

"Hi," I reply to his broad chest. When he lets me go, I turn to his wife and say hello. Felicia doesn't look me in the eye, but she greets me in return. Felicia and Dale don't seem like they'd fit together, but they're a perfect match.

He lost the lower part of one leg in a construction accident when he was overseas with the army and came home with a healthy dose of PTSD. She's a brilliant data analyst who's on the autism spectrum. You'd think the odds were stacked against them. However, because of their respective issues, they have dedicated themselves to communicating about everything and I've never known a stronger couple.

We watch on and talk quietly while they feel each other out in the kitchen, taking each others' measure. When Isabel finishes her sandwich, Emme asks, "So, do you wanna go see my room? Well, I guess if you decide to stay, it'll be our room."

Isabel looks at her cousin, who nods.

"Excellent!" Emme says and takes Isabel by the hand, practically dragging her off her stool. They go upstairs with Emme chattering the entire way.

"Be quiet," Roni says, just loud enough for them to hear. "The other kids are in bed."

Emme lowers her voice, but doesn't stop talking. Those of us lurking in the wings move into the kitchen. While Isabel is upstairs, I want to make sure they know exactly what they're getting into.

"Maggie, I think it's important that they have the complete picture, so I'm going to tell them everything. I don't feel that's betraying Isabel's trust, but if you think it is, I won't say anything."

After a moment's thought and a look over her shoulder to where her cousin disappeared, she says, "No, you're right. They need to know what they're up against."

When I finish telling them in quick, clipped sentences exactly what Isabel has been through over the past two years and what has transpired over the past few days, Jack hisses out an oath. He begins to pace around the perimeter of the kitchen.

"That poor baby," Beth breathes.

"I want to dig up some evidence on the man and I know some trustworthy law enforcement officers I can hand it over to. However, my first order of business is to get her little sister pulled from the home as well, because Isabel is fearful that her mother will allow her sister to become her replacement. It's my hope that we can have the same type of temporary guardianship executed by her mother. If not, I'll get DHS involved."

Without hesitation, Takoda says, "If you do, bring her here." Roni gives him a warm, mushy look and leans into him.

"Thank you," I reply. "Once we're finished with the last couple of weeks of school, we'll have more freedom."

"If you're going to be involved in investigating, perhaps Maggie should come here, too, when she's finished with classes. We could put the three of them into the Manager's house here on the property," Roni says. "It's empty right now and that would let them have some privacy and be able to stay together until the situation is resolved."

"I could resolve it real quick," Jack grumbles.

"You *could*, but you won't," Sarah says sternly. He just winks at her in response.

As much as I hate to admit that I have that kind of darkness in me, I would be perfectly fine if Mr. King, or whatever his name is, simply disappeared off the face of the earth. Anyone who would hurt a child like that is worse than scum, and pedophiles don't ever stop being pedophiles.

"It would be helpful if you could trace the money," Felicia says, ever focused on the data. "At least that's what they say on TV. Those police officers have to be getting paid. Who knows what all you could find when you start digging into the data? I could analyze it if you had it, but I don't have the skills to get it without being caught."

Vance speaks for the first time since we arrived. "I might know a way, but it probably wouldn't be admissible in court."

Jack levels a look at him and raises an eyebrow.

Vance runs a meaty hand over the back of his neck. "I know someone who knows someone. He called the guy, the Crow or the Raven or some such. He, or heck, it could be a she, no one knows, for sure, is a dark web gray hat hacker. The word from my friend is that he is a hacker for hire, but if someone does something he doesn't like, he goes after them. It's kind of like that Anonymous crew. Sometimes the subjects of their searches get disappeared."

"The Crow?" Sarah asks, sounding amused. "Wasn't that the name of some nineties grunge movie?"

"So..." Dale starts, but stops when the girls appear at the top of the stairs and start coming down. Emme is still chattering up a storm.

When they come back in among the adults, Maggie asks her, "So what do you think?"

Isabel nods and I can see the relief in Maggie as her shoulders relax and come down from around her ears.

"I'll be okay here and you need to go back to school," Isabel says, speaking for the first time.

I know she's putting on a brave face for Maggie's sake, but whether or not she feels it right now, she speaks the truth. With

Isabel here, we won't have to worry about her. There are plenty of good people here to watch over her and keep her safe.

"You have school tomorrow, so you need to go home so you can get a good night's rest," Isabel continues, doing a role swap on her cousin.

Maggie chuckles and teases, "I see how you are. Now that you're here with other kids and some dogs, you don't need me anymore." She rises out of her chair. "Give me a hug and I'll let you get settled in for the night. If you need me, call me."

"I will," Isabel replies as Maggie wraps her up. Now that the time has come to leave her here, Maggie hesitates, but Isabel pushes her away, maintaining her brave face. "Go already."

"Te amo mucho, prima," Maggie says.

"Love you, too."

Chapter 12

Vance

Maggie was hesitant to leave, so it took some time for everyone to say their goodbyes. Eventually, Isabel, mask of bravery in place, practically pushed her cousin out the door, assuring her she'll be fine. It seemed as if Serena would have liked to linger with her brother, too, especially when Jack and Sarah asked if I'd mind riding back with Serena so they can stop by Sarah's sister's house.

I was fine with it, though, because I'd intended to talk my way into Serena's car, anyway. It was interesting meeting her brother. Based on their friendliness toward each other, I think he must be the half-brother she told me about before because she didn't have much contact with her other two brothers.

"It's amazing those people would take Isabel in even though they don't know her," Magdalena says from the back seat.

"They're good people," Serena replies. "At least that's what my brother tells me. I've met most of his wife's family, but I don't know them all that well. His word is good enough for me, though."

"We haven't known many good people in our lives."

"With Isabel safe, you can either go back to your apartment, or you're welcome to stay with me through the end of school."

"I don't have an apartment," Maggie answers. "Mostly, I've been sleeping on the couch at a friend's house."

Serena doesn't respond right away, as if she's not sure she heard correctly.

"Well, that settles that. You're staying with me. Once school's finished, we'll see what you want to do then. Okay? Should we swing by your friend's place to pick up your things?"

Maggie doesn't answer, so I turn in my seat and look back at her. She's fallen asleep. Who knows when the last time was that she got a good night's sleep? Serena is watching her in the rearview mirror and from the look on her face, it seems she might be thinking the same thing.

"It's going to be all right," I tell her, keeping my voice low.

"How is it that people have children they don't take care of?"

"There are some fucked up people in this world."

One reason I left the force is because seeing the evidence of those people day in and day out was wearing me down. Sometimes they do terrible things to themselves, but most often to others. Way too often, the children are caught in the middle if they're not the direct victims.

That's why this job with Carver Security appealed so much to me. I'll have a hand in helping to keep people safe. Hopefully, before anything bad can happen to them.

"I heard about what happened in Atlanta. That was so unbelievable. I tried to check on you after it happened, but you just packed up and disappeared. Is that when you came to Oklahoma?"

If I hadn't been observing her, I would have missed the way her hands tightened on the steering wheel.

"Yes. I'd heard about a teaching opening in the law school up here, so I applied and was awarded the position."

"I thought maybe your brother was part of the lure."

"He was still in the military when I came here. Me being here was part of the reason why he moved to Oklahoma. When he was in the hospital recovering after he lost part of his leg, he shared a room with Sarah's brother. She went out there to Baltimore and when she brought her brother home, Dale came with them. He met Felicia, and that was it for him."

"Felicia and Roni are sisters, right?"

"Yes."

She tells me about all the connections between Sarah's family and Felicia's. There are a lot of names to keep up with, so mostly I just get the gist of it. There are four sisters who are cousins to Sarah's sister's husband, and all of them are close.

"It's probably nice to have such a close extended family," I say. "When I was growing up, it was just Mom and me. Dad left before I was out of diapers."

"I remember you saying that before."

"And I remember you telling me that you didn't know if it was better to have a father who left or one who didn't but was an asshole."

She chuckles, but there's no humor in it. "Yeah, I did. So what brought you here?"

"Mom. She moved up here to live with her sister a few years ago. They're not getting any younger and needed someone to look out for them. My kids are in college now. Tamara is at Howard and wants to go into medicine. Tyrone got a baseball scholarship to Arizona State. With the kids grown, my wife and I divorced. I was ready for a change and didn't see a reason to stay in Atlanta, so I sold everything and moved up here."

We go quiet when Maggie shifts in the back seat. She mumbles something, but I can't make out what it is. I look over at Serena, who is also listening intently. She looks back at me and shrugs, showing she didn't catch it either.

"When are you going to go to the mother's house?" I ask.

"Tomorrow after classes, I think. The sooner the better because the longer she stays there, the more time Mr. King, or whatever his real name is, will have to finagle the girl into his clutches."

I nod. "Yeah. First things first. Get the sister to a safe place, then we can start digging."

"We?"

"I can help with the digging."

"You don't have to."

A frown creases my brow. "I know I don't have to, but I'd like to."

"Okay," she replies, but not like she believes me.

When we get back into Norman, I direct her to the Carver Security offices so I can get my car.

We're just a few blocks away, so I finally ask the question that's been niggling at the back of my brain. "Are you sure you all should stay alone at your house?"

"We should be fine. I'll make sure we set the alarm as soon as we get home."

She pulls into the parking lot and stops next to my car.

"Unlock your phone and give it to me. I'll put my number in so you can call me if you need anything. And I do mean anything. I'm just over in Del City, so not that far away."

She does as I ask, and I hand it back to her after inputting my information. Before I let it go, I catch her eye.

"If you want someone to go with you to the mother's house tomorrow, let me know. I know Jack won't mind me taking time out to accompany you. Even if I just sit in the car waiting to see if I'm needed, I'd rather you have some protection available."

She nods. "I appreciate that, and I'll let you know."

I open my door and get out of the car, standing in the parking lot watching until I can't see her anymore. Today has brought all kinds of surprises, with the biggest being finding Serena Chilton in Oklahoma, of all places.

That one was a pleasant surprise and I can't wait to see where it takes us. She's changed, but so have I. However, I'd still like to know what's happened in the past eight years to make her so reserved.

She used to be quick with a smile, but now, they're like buried treasure and I intend to excavate as many as I can.

Chapter 13

Serena

No sooner does the car door close than Maggie sits up, rubbing her eyes. "He seems like a nice guy."

"He is."

"Handsome, too, for an old guy."

"Magdalena!"

Her low laugh seeps over the seat.

Thankfully, there are no police cars waiting when we arrive back at my house. Maggie goes to her room and I don't see her again for the rest of the evening. As promised, I set the alarm and double check the locks on all the doors and windows.

Although I know we're locked up tight, my sleep is uneasy as my mind reels. Sophie is our next order of business, but plans for how to proceed after that are dancing in my brain like an ethereal game of Tetris trying to fit all the pieces together.

Finally, around four in the morning, I give up and get up. Once I pull on my robe, I slip down the hall to my office at home and start writing down the thoughts that kept me from sleeping. I probably should have done it when I first found sleep elusive because now that it's done, I feel like I could sleep.

Too late now, though. With a yawn, I go to the kitchen and start the coffeemaker, then start pulling items from the fridge. I'm just dumping everything into the blender for my morning protein shake when Maggie shuffles in, freshly showered and fully dressed.

"Want some breakfast?" I ask as she fills a travel mug with coffee and doctors it with sugar and creamer.

"No, thank you. I'm going to stop by my friend's house this morning to get my things if you're really okay with me staying here."

"I am. Today I'll be finished with classes at four-thirty. We should go see your aunt today about Sophie, if possible."

She nods. "Yeah. I'd like to get her out of there as soon as possible."

"We also need to find out if Mr. King is really the name of the attorney. If it's not, we'll need to find out what his real name is so that we can start pulling information together."

"Okay. I'll meet you at your office at four-thirty."

"Great."

She hefts her backpack onto her shoulder and leaves with nothing for breakfast but the coffee in her mug. I can't say much. When I was her age, caffeine was my primary source of sustenance, too.

She's in my class as she's supposed to be, bright-eyed and attentive, then shows back up right on time. On the way to her aunt's house, Maggie is fidgety. I'd probably be nervous, too.

As much as she understands the need for getting and keeping both girls out of their mother's house, she's a college student being given legal guardianship of two young girls. If anything happened to her aunt, she'd be the one to take care of them.

Based on the fact that she's been sleeping on a friend's couch and just lost her job because of all this, she's in no position to take on that kind of responsibility.

One step at a time, Serena.

Get the girls. Get some solid evidence. Get the money trail.

Once those things are done, we'll cross the next bridge.

The apartment complex we pull up to is exactly what I expected it to be and run down isn't a strong enough descriptor for the building. It's the kind of place where you don't go outside at night. Instead, you lock yourself inside with the cockroaches where you don't hear or see anything that goes on outside.

Maggie knocks on the door, and it is opened quickly by Sophie. When she sees her cousin instead of whomever she was expecting, her face lights up.

"I'm so glad it's you! Mama is expecting company soon, so I figured they were early."

"Is it Mr. King she's expecting?" Maggie whispers.

"No. He was here yesterday looking for Isabel. They had an argument, and he yelled at her for a long time. I had a pillow over my head so I couldn't hear everything, but I heard some parts were about money and paying him back."

"Is she home now?"

"Yeah, kinda," she breathes, looking over her shoulder.

Her mom calls from deeper in the apartment, but I can't distinguish her words. Sophie steps back and opens the door wider, allowing us in.

"It's Prima Magdalena, Mama," Sophie calls back, then whispers as we pass by. "She's in her bedroom."

We walk through the apartment, and I have to work hard to school my face. Despite the condition of the outside, the inside is neat and as clean as it can be. However, there is a pervasive smell that makes me wonder if there's a problem with the sewer system.

In her bedroom, Maggie's aunt is dressed in scanty lingerie. When she sees us enter, she snatches up a robe from the end of her bed. Is she planning on entertaining whomever is on their way here with Sophie in the house?

"Whatchoo want?" her aunt asks, her words slurring. She's high or drunk, or maybe a bit of both.

"Tia, I wanted to let you know Isabel is safe. I've arranged for her to stay with some people who will look after her until I'm finished with school."

Her aunt nods. "Thank you, Magdalena. I knew I could count on you."

"So, I understand that Mr. King was here last night. Did he ask for Sophie?"

She doesn't answer, but when she looks away, that's answer enough.

"Tia, I know you feel like he has you backed into a corner, but that's just scare tactics. You could do the same thing with Sophie that you did with Isabel. I can take her to the same safe place. We're going to work on bringing Mr. King down and then you won't have to worry about him anymore."

Tears are streaming down her aunt's face. "He's too powerful. There are cops in his pocket."

"I know. They tried to come take us before I got Isabel safe, but they were scared off."

"How'd you manage that?"

Maggie turns to take my hand in hers and pulls me forward.

"She did it. This is one of my law professors at college. They were trying to bully their way into her house and she shut them down so hard they scurried away with their tails between their legs."

Her aunt's chuckle is rusty. Because Maggie doesn't use my name, I figure there must be a reason, so I don't offer to introduce myself formally, either.

"If you don't let us take Sophie to be safe with Isabel, you know they're going to come take her because they think you're powerless to do anything about it," Maggie says gently.

The woman doesn't respond for so long, I'm sure she's going to refuse. My temptation is to tell her that if she doesn't let Sophie go with us now, I'll be back tomorrow with DHS, but she's been threatened so much that what she needs right now is an ally.

"You're sure they'll be safe?" she finally breathes into the room.

"Positive. It's a wonderful place with a family with children and a couple of dogs. As soon as the danger has passed, we can bring them right back home to you."

She goes quiet again. Sophie steps into the room. "Please mama, I don't want those gross men to hurt me like they did Izzy."

That breaks her and the tears flow harder. She doesn't speak, but she nods. From my bag, I pull out a piece of paper I prepared today. It's a bit more formal than what they prepared in haste at the hospital, and it covers temporary custody for both girls.

Bringing a notary to witness the signing would probably have spooked the aunt, so I sign as witness. It's better than nothing and would certainly hold up more than some shoddy attorney demanding the girls because he said so.

"Go pack your things," Maggie says to Isabel, handing the girl her new backpack, which she must have emptied before we left school. I make a mental note to get her another one.

Before the ink is even dry on the page, there's a pounding on the door. "Keep them safe," the aunt says, scurrying toward the door, but Maggie grabs her arm.

"Mr. King, what's his real name?" she asks.

"There are mainly two of them. Mr. King's real last name is Graham. The other one has never been here, but I know they're partners and both take part and share. I've only met him a couple of times and his last name is Makowski or something like that. Now get out of here. I've got company."

She goes to answer the door while we gather Sophie, who is packed and ready to go. The backpack isn't even close to being full. We usher her out the door as her mother ushers her company to the bedroom.

As soon as we're in the car, I call the number I have for Veronica Nomee to let her know we're on our way with Sophie.

Chapter 14

Serena

Once we're in the car and headed south, Sophie warms up and chatters with Maggie. I'm thrilled things went so smoothly because it wouldn't have taken long in the clutches of those bastard pedophiles for her to shut down like her sister has.

Getting all three of them some counseling is high on my priority list. Although Maggie didn't fall prey to the same men, by all appearances, her life hasn't been all rainbows and unicorns either.

One step at a time, Serena.

After Sophie is settled with the Nomee family, we'll get to work finishing the semester and starting to dig. Sophie is ecstatic about her new temporary home as soon as she sees the dogs. She practically jumps out of the car before we stop.

When their big white dog starts to lick her face as she tries to hug it, the girl bursts into giggles. The back door of the house is flung open and both Isabel and Emme come racing out. Isabel wraps her sister up in a hug and squeezes her so tight, Sophie complains and squirms to break free.

I look up and see Roni and her husband watching, so I go join them on the porch. The three girls are chattering up a storm and the dog, caught up in their enthusiasm, barks to add her opinion to the mix.

"That was quick," Roni says.

"Yeah. It could have been a very different outcome, though. The attorney had already been there last night pressuring their mother to let him take Sophie. Thankfully, she refused, and we convinced her to sign over temporary custody of Sophie, too. I prepped a new document for both girls that, although it's not ironclad, it stronger than what they'd done in the hospital."

"Do you all want some supper?"

Maggie steps up on the porch with us, so I look to her for her preference. I'd rather get back to Norman, but if she wants to spend a little more time with her cousins, I won't deny her that. She looks back to the yard where the girls are playing with the dog and shakes her head.

"No, thank you. I think it would be better if we kept this visit short. Getting Sophie here was a giant accomplishment, and I will never be able to thank you enough for letting the girls stay here. However, I think it will be better for Sophie if there's not a long, drawn out goodbye."

Takoda nods. "I understand. We'll watch over them for you, but you are welcome anytime you want to visit until this is settled. Also, the offer still stands for you to come stay here, too, once you're finished with school."

A look of longing crosses her face, but it's quickly banished by a stubborn set of her jaw.

"Thank you," Maggie replies.

I'm going to have to work that out of her over the next two weeks. She will be much better off down here with her cousins than in Norman helping me investigate. Helping *us* investigate. Vance is a former detective, so his help will be invaluable.

He knows exactly what kind of evidence is needed by the police to bring these pedophiles to trial and put them away for...well, hopefully the rest of their lives. That will take a boat-load of evidence, but men like them have probably perfected their approach through the years, leaving a trail of tragedy in their wake.

"Go say goodbye," I tell her.

With slow steps, she leaves the porch and goes to her cousins, hugging them both. She speaks to them too low to carry to us and says something to Emme, too. Emme nods, her eyes wide, and says something back. One more hug and she leaves them to move toward the car.

"Thank you," I say to Roni and Takoda.

"They'll be safe here," Takoda assures me.

"I know," I say. "That will help Maggie rest easy while we track down something to take these deviants off the streets so they can no longer do harm."

I join Maggie in the car and stay quiet as we back out of our parking place. She turns to the window and returns the waves of the three girls still in the yard. The somber mood sticks with us the rest of the way back to my house.

It feels as if the daunting prospect of what lies ahead is a dark cloud hanging over both of us.

As soon as we get home, I go to the kitchen and fix myself a sandwich. I offer to make one for Maggie, too, but she declines and says she needs to study for her upcoming final exams. Rather than trying to coax her, I trust that if she's hungry, she'll eat.

Taking my food to my office, I turn my attention to work and grading the stack of papers I pull from my tote bag. My cell phone catches my eye and I remember I promised to let Vance know today's outcome.

Me: *Getting Sophie out was a success. Paperwork in place for her, too, and she's been delivered down south.*

Vance: *Hi there. That's good news. How's Maggie doing?*

It's kind of him to ask about her. I remember that about him. Although it seemed he was always good-natured, he wasn't the most outgoing or gregarious of men. He was an observer who always seemed to notice those around him.

There were several times I'd seen him offer a kind word to someone who needed it, or a steady shoulder for them to lean on. I always thought he'd be a good friend to have and would have liked it if we'd been able to develop a friendship, but once he went back to his wife, I thought it best to back off.

Me: *She seems ok mostly, but she's struggling with the enormity of everything, I think.*

Vance: *Understandable. How are you?*

I smile at my phone. It has been forever since someone was concerned about my well-being. Sure, my brother checks on me from time to time, but he's my closest family, so he's obligated and his concern for me is still fairly recent.

Mama passed soon after I was introduced to society at my debutante ball at sixteen. It was almost as if she was waiting to see me to that milestone before she gave in to the leukemia that had plagued her since she was a girl.

I think she finally got tired of fighting against her ravaged immune system and let the last bout of pneumonia take her away. Daddy, who had always been a hard man given to a sullen approach to life and his children became even harder.

By that time, Dale had learned to stay quiet and keep his head down, but he was still my safe harbor when I needed someone to talk to. I was left with my two full-sibling brothers who were just as bad as Daddy. Once Mama was gone, there was no more tenderness in our home and none of the men knew how to relate to a teenage girl, so I had to learn to take care of myself.

Me: *I'm fine, thanks. Trying to stay focused on taking a step at a time and not get ahead of myself.*

Vance: *Speaking of, want to have lunch tomorrow to talk about how we'll proceed?*

A thrill shivers through me at the thought of seeing him again.

Me: *Lunch sounds good. I have a break at 1. Louie's at the corner of Asp and Boyd. I'll meet you there.*

Vance: *Perfect. See you tomorrow. Good night, Serena.*

Me: *Good night, Vance.*

Oh, Lord Jesus, I have a lunch date.

No...it's not a date. It's two colleagues getting together to discuss evidence gathering. Definitely not a date.

With that taken care of and pushed out of my mind, I turn my attention to grading. When I next look up, it's nearing midnight, and it's no wonder my eyes are so tired. I put everything away so it's ready to go for the morning and take my dirty dishes back to the kitchen.

There are signs that Maggie fixed herself something to eat, so that's good. If she didn't eat something soon, I was going to start worrying or maybe sit on her until she had a meal. I have no idea how to mother someone and she's not a child.

Turning off the lights, I take my weary bones to bed, but can't help thinking about what I should wear tomorrow to make a good impression on my not-date.

Chapter 15

Vance

As soon as I walk into the building the next morning, Jack calls me into his office. "What's up, boss?" I ask when I step inside.

"Now that both of the younger girls are safe, I want you to do whatever is needed to help Serena."

I probably shouldn't be surprised after seeing how a family with only tenuous ties to Serena, and no reason to do her a favor, stepped up to help two little girls in trouble. "Are you sure?"

"Yep. Serena's Dale's sister, so she's family. She needs help protecting those girls, and we're going to help her. If I could spend all day, every day, saving kids from predators, I'd do it. For now, we help save two of them."

"Copy. I'm having lunch with her today to talk about how we're going to proceed. Also, I put a call into my buddy who knows the hacker, but we can't turn him loose on the money trail until we know more about the attorney. I'm hoping Serena discovered some more information to go on."

He nods. "Great, just keep us informed and let us know if we're needed. Otherwise, I'll let you handle things with Serena on the investigation side of things."

With a lift of my chin, I turn to go find my trainer for the day. This morning, I'm shadowing Moses on an install. Although I don't know all the ins and outs of the security systems yet, it's starting to come together. I wasn't hired for my technical skills, but Jerald wants all of us cross-trained.

We all have an area of specialization, but there will be times when we'll all need to pitch in to get something done on a project. I have always enjoyed learning new things, and this is the same.

Moses is an excellent teacher. Even though I know he is, he doesn't make it too obvious that he's dumbing things down for me. He's very patient and lets me try things but offers gentle correction if I start to go astray.

We get back to the office just in time for me to head to my lunch date with Serena. I'm excited to see her.

Using the navigation system makes it easy to find the restaurant, but not so much on parking. There seem to be several restaurants and bars in this area, which isn't surprising since it's right across the street from the campus. But until I turn the corner, I'm cursing at the lack of parking.

When I was thinking about meeting her today, I was tempted to pick up some kind of flower to surprise her with. I thought better of it, though. This isn't a date.

Hell, for all I know, she could have a boyfriend. I hope she doesn't, but I haven't had a chance to talk with her about anything personal. We'll be spending a lot of time together, so there's time for all that.

If she is single, I'll be shocked because she's such an accomplished, smart, desirable woman. That she's beautiful with a body that has more curves than a racetrack is just icing. Maybe men up here don't appreciate a woman like her, which is all the better for me.

I ain't no fool. Back when we knew each other in Atlanta, I knew Serena Chilton was a good woman, the kind that's hard to find. To have known her once was a gift, but to have a second chance with her would be a miracle.

When I round the corner, from where I parked my car, I see her standing at the light, waiting to cross the street. She seems to be lost in thought, so I step back into the shade and watch her.

Did she walk here? Probably so, based on the sneakers on her feet. From the ankles up though, she's pure professional in a dress that is simple, but the vibrant purple color makes her stand out.

When I knew her before, she kept her hair longer, but I like this shorter style on her. It makes her look sassy and full of spunk. The light changes and she starts to move. Our eyes meet as she walks toward me, and a gorgeous smile spreads across her face.

She draws near, and I put my hand on her elbow to lean in and kiss her cheek. "Hi there," I say, pulling back and returning her smile.

"Hi yourself," she replies, still smiling.

I guide her to the door, my hand still on her elbow. This lets me stick close to her, and she's not pulling away, so that's a good sign. Inside, the place is more crowded than I expected it to be since it's after the main lunch hour, but being across the street from the university probably keeps a steady flow of customers coming and going.

The host leads us toward a booth, but Serena points to a different booth, away from other customers and asks if we can have it instead. "We need to have a private conversation about a student," she says.

That's true, but it lets the hostess infer any number of scenarios. She agrees and seats us, telling us our server will be by soon. After that, we're mostly left alone, other than placing our orders.

In that time, Serena tells me about the day before, including the visit with Isabel's mother and delivering Sophie to the Nomee's ranch. We're talking in quiet voices when the server arrives and all conversation stops.

Once the server refills our glasses and leaves, Serena hands me a piece of paper. "These are the names of the two lawyers and the two police officers who visited my home. The officers have to be getting paid, and it's my bet that it's by one or both of the attorneys."

"I talked to my buddy, and he gave me a web address, but it's not like a usual URL, it's just a bunch of numbers. When I went there, it was a blank page with a contact form."

"Dark web?" she asks.

"I think so. Because I didn't have the names, I just exited out of the page, figuring I'd go back after we met today and plug in the information."

Her eyes light up. "Or we could go back to my office and do it now."

I flag down our server and tell him that something's come up and ask if our food can be boxed up. We go get my car instead of walking since there's parking near her building and we talk as I drive.

"Once we send the message to the hacker, what do you think we should do next?" I ask.

"I've been thinking about that," she replies. "A lot of the court system's records are online, so I was thinking we start with pulling all the cases for the attorneys in question. Then we go through them to analyze for patterns involving female clients."

"That's what I was thinking, too. How do you want to work on this? I'd say you could come to my house, but considering I'm living with two elderly and nosy women until I find something I want to buy, that might not be the best idea."

She chuckles. "You can come to my house. I have classes for the rest of this week. Next week is primarily final exams. I'll start pulling information and if you don't have plans, you can come over this weekend and we can start organizing it. Once next week is over, I'll be able to focus on this. I want to get the police involved as soon as possible so the girls won't have to worry."

She directs me to a parking lot and points out the building we're aiming for.

"Jack gave me the green light this morning to spend whatever time with you is needed until this is settled."

"He did?" Based on her tone, she's clearly surprised. I was, too.

I relay our conversation from earlier and surprise her again.

"He considers me family?"

"Apparently. From what I saw the other day, they're a very welcoming sort."

"That's what Dale has said. He has invited me to their goings on several times. Maybe I need to start taking him up on the invitations."

"Maybe you should. They seem nice."

I put the car in park, and we gather up our things. When we enter the building, it's exactly what I expected. Although it's newer construction, there's lots of wood paneling and heavy wood furniture, and tables topped with lamps with green glass shades in the open space when you first walk in. However, it's balanced well with enormous windows that allow plenty of natural light inside.

From there, we enter a maze of hallways that twist and turn until we come to a door with frosted glass in a line of doors with frosted glass. The nameplate says Professor Serena Chilton, esq., so we're in the right place. I don't think I'd be able to find my way back here again on my own, though, after all those turns.

Other than a stack of papers on the corner of her desk, it's neat as a pin. Bookcases line the walls and they're full of what appear to be mostly law books, which makes sense.

It's surprising that there's nothing of her here. There are no personal photos or knick knacks. No art on the walls. That part doesn't seem like her at all.

She takes a seat behind her desk and hits a button on her keyboard to wake up her computer. While she gets logged in, I put the bag with our food, surely cold by now, on the corner of the desk and unpack it.

"I'm ready," she says.

Pulling my phone out, I unlock the screen and find the text from my buddy. Carefully, I read the web address to her as I move around her desk so I can see her screen. She gets the same contact form page that I did.

Hesitating, she draws in a deep breath, then looks up at me. "What do I say?"

"Just tell him what we know, but need someone to follow the money and identify payouts."

Serena begins typing, then back spaces to erase it. She pauses, then begins typing again. "I'm not sure if I can do this."

I think I understand. She's spent the better part of her life pursuing a career in law and submitting that form would be skirting the edge of legality. We're not doing anything against the law, but we'd be asking someone else to break the law on our behalf.

"It's okay. I'll take care of it."

The look she gives me is apologetic, but she's clearly relieved.

Pulling up the site on my phone, I type in my details, using a generic online dummy email I set up just for this purpose, then fill out the space provided for information. It takes a while for my big fingers to type out everything on my phone screen, but I get it done, then read it back to her.

With a nod, she says, "I think that's everything."

"All right, then," I reply and stab a finger at the screen to hit submit. The screen goes black except for one sentence.

Thank you for your submission.

Then the site disappears and I'm back on the home screen of my phone. That was weird.

"Now we wait," I say. "In the meantime, I'm starving."

Chapter 16

Serena

I should have known I'd be unable to submit that request. It's too close to skirting the edge of the law by asking someone else to break it. Although I know full well that's how this person makes their money every day, that's not a justification for asking them to perpetuate that way of life on my behalf.

Vance moves to the other side of the desk and slides into a chair, taking his container of food in hand. As we eat, we get reacquainted with each other. I ask him about moving to Oklahoma and have to laugh when he talks about living with his mother and aunt. They sound like they're quite the characters.

"Let's just say I'll be glad to have my own space again. I love those women, but they are way too invested in the goings on in my life."

Thankfully, he doesn't ask about my move to Oklahoma. He partly knows about Mrs. Jackson and what happened in Atlanta, but doesn't push for more information, although I know he's probably curious.

As much as I want to connect with him, I feel the need to be cautious. I think it probably has to do with the fact that just a few days ago, I thought I was in a relationship with Diondre and was completely wrong. With everything going on with the girls, there hasn't been time to examine it, but seeing him on that stage on Sunday stung.

He's the first man I felt a connection to since moving here. We probably would have broken up anyway because I was getting frustrated with how our relationship had devolved into him showing up whenever it was convenient for him.

Now I know why he had pushed us in that direction and he played me for a fool. Instead of being someone special, I'd become his side piece, and that was humiliating.

"Serena?"

My eyes snap up to Vance's. "I'm so sorry, Vance. The last few weeks of school are always taxing, but with the goings on of the last few days..."

I trail off, but instead of being bothered, his eyes go soft.

"It's understandable that you'd be distracted. Do what you need to do. If I hear from the hacker, I'll let you know and if you want to get together between now and the end of next week, call me and I'll come over or we can meet somewhere else."

Tears prickle in my eyes at the grace he's giving me. Why on earth am I so emotional? Probably because I haven't had any time to deal with the emotional fallout of my relationship with Diondre. He might not have given two shits about me, but I actually cared for him, even if things weren't the best between us.

I nod. "Thank you, Vance. I promise I'll call once I have some stuff for us to start sorting through."

With a wink, he says, "You better." He rises and turns toward the door, but pauses before leaving, casting me a look over his shoulder. The corner of his mouth tilts up when he catches me looking at the way his pants fit over his butt. "It's good to see you again, Serena."

Heat crawls up my neck. Good thing my darker skin tone doesn't show my blush. "You, too, Vance."

By the time my last class is done on Friday, I am ready for the weekend break. The days have been long in the classroom, and when I've gone home, I fix myself some supper, then go to my home office and start working on pulling information on cases worked by the two attorneys whose names we have.

They've been busy, so the volume of data is enormous. I wish there was an easier way, but it's the nature of the beast and I cut my teeth in law school on skulking through old case law that wasn't always stored with care.

For one case back then, I had to go to a small county to pull cases and the files I needed were stored in an outdoor shed. As if that weren't bad enough, the shed was infested with squirrels. When I asked about the cases, the court clerk actually told me, "Oh, those are out in the squirrel shed." No joke.

Well, the clerk laughed, but I didn't think it was funny. Not at all.

Maggie and I get home about the same time late Friday afternoon. "I haven't had a chance to go to the grocery, so I'm thinking I'll order a pizza. How does that sound?"

She looks about as tired as I am when she replies, "Perfect. I am staying in and going to bed early tonight so I can get to the library before it gets crowded. That's where I'll be most of the weekend studying for finals."

"Sounds like a good plan," I tell her.

Once I call in our order, I go to my room and change into something more comfortable. Although I didn't think I took that long, the doorbell rings with the pizza delivery. The door to Maggie's room opens behind me and soon after, she opens the fridge to get a pop.

On my way to the door, I snag the money I set out for a tip and open the door with a smile on my face. But it's not the pizza delivery person. It's the appetite-killing ex-philanderer, Diondre.

My lip curls in distaste. "What are you doing here? Shouldn't you be at home with your wife?"

"Please, Serena, can we talk?"

"No," I say and push the door to close it, but he puts a hand up and forces it open.

"I just want to talk, baby."

"No, I said, and I am not your baby. Diondre, leave. I'm not here alone."

Of course, he uses that statement to muster up righteous indignation, his mind immediately assuming I have a man here. Either way, it's none of his business.

"What do you mean, you're not alone? You've already moved on to a new man?" he huffs as he walks toward the noise he hears from the kitchen created by Maggie taking down dishes from the cabinet and setting them on the counter.

He stops in the doorway. "Who are you?"

Maggie's looking at him with eyes as big as saucers and she's frozen in place.

"That's none of your business," I supply. "Now please leave Diondre. We have nothing to talk about."

Spinning, he growls at me. "Yes, we do."

I put my hand on his arm and pull him back to the front door. When we reach the foyer, I lower my voice and snarl at him.

"You are married and I am no one's side piece. For months, you lied to and played me for a fool, which was humiliating while I watched you up on that stage with the daughter you refused to even talk to me about. Go home to your wife because I'll never see you or sleep with you again."

"Baby..." he croons.

"Never, Diondre. Now leave before I call the police."

"Who's that girl?"

"None. Of. Your. Business."

The doorbell rings so I put my hand on his wrist and pull him to the front door. When it opens, I push him out, him practically trampling the young man holding our pizza box. Taking the box from the boy, I hand him the money.

"Thank you," I say to the driver, then close the door firmly, turning the deadbolt.

Chapter closed. It's time to move on.

Chapter 17

Magdalena

When Serena comes back into the kitchen, I can tell she's upset. That man seemed as if he might be her boyfriend or maybe ex-boyfriend and as much as I want to ask if she's all right, I feel as if I should stay out of it.

"Sorry about that," she says, as she puts the pizza box on the counter, then turns to take her bottle of wine out of the refrigerator. She drinks, but only seems to have one glass of wine when she does.

When I first saw her pour a glass, I was worried. My dad was a drinker and once he started, there was no stopping until the bottle was empty. Soon, drinking wasn't enough, and he turned to harder vices.

That's one reason I'm willing to do whatever it takes to make something of myself. I refuse to perpetuate my family's cycle of poverty and addiction. To that end, I have never taken a drink or done any drugs, not even smoking a blunt. Just one step across the line could be enough to drag me down.

"It's okay," I say, figuring she opened the door, so I'll ask. "Is he your boyfriend?"

"Was," she replies, putting two pieces of pizza onto a plate.

"I'm sorry."

"Thank you, but don't worry about him. He's a dog and I'm better off without him."

All right then.

Instead of going to her office like she usually does, she slides onto one of the stools at the kitchen island. Since I've been here, I've mostly tried to stay out of her way because I don't want to do anything that might make her think twice about letting me stay.

I'm incredibly grateful to her for what she's done and want to be as minimal a burden as possible. Who am I kidding? She's taken on a whole lot of trouble that isn't hers to deal with.

Most people would have shut the door in our faces.

"How are you feeling about your final exams?" she asks.

"Good mostly, I think, but I never really feel like I've prepared enough."

She nods her head and takes a sip of her wine.

"I remember how that felt, but you'll do fine. Vance sent a message to someone yesterday to see if they can trace payoffs to the two officers who were here. While we're waiting for that information and for school to be finished, I'm pulling data on cases that we'll start going through. If we can find a pattern, we can hand it over to a couple of officers I know who are good guys."

I don't want to be skeptical. A good cop is not someone I've had any experience with, so I make an ambiguous noise like my mom used to when my dad would say something she might not actually agree with.

"So, you're going to be working with Vance on this?" I ask.

"Yes. I'm mostly pulling the information, but he's going to help me go through it."

"He seems nice. Did you know him before Monday?"

She hesitates for a moment. "I did. We met when I still lived in Atlanta."

"I think he likes you."

Her hand holding the wine glass pauses halfway to her mouth. "What makes you say that?"

I shrug as I rinse my plate before putting it into the dishwasher. "Just the way he looks at you."

It's her turn to make a non-committal noise, and it makes my lips tick up on one side. I toss my empty pop bottle into the recycling bin and when I start putting the leftover pizza away, she tells me she'll take care of it.

"Okay, thanks. Well, I'm gonna go study. Just holler if you need me."

When I go to the kitchen for a glass of water a few hours later, the light is shining under the door of her office. She must still be in there working. Maybe she and Mr. Vance will get together. She's too young to spend all her time working.

The next morning, Serena is up and out of the house before I roll out of bed. On the kitchen island, she has left a key with a sticky note giving me the alarm code.

I meant to give this to you the other day. We're likely going to be coming and going at different times this weekend, so please just remember to set the alarm if you leave or if you're home alone.

Tears prickle in my eyes. The fact that she trusts me is incredible. Other than being one of her students, she doesn't really know me, but here she is giving me a key to her home.

She's already done so much for me and my family. Once this is all over, I'm going to have to find some way to say thank you because words simply won't be enough.

Hours later, my eyes are tired, and my stomach is growling. I gather up my things to go outside into the sunny day to eat the sandwich I brought. As soon as I push through the doors of the law library, I turn my face to the sun. It feels good after being in the chilly building.

While I eat, I people watch. There isn't a lot of foot traffic this morning. Maybe all the students are closed away doing their own cram sessions for finals.

There are the usual walkers and bikers wending their way through campus, but most of them seem to be doing it for enjoyment or exercise rather than a need to get somewhere. Maybe I should start exercising more.

What I need to do is get another job, but I can't do that, at least not right now. I'll be through with finals on Thursday and then I'll have to figure out what to do with the girls. I could go down to the ranch with them.

Maybe I could get a job down there for the summer or for however long it takes for Serena and Vance to dig up the dirt they need. Surely, with all the people who are connected with Roni and Takoda, someone would need a helping hand in exchange for a modest hourly rate.

Because there are few people to watch, the two police officers rounding the corner from the west parking lot catch my eye. It's normal to see campus police roaming around at all hours of the day and night, but the uniforms of these officers aren't the same as campus police.

They go into the law center and suddenly, I feel the urge to go study somewhere else.

Chapter 18

Vance

I agreed to meet Serena at her office this morning. She said she had pulled a lot of information and we could use a conference room if we wanted to print it and spread out. We've spent hours filtering through cases and we're starting to see some patterns.

Based on the shoddy job they've done in covering their tracks, I'm surprised no one has caught on before. However, when you have the money and muscle to bully people into silence, it is difficult for someone to step up and say something.

I text her when I arrive at the building and wait for her in the large room with all the tables and green lamps. It will probably take me a few times of navigating the hallways to be able to find her office on my own.

There are only a few people in the room, and my presence gets me some curious looks. Most of them have books, laptops, and notepads open around them, so I assume they're students. Once they give me a once over, they go back to studying or whatever it is they're doing.

As soon as she enters the room, I know it. She draws my gaze like she's the sun and I've been too long in the dark. I couldn't stop the smile that spreads across my face if I wanted to.

She smiles back, if a little shyly. As I move to meet her halfway, I take her in. Today, she's dressed more casually than she was the last time we saw each other, but she's still put together and looking professorial.

I want to get her into a position to relax completely and let her hair down, so to speak. Thinking about getting her into positions waylays my train of thought and I have to drag it back onto safer ground before I take her back to her office and make out with her.

"Hi," I say when she draws close.

"Hi," she says back, then cocks her head in the direction from which she came. "Are you ready to get to work?"

"Absolutely."

She leads me through the maze of hallways and I try to track our path better than I did last time. Inside, she gathers up a stack of papers and hands them to me, then she picks up another stack and urges me back toward the door.

"You've been busy," I say, as we start spreading out the papers.

"You'd think, but this is just a quick and dirty data dump. I intended to do more digging on each case, but it was taking too long and between school and the girls, I'm too distracted to trust myself to filter through it alone."

"That's why you've got me," I tell her with a grin. "When you're ready to turn your quick and dirty into something substantial, I'm your man."

Yeah, I totally meant to slide a double entendre in there. In response, she just chuckles and gives a non-committal, "Mmm hmm." But I can see the corner of her mouth tucked up with mirth, so my arrow hit its mark.

She's had a lot of heavy stuff to deal with over the past couple of weeks and all in the name of three girls who had no one else to help them. I admire her for that because a lot of people would have walked away.

Once the younger girls were safe, she could have stopped it there, but instead, Maggie was welcomed into her home simply because Serena sees potential in the girl. As for me, I see potential in Serena. She was a beautiful and amazing woman when we knew each other in Atlanta, and she's even more so now.

We talk over our approach and start sorting through the stacks of paper. Hours later, we've made a dent in the material, but that's all, just a dent. "I don't know about you," Serena says, "but I am ready for a break. Want to grab something for lunch?"

"That sounds like an excellent plan."

Serena locks the conference room and slides a marker on the outside from *Available* to *In Use*. Although there doesn't seem to be a lot of traffic in this area of the building from professors, it's probably better to hedge our bets.

As we make our way toward the exit, neither of us speaks. It seems we're both trying to let our brains decompress from staring at endless pages of black and white. The moment she stiffens, I sense it.

"What's wrong?"

With a slight incline of her head, she directs my attention to the front of the large room near the front of the building. Two police officers are making their way through the room from student to student. They don't speak to them, but make a point to get a good look at each one.

"Those are the officers who came to my door looking for a missing child," she breathes.

I'm about to ask her if she wants to go say hello, when her back goes ramrod straight and she strides purposefully across the room. The men are almost like that vintage television pair Laurel and Hardy.

One is large and beefy, with a gut that says he probably wouldn't be able to chase a suspect down if he tried. He must be the one she said was the bad cop at their first meeting.

She walks toward the other officer. He's smaller in stature and has a weasel-like appearance with his sparse dark hair slicked back, beady, almost black eyes set too close together, narrow face and prominent nose.

"Officer Draper," she says when she draws near, "may I ask what you're doing here?"

The man's head snaps up in startlement, but he recovers quickly. "I'm doing my job, ma'am."

Her head tilts to the side. "What job does an Oklahoma City police officer have to do in Norman?"

"We're still looking for that missing child, ma'am."

"Hmm," she says. "I still haven't seen any kind of Amber alert and I even searched the local news stations and couldn't find a single thing about a missing child. The individuals here are students and, therefore, all over eighteen. So I ask again, what are you doing here?"

The man's face darkens, so I step up next to Serena. "It's customary for local law enforcement to check in with campus security. Perhaps we should just call them and make sure they're aware of the officer's presence so far outside their jurisdiction."

He looks me up and down. As he does, his partner makes his way over, puffing up his chest and considerable gut, posturing. Part of me wants to laugh. As if this out of shape fathead would stand a chance.

"Is there a problem?" Fathead asks.

"Yes," Serena answers. "You're harassing students in the name of some non-existent missing child, and doing so for the second time well outside the bounds of your authority. I've half a mind to contact your supervisors and let them know what you've been up to."

Fear flickers through the weasel's eyes. Fathead seems too stupid to be afraid. If I were in his shoes, I would be, but they don't know Serena like I do.

"Listen here," Fathead starts.

"Choose your words carefully," I interrupt him to say.

"Who the fuck are you?" Weasel asks.

I put an index finger to the middle of my chest. "Former homicide detective."

Weasel's lip curls in a snarl. "So the failed judge has a failed cop for a boyfriend. That figures."

I don't react, but Weasel doesn't miss Serena's flinch and his snarl morphs into a shark's smile. He cocks his elbow and lightly smacks his buddy's chest with the back of his hand. "Come on, Pierce. Let's be on our way."

His attention turns back to Serena. "It would probably be a good idea if, the next time you see us, you go the other direction."

Serena's eyes just narrow in response as they turn and head toward the exit. We follow because that's where we were going anyway, but I'm curious to see if they are in a cruiser or an unmarked vehicle.

If they really are doing their own thing and aren't under orders, it would be bad enough that they're doing it in uniform, even worse if they're using a city-owned squad car. The two men are talking, oblivious to our being behind them, but we're not close enough to hear what they're saying.

That's too bad because I'd love to know what they're talking about. Their dislike of Serena is clear, and it makes me afraid that they'll do something to harm her. We need to sort this out and do it quickly.

Chapter 19

Serena

Those two knuckleheads have done gone and pissed me off. How dare he speak to us that way? Those idiots have no idea who they're fucking with, but they gon' learn, as my brother would say.

I watch the backs of the two officers, and I use that term only loosely, not even caring if they notice us behind them. If they're aware, they aren't showing it. The cruiser they are driving comes into view and on a whim, I quickly pull out my phone to take a photo of them getting inside.

As we walk past their car, I resist the urge to raise my middle finger to the two assholes. However, it's just as much of a fuck you to them when I send the photos to my friends, Cait and Alicia, to pass along to their significant others.

The photo along with the officer's names are included, but I don't get into too many details because I don't want the bad actors to know to what depths we're onto them. Keeping it simple, I ask why two OKCPD officers would be in Norman searching for an unidentified missing child.

"So, where are we going?" Vance asks when I drop my phone back in my bag.

"Let's get away from campus and go downtown."

I take him to a deli I like on the downtown strip. Once we're seated with our orders, he asks. "Who did you send the picture to?"

"Some friends. Their partners are on the police force in Oklahoma City. One in homicide and the other in gangs. They're good guys."

"You have an amazing network of connections up here."

"That is a recent development. For years, I lived quite solitary. After what happened in Atlanta, I became positively hermit-like. Then Dale moved up here and suddenly, I had family again."

I tell him about the invitation I received from the Belladonna Society that brought me a new circle of friends.

"It has taken me some time to open up and get more involved, but I'm glad I have. Demi, Cait, Gabriella, and Alicia have become dear to me."

"That's good Serena. It sounds like you've found a new home."

Have I? Since Mama died, I've felt unmoored, a girl without a home. Papa only cared for his sons and once he died, my greedy brothers made it their mission to be rid of both Dale and me once the will was executed.

They fired Dale from our father's construction company and sent him packing with his small inheritance, despite having tried to take that from him, too. They at least didn't try to take the money my father left me as long as I left them alone, so I enrolled in college, then law school, then went to work.

"I think this could be home, but it has been a long time since any place has felt that way."

He cocks his head at my statement as if processing it.

"Why do you think that is?" he asks.

I know why it is, but I don't want to tell him, but when he puts a hand over mine, I can't stop myself.

"Ever since Atlanta, I've guarded myself from connecting with people. The men I've dated, I've kept at arm's length until recently and my last relationship was a lie. Until the Society, I haven't made any friends and even with them, I was slow to warm."

"I think you're more connected than you believe you are. If you weren't, would you have been willing to take such a risk for Maggie and her cousins?"

His ability to look on the positive side of things is something I remember about him. I give him a small smile. "Perhaps you're right. So how are things with the new job?"

I'm ready to get the spotlight off myself and onto lighter topics. That meeting with the officers has thrown me off kilter for some reason, and I don't enjoy feeling this way.

"This old dog is learning some new tricks, that's for sure, and it's certainly been electrifying."

"What?" I ask, half laughing, but I'm not so sure he's teasing.

"Yeah, my first time out with Moses, the tech genius, I just watched what he did. The next time, he let me try it on my own because I was feeling all cocky and told him I had it. Little did I know, I skipped one key component–I forgot to flip the breaker."

"Oh, no!" I exclaim, sure I know what's coming.

"That's right. I grabbed that wire, and it lit up my life like nothing I've felt before. Thankfully, Moses knocked me loose before it killed me. But for the rest of the day, the asshole kept poking me in the side and going bzzt! Later that day, I got him back when he had to get on the mats with me for hand-to-hand training."

I can't help it; laughter bubbles out of me. He keeps making me laugh with stories from learning his new job. It feels good to laugh like that, especially since I can't remember the last time I did.

As we're driving back to my building, Vance says, "You know he was full of shit, don't you?"

"Who?"

"The weasel cop. He was just baiting you and had no idea what he was talking about with that comment he made."

"Oh, I believe that about you being a failed cop, but he was right on the nose when he said I was a failed judge. Mrs. Jackson was just the straw that broke the camel's back, but I had been faltering for some time."

There it is. An admission of the biggest shortcoming of my life. I'd worked so hard to achieve my goal of becoming a judge only to get there and realize it wasn't what I wanted after all. How messed up is that?

I failed spectacularly, then retreated into a cave like a bear entering hibernation, cutting myself off physically, emotionally, and mentally from everything and everyone. That has gotten me exactly nowhere and, frankly, I'm sick of my own shit and ready for change.

Chapter 20

Vance

S erena's comments were enlightening. They struck home with me in a lot of ways. To know that she cut herself off after what happened in Atlanta makes me hurt for her, but I can relate.

At the time it happened, I wondered if anyone had been there for her. If she'd had anyone to help her through such a horrific thing happening right in front of her. Now I know. She didn't. She was all alone in the tragedy and slogged through the impact as best she could.

It was accomplished by moving to a new location and not allowing herself to get close to anyone. I chose to go back to my wife for the sake of my kids and it was the right decision to make, but I was also alone in a lot of ways and in a holding pattern until the kids were grown.

It's almost as if we were both waiting for the pieces to come together to start living life again. Maybe we're each other's missing piece and the universe was just holding onto us until it was the right time to throw us onto the board.

When the mood got so somber, I had to do something to take that sadness out of her eyes. I probably should have stopped when I had her laughing, but no, I had to go and drag the mood back down. Something inside me had to say it, though, because I saw how much that asshole's comment stung her.

There have been glimpses of the fiery woman I used to know, like today, with that cop, until he fired off a particularly well-aimed barb. I saw her when she transformed into a woman of steel intent on protecting those girls no matter what. She's still in there and I'm excited to see her come to life again.

Serena opens the conference room and lets out a sigh at the stacks of paper. "I can't believe I used to love this kind of thing. That was a long time ago, though."

"In cop land, this is just another day. I have faith that we'll get there."

"I know, but I want it to all come together quickly, so no more girls get hurt."

"We could always go with Jack's method," I say, only half teasing.

She chuckles. "Tempting."

But she just picks up another stack of paper and goes to sit on the far side of the conference table, grabbing her notepad on the way. I sit in front of the stack I'd been going through before we left for lunch.

A few hours later, I ask, "Have you noticed how almost all his clients are women?"

"Yes. I've come across a few men, but only a few. Those few are getting listed on the side to compare surnames. Although there's nothing that says the men will follow the same pattern as Isabel's parents."

"It's worth checking out, though."

She nods and hums in response while she turns over another piece of paper. Another hour goes by in silence, both of us making our way through the papers when my stomach decides to tell me it's time for supper.

"Sorry," I say, sheepishly.

"Oh, thank you Jesus," she says with a laugh. "I was about to go cross-eyed but didn't want to quit if you weren't ready to."

I start stacking pages. "Here, let's get this into some sort of order and go find some supper."

She's quiet while we organize our stacks, not responding to my comment. I'm just about to say something when she says, "I have some chicken marinating that I was going to grill for supper if you'd like to come to the house. Maggie and I have been passing each other at the beginning and end of each day, so I'm hoping she's home so we can sit down together."

"Thank you. I'd like that, Serena. I enjoy spending time with you."

She pauses briefly, but doesn't reply. It makes me wonder what she's thinking. Unfortunately, I've never been able to read minds, and she doesn't appear to be inclined to share, so I'll just have to bide my time.

Thinking of how she's cut herself off, she's going to be a tough nut to crack, but that's fine. The best things in life are hard won and if I can accomplish nothing more than setting a match to the fuse that will return the light to her eyes she used to have, it will be worth the effort. Of course, I'm hoping for a lot more.

I follow her to her house, then follow her inside. When we step into the kitchen, Maggie is standing there with the refrigerator door open. She looks up, "Oh, hi! Hello again, Mr. Douglas."

"Please call me Vance. Calling me Mr. Douglas makes me feel old. Hello back, Maggie. How are your studies going?"

She smiles. "They're going well. I got a lot of cramming done at the law library today. Speaking of which, while I was eating a sandwich on a bench outside, I saw those same two cops again. As soon as I saw them, I came home."

"We saw them, too," I tell her. "Serena stepped right up and confronted them. They tucked tail and left."

Maggie looks at Serena. "Do you think they were looking for me?"

"Yes, I honestly think they were," Serena answers, her voice soft. "I sent pictures of them to the friends I told you about that work for the Oklahoma City police department, so perhaps they'll get a reprimand and will be forced to stay in their jurisdiction from now on."

"We can hope," I add. However, I doubt it.

Those guys have crossed too many lines to be afraid of a simple reprimand. Isabel had said that she went to the police and a few days later, the officer she spoke with showed up at the house where she was being kept and was allowed to use her.

I wonder if it was one of those two. My money is on the weasel. He looks the type that would get off on hurting little girls. Or hell, it could be both of them which makes me inclined to join Jack and go pervert hunting.

Chapter 21

Isabel

These first few days at the Nomee's house have been awkward and a little weird. They've done everything they could to help me settle in and feel welcome, but I didn't know how to act.

At my house, I pretty much just stayed quiet and out of the way, so I tried to do that here, too. They were all loud and outgoing, constantly cracking jokes and playfully teasing each other. All of them except the dad, Takoda.

He was mostly quiet, observant, taking it all in. Taking me in. It wasn't in a pervy way, but it was as if he was seeing underneath my skin. Seeing all the things I hid there, both the treasures and the scars.

There are a lot of scars and I don't like the feeling that he can see them. So far, he hasn't told me to get out, so that's good. I'm not sure why, because anyone who knew the things I'd done, well, they wouldn't want me around their happy, healthy kids. Their normal kids.

When Sophie came, everything was better. She is all sunshine and rainbows, with an outgoing personality like Emme. With her to draw the attention, I can fade back into the shadows, trying not to do anything that would make them want to tell me to leave.

They were going to put Sophie and me in a room together, but Emme wouldn't hear of it. Instead, she asked her parents if there was a way to put three beds into her room so all of us older girls could stay together.

That's all it took. She asked and the next day, they made it happen. They took one of the twin sized beds from the room they were going to put Sophie and me into and squeezed it into Emme's room. She said she'd sleep on the smaller bed so my sister and me could sleep in the bigger one.

I never knew that parents would act that way and just give their kids something they wanted without giving a million reasons why it couldn't be done.

"Are you guys going to stay here forever?" Emme whispers into the dark as we're trying to fall asleep.

"I don't know," I reply honestly. "We have a mom."

Sure, it's nice here with three meals a day and comfortable beds instead of a pancake of a mattress on the floor. There are no men coming and going paying money to go to mom's room for sex. Lately, more of that money goes into her veins than into the grocery store. But mostly, there's no Mr. King.

"Yeah, but she gave us to Maggie," Sophie says beside me.

"That's just something temporary."

"I hope we get to stay because I like it here."

I like it, too, but I'd never say it out loud. That would be too much like hope and hoping too much only gets you hurt.

"Go to sleep, Soph," I grumble as I turn onto my side, giving her my back.

Today, they're taking us shopping for clothes and shoes and boots.

We've been helping Emme with chores on the ranch and Miss Roni says we need boots because our sneakers will get ruined. She also says we need more than two pairs of pants and shirts each.

I think they must be from Mars or something because normal people don't do nice things like this. Well, except for Christmas. Our names are usually on an angel tree somewhere and we'll get presents. Mom would let us keep the clothes, but toys and other stuff were always sold to support her habit.

Instead of going to a thrift store, like I expected, that's where mom always shopped for us, we pull up to a regular store. We try on about a million pairs of boots and jeans and shirts.

Emme hasn't asked for anything the whole time we've been in the store, but as she's looking through shirts, she sees one she likes and holds it up. "Izzy," that's what she's taken to calling me, "this is cute, huh?"

I look over to see her holding up a purple, white and black plaid western shirt. At least it's not pink. "Yeah."

"Mom," she calls out to Miss Roni, "can the three of us get these shirts? We'd be matching. How cute would that be?"

Her mom doesn't even look up. "Only if they have one small enough for your sister, too. You'll need to find a shirt for your brother, as well. Heaven forbid one of you gets something and the others don't."

Her words make it seem like she's bothered, but her tone sounds like she's half laughing. Like I said, Mars. It has to be something like that.

Bags are piled into the back of an SUV with the ranch's logo on the door and I'm happy at the thought of going back to the room. Maybe I'll take Daisy and go for a walk. She seems to enjoy wandering through the woods with me.

I've never been outside of Oklahoma City and didn't think I'd like the country, but I was surprised to find I do. With Daisy there to keep me safe, I like it because it's quiet. No one wants anything from me and there's nothing and no one to be afraid of. I haven't had that feeling very often in my life.

Unfortunately, there's no walk in the woods in my near future because we're not done. Next we go to Wal-mart for socks and panties and Miss Roni makes me get a bra. Gag. But she's been nice, so I let her talk me into getting one.

Mom always said we were part of the itty bitty tittie committee and didn't need to wear one. Hers weren't that itty bitty if you ask me, but I think she just didn't like wearing a bra. I don't think I'm going to like it either.

Just when I think we're going to be done again, we go over to the grocery section. Miss Roni is on the phone with someone and when she hangs up, we start piling food into the basket. A lot of it is what she says is junk food, but to us it's just normal food we had every day because it was cheap, so the day's looking up.

After all that shopping, we take pizza home for lunch. I'm so tired I go upstairs for a nap after we eat. Ever since I woke up in the hospital, it's like I can't ever get enough rest. Maybe I'm catching up from the years of being too afraid to sleep.

Chapter 22

Magdalena

Serena, Vance, and I grill chicken and some corn, and I chop up some stuff for a salad. Although at first she only had the makings for sandwiches, since Izzy and I arrived, she's kept the fridge stocked. Now, there's always healthy food here and I really like that.

Always having food in the refrigerator is great because I'm down to my last few dollars saved from when I was working. And it seemed that the professor was just waiting for someone to cook for.

I couldn't eat out even if I wanted to, but I need to save those dollars to put in the gas tank to get me down to the ranch at the end of the week to get the girls. Where we go after that, I don't know. Getting a job will be the first order of business, though. We can't survive on air.

We're halfway through supper when all our phones go off at the same time. I look between them and they're looking at each other and me, just like I am. A laugh bubbles out of me.

"That's creepy," I say as I pull out my phone.

It's from an unknown number, but the message is anything but ominous. I read the message out lout.

Sorry for the late notice. We do a family lunch every Sunday and thought y'all might like to come.

The message gives us details about location and time and is signed by Roni. Vance is looking at his phone and confirms he received the same message. "What do you say, ladies? Want to go to a bar-b-que tomorrow?"

"Hmm," Serena humphs. "You know they don't have real bar-b-que here."

I laugh. "What does that mean?"

"In Georgia, the sauce is mustard based instead of tomato based like it is here. Which is better is a hotly debated topic," Vance explains with a grin. "Personally, I like both, so it makes no never mind to me as long as what you're putting it on tastes good."

He rises and takes his plate to the sink, rinsing it and putting it in the dishwasher. Serena and I get up and do the same, then start to put away the leftovers. Once everything is dealt with and the kitchen clean, I leave them alone.

The murmur of their voices follows me down the hallway, but I can't make out what they're saying. He likes her; that's plain to see. Every look, every move he makes, he's attuned to and focused on her.

I hope she realizes it. They both seem to be wonderful people and he's so much better than that other guy that came to the house. Her ex. It only took me ten seconds to see him for the asshole he is.

I just wonder why she didn't. Maybe she was lonely. Loneliness can make people do strange things.

I'm surrounded by books when a quiet knock sounds on the door. There's no way I'll be able to get up without losing my place, so I call out, "Come in."

Serena opens the door and steps in. She places an envelope on the dresser. "I know you said you had to leave your job because of taking Isabel from the hospital. This should tide you over for a little while until you're finished with finals and decide what you want to do after."

I stare at the envelope. Was she reading my mind earlier? "Thank you, Serena. I'll pay you back, I promise."

She waves a hand in the air and, as she's closing the door, says, "Nonsense. Good night Maggie."

When I got the invitation to come to lunch today, I didn't expect there to be so many people. Glad I drove my own car, thanks to Serena's gift of more money than I used to make in a month, I'm tempted to turn around and go back home. Only my extreme desire to see the girls makes me pull in and park.

We're not at the ranch, but we're not far away from it. I think it's just around the corner. This house has lots of open space around it and enormous garden areas set back a short distance from the road. With a deep breath, I get out, steeling myself for the sea of strangers.

Voices and music carry from the back of the house, so I walk around instead of going to the front door. I see Serena's car, so I know I'm in the right place. As soon as I round the corner, a high-pitched squeal breaks the air and, in a flash, I'm almost tackled by Sophie.

"Prima! I'm so happy to see you. Come on," she says, taking me by the hand and dragging me behind, "you have to meet everyone."

She's smiling and laughing. I can't remember the last time I saw her do that. With an attempt to be inconspicuous, I dash my fingers at the tears I can't keep from falling.

Now that I'm looking around, I recognize some faces from the first night we brought Isabel here. The names don't come so easily, but at least I'm not surrounded by complete strangers.

"Hi," Roni says and pulls me into a hug. She catches me off guard, but it's not weird at all, so I hug her back. "We're so glad you came. Some folks you know, but pretty much everyone is family."

"This is your family?" I ask, looking around at the crowd.

"By blood or by choice, yes." She points out her three sisters to me. I recognize the one that's married to Serena's brother and see Serena and Vance nearby talking with them. There are people and children everywhere, but I don't see Isabel.

"She's in the house with my cousin's wife. I think the crowd was a little overwhelming for her," Roni says when she sees me looking around.

I can imagine it was. She points me toward the back door, and I thank her before turning that way. As I step inside, the cool air from the air conditioner washes over me, along with the scent of fresh-baked bread and some kind of baked fruit. "Hi there," I say to Isabel.

She's sitting at a small kitchen table with a piece of the bread I smell, slathered with butter. A short, curvy woman with auburn hair and skin tanned by the sun smiles up at me from where she's arranging pies on a rack to cool.

Coming around the kitchen island, she extends a hand to me. "Hi there. You must be Magdalena. I'm Miriam. Isabel was just keeping me company while I pulled the pies out of the oven."

She looks around as if checking to ensure everything is as it should be, then unties her apron, taking it off and hanging it on a hook on the wall. "How about we go outside and see what everyone is up to? You can bring your bread if you like, Isabel. The food should be done soon."

As soon as we step outside, Emme calls out. "There you are!" She takes Isabel by the hand and drags her away, but Isabel doesn't seem too bothered by it. It's only now that I realize they're wearing matching shirts.

When it's time to eat, I find the table the girls are sitting at with Emme, her little sister Tamaya, and a boy with long black hair woven into a braid down his back. All four of the girls have matching shirts and it's one of the cutest things I've ever seen, so I snap a photo with my phone.

The boy, Solomon, is Miriam's son. As soon as I sit at the picnic table with them, he dramatically brushes his hand over his forehead and says, "Whew! I thought I was the only one who didn't get the text about the dress code."

He keeps us entertained throughout lunch, cracking jokes and acting silly. The instant they're finished eating, all the kids but Isabel take off to go play. Emme tries to cajole her into coming with them, but Isabel says she wants to visit with me.

"How are you liking it here?" I ask her.

She shrugs.

"I need your words, Isabel. School will be finished in a week, and I need you to tell me how you're feeling here."

She looks down at her hands but finally says, "Safe. They're nice, but weird. I can sleep at night here and there's always food."

Concern tickles up my spine. "How are they weird?"

She shrugs again. "Like these shirts. Emme asked, and Miss Roni just bought them for us. Emme wanted to be in the same room with my hermana and me, so they crammed another bed into Emme's room. I mean, they don't give her everything she wants, but..."

My smile is wan. Of course, parents taking care of their children would be a foreign concept to her. "I understand."

A hand squeezes my shoulder, making me jump. "I apologize," Serena says. "I thought you heard me. We're going to go inside to talk about what's happened since we brought Sophie here and I thought you'd like to come."

I maneuver my way out of the picnic table and smooth down my shorts. When Isabel stands, too, I'm surprised. "I'm coming, too," she says with a hitch of her chin.

Much as I hate it, she's not a little girl anymore and deserves to hear what's happening and what's being done on her behalf. I nod and take her hand in mine as we go toward the house.

Chapter 23

Serena

For a moment, I question Maggie's decision to allow Isabel to come inside with the adults. My instinct was to shield and protect her, but she has already faced far worse than what we'd be talking about.

I tilted my head toward the house and said, "Let's go, ladies."

Isabel puts herself between us and puts her free hand in mine. I give her a reassuring squeeze and smile down over at her when she looks at me. Her return smile is barely a curve of the corners of her lips, but it's there.

Being at the ranch has been good for her. That was an almost smile and her eyes have lost the haunted look they had only a week ago. It's amazing what a feeling of safety and security can do to create a space for healing to begin.

Inside the house, the same people who were there when we delivered Isabel to the Nomee's house are perched on sofas and chairs and the fireplace hearth except for two new faces. I've met them, but they'll be new to Vance, Maggie, and Isabel.

Vance is sitting on a sofa alone, so I go sit next to him with Isabel and Maggie sliding in beside me. With four of us, we're quite snug and I'm pressed up against Vance's side. He raises his arm and puts it across the back of the couch to give me a little more room. The scent of his cologne teases me, making me want to lean in closer to get a better whiff.

"Serena," Jack says from his seat in an armchair with his girl-friend on his lap, "why don't you update us on what's happened since Monday?"

I look up to see my brother's eyes scrutinizing me, a hint of mirth crinkling the corners of his eyes. Heat climbs up my neck, and I shift a fraction of an inch away from Vance.

"Sure," I reply. "However, while I know Heather and Sean, not everyone does. Isabel, Maggie, and Vance, the newcomers to the group perched on the hearth, are Heather Priddy, Roni's sister, and her partner Sean Martelle. Heather worked as a coun-ty sheriff's deputy for many years and is now with tribal law enforcement, and Sean was an OSBI agent for several years who now shapes the minds of students and arms of pitchers at the local university."

With the introductions made, in concise statements, I relay visiting Magdalena's aunt and convincing her to let us remove Sophie from the home and getting signatures on the temporary custody documents.

When I talk about the police officers showing up on campus yesterday, I feel Isabel tense next to me. Purely on instinct, I put my arm around her and pull her close. Instead of pulling away, she snuggles in closer to me and it makes my heart squeeze.

Seeing that I'm focused on Isabel, Vance smoothly takes up the narrative. "We went through a lot of cases yesterday and are starting to identify some patterns and possible former victims. Almost his entire caseload is women. I also reached out to the contact we discussed, but haven't had a response yet."

"Maggie, how are you doing?" Roni asks.

"I'm okay. Staying with Serena has been wonderful. Thankfully, I was outside eating lunch when the cops showed up on campus yesterday. I saw them and left to go home before they saw me, which is lucky because I think I was the target of their search."

"Do you think you'll want to come here when you're finished with your exams?"

Maggie hesitates.

"We have plenty of room, and it would appear that since they can't get to the girls that they might be trying to snare you to use you as leverage to get them back."

"I'm afraid of that, too," Maggie says, sounding very young.

"What is your hesitancy?" Roni's husband, Takoda, asks. He's usually the quiet observer and only rarely interjects his voice into the conversation.

I look over at Maggie and give her a reassuring nod.

She sighs and looks at her hands in her lap as she speaks. "You all have been so kind and given so much already. I just...Well, I don't know how I would ever be able to repay you."

Takoda waves a hand as Roni gasps, then he levels his gaze at Maggie. "Little sister, this gift has no strings or expectations. We have the means to keep you safe and are willing to do so."

Then Roni grins, "Although, after talking to Serena and learning how smart you are, I fully intend to put you to work. Paid, of course. Also, if you'll commit to staying the summer, in addition to a guaranteed job, we have a friend who is a child therapist would be willing to come to the ranch once a week to visit with the girls. I was given a great blessing a few years ago and want nothing more than to pay that forward with you and your cousins."

"Thank you. However, it's not my decision to make alone. Would it be okay if I had a moment to talk with Isabel and Sophie? Serena, I'd like for you to be there, too, and your brother Dale and Mister Vance."

"That is more than reasonable," Takoda says. "Dale, why don't you take them to the resting room? We'll go outside to bring Sophie in."

Dale stands and gives his wife, Felicia, a kiss on the cheek and everyone else rises to go back outside. Isabel squeezes my hand and I look down at her. "What's a resting room? Is it like the bathroom?"

"That, petit," my brother says, "is a place where folks can go to rest for a minute when they feel overwhelmed."

He raises his pant leg and shows her his prosthetic, then drops it and leads us down the hall. "I was hurt in the military and sometimes this big old group of people can get to be too noisy, so I go take a break. My wife and a few others in our family need to take breaks, too, so this is the place for it."

He flips on the light to reveal a room that could be used as a guest room, but also has a cushioned bench at the end of the bed, and a couple of comfortable chairs. Dale sits on the bench and Isabel leads me to perch on the bed, not letting go of my hand.

Vance and Maggie take the chairs. Several minutes later, a sweaty Sophie is let into the room by Takoda and bounces over to squeeze in next to Maggie. "Hey squirt!" she says, putting her arms around the girl. "How are you liking it here?"

Sophie squirms out of Maggie's embrace with an uttered, "Too hot." Once she's sitting on the floor, she answers, "I like it. They've bought us stuff, and it's fun with the other kids. Plus, there's always food. I like the dogs, too."

My heart squeezes for all these girls have gone through.

"What about you, Isabel?" Maggie asks.

She shrugs. "It's okay. What she says is true, but it's too noisy sometimes, so I have to take Daisy and go for a walk." Her eyes flick over to Dale. "Even though I think they might be from Mars, it seems safe here."

I can't help the laugh that bubbles up out of my throat. "What? Mars?"

Isabel looks up at me, one corner of her mouth tucked in, almost smiling. "Yeah. They're so nice all the time that they've gotta be aliens or something."

So our little Miss Isabel has a sense of humor lurking under all that pain.

Dale chuckles. "I thought that, too, when they first asked if I wanted to come here. When I got hurt, I was in the hospital with Miss Miriam and Miss Sarah's brother. Sarah invited me to come here. Now I'm married, have reunited with my sister, and have a whole enormous family surrounding me. Loving me."

"So, you trust them?" Maggie asks.

Dale's normally jovial demeanor turns serious as he replies, "With my life. They're not perfect, but I've never known a better group of people."

Maggie absorbs that, then takes a deep breath. "So, Isabel and Sophie, what do you think about me coming here, too, and all three of us staying for the summer?"

"Yeah!" Sophie squeals. "That would be awesome!"

"Isabel?"

Her eyes slide to her sister for long moments. I lean down and speak only loud enough for her to hear. "It's okay to be honest."

She sighs. "For the summer, yeah, but I don't want to stay here forever. I'd rather go back to Serena's house, but I know it's not safe right now, especially since Mr. Vance and her are working to put the pervert in jail."

Maggie nods. "All right, then. When I'm finished with classes next week, I'll come down here and we'll stay for the summer until it's time to go back to school. At that time, we'll talk again and see what's changed and what we want to do. However, if anything changes with how you feel, I want you to talk to me about it."

That last bit was said with her looking directly at Isabel. I'm glad she's giving the most power to the one most wounded and affected by their living arrangements because of her emotional fragility.

"Does that mean we won't see you all summer?" Isabel asks me.

I'm so shocked and touched by her wanting to be close to me. We spent so little time together that I wouldn't have thought she bonded with me that much, but I guess I was wrong.

"That's an excellent question, petit," Dale says, using a French term for the girl. "I think Miss Serena should come down for Sunday lunches so you can see her each week, don't you?"

I want to sigh, but the hope in Isabel's eyes stops me cold. Considering he's been trying to get me to do just that ever since he moved down here, I'm not surprised by his loving manipulation.

"I think I can manage that," I say, resigned.

"You have to bring Mr. Vance, too," Maggie says, an ornery glint in her eye.

"Absolutely," Dale agrees with a brilliant grin splitting his face. "There's always plenty of room and plenty of food."

Vance, who's been quiet this entire time, chuckles, and says, "I guess I know where I'll be spending my Sundays for the next few months. Thank you for the invite."

Once we talk with Roni and Takoda to relay the decision made by Maggie and the girls, we linger for a while longer.

Maggie and I don't have classes tomorrow, but Vance has to work. By late afternoon, the crowd has dwindled, so Vance and I say our goodbyes.

"I'm going to stay a while longer and hang out with the girls, but I promise I won't be home too late," Maggie says.

This time of year, the sun doesn't go down until late evening, so I'm not too concerned about her being on the road, only that she'll be traveling it alone.

As much as I want to fuss, she's an adult, so I treat her as one. "Okay. Just be safe and if anything happens, call me."

With a warm smile for my concern, she says, "I will."

Then she shocks me and pulls me into a hug. "Thank you," she whispers. "We would have been lost without your help." These girls are not only regularly invading my personal space, but my heart, too.

I squeeze her back, but I am absolutely not tearing up.

We're about halfway home when I finally speak into the silence of the car, the thought that's been spinning in my mind. "Why do you think Isabel seems so attached to me? I mean, we were only together a short time before we brought her down here."

Vance doesn't answer right away, thinking over my question. "Perhaps it was because being with you was the first time she has felt safe since she was a little girl. Not only did you take them in, you called in the cavalry to protect them while you go off to slay their personal demon."

I bark out a laugh. "That's a bit of a romanticized version of things, and I'm not doing it alone."

He reaches over and puts a hand on my arm. "Yes, but you're the heroine of the story. The rest of us are merely privates in the ranks. You're the one leading the charge."

Pleasure mingled with disbelief washes through me. Surely he can't be right, but it warms me that he thinks so. When he pulls his hand away, my skin tingles in its wake.

Chapter 24

Vance

As we turn the corner onto her street, Serena goes quiet and stiffens, her knuckles lightening because her grip is so tight on the wheel. "What's wrong?" I ask, then I see the car parked in front of her house. "Who's that?"

"The past," she replies. "Please, just let me handle it."

She clicks the button for her garage door, then pulls inside. As quickly as she can put the car into park, she's out of her door, stalking down the driveway toward a man walking up toward the house.

She'd said he was the past. Is he an ex-boyfriend? I know she can handle herself, but when he wraps a hand around her upper arm and won't let her pull away, I get out of the car.

He sees me when I step around the car. "Who's this? You already moved on to fucking someone else?"

With him distracted by me, she wrenches her arm free and walks back to me, standing by my side. "It's none of your business what I'm doing. I told you, Diondre, we're done. Knowing you were merely separated and not divorced, from the beginning, I told you I didn't get involved with married men, which you are. You lied to me."

He rubs a hand over his bald head. "I didn't lie. I just didn't tell you when we got back together."

Oh shit. Is this guy for real? I want to laugh, but I keep my mouth shut and expression closed.

"A lie by omission is still a lie, Diondre. Leave and don't come back. Ever. I'll get a restraining order if I see you again. Or better yet, I'll call your wife. Or maybe have a talk with your good buddy, the pastor."

She shocks the shit out of me when she leans against my side and slides an arm around my waist. I put my arm around her shoulders, pulling her tight against me. The dude scowls at me, but I keep my face set like stone, then tilt my head to one side as if inviting him to try something.

Part of me wishes he would because I'd love to give him a beat down. He's a married man, for fuck's sake. Did he really think he'd get away with lying to Serena? I guess he's a stupid married man.

When he doesn't move, Serena says again, "Leave Diondre, and don't come back."

He tosses one last glare at me and turns on his heel. Like a pissed off teenager, he slams his car door and peels away from the curb. I can't hold back any longer and let the laughter flow.

Serena swats me on my abs. "I'm glad you find this funny."

"Is he for real? I hope he was good in bed because I don't know what else you could have seen in him."

She stares in the direction his car went and admits, "No, he really wasn't."

I laugh again, and she swats me again. Then she starts laughing, too.

My laughter fades when she tiptoes up and presses her lips to my cheek. With everything in me, I want to turn to her and kiss her for real, but after that asshole, I know I need to take it easy.

I do kiss her, but only on the forehead, then I pull back and look down at her. "I'm going to get going because I know you have a lot of prep work to do for the coming week. If that guy comes back, or if you need anything, just let me know and I'll be right over."

With a brief squeeze of a hug, I let her go and turn toward my car. "Good night, Vance. Thanks for going with me today."

I grin at her over the hood of my car. "Good night, Serena."

Instead of going home, I go to the office. I'm too keyed up to sleep and need to burn off some energy. We all have access to the office twenty-four-seven in case we need to pick up equipment or just want to work out.

There's a car in the parking lot when I arrive and I'm glad to see it. Maybe Jack will spar with me. That would be more of a workout in a few minutes than I'd get from lifting weights for an hour.

I grab my bag from the back seat and head inside. "Hey Jack," I say, closing the exterior door behind me.

"Hey, Vance. Wanna spar?"

"I was hoping you'd say that."

My phone buzzes. I figure it's probably just my mom, but maybe that asshole saw me leave and decided to return to Serena's house. It's an unknown number and that makes me frown.

No one has my number but family, friends, and my employer. Maybe it's just a spam caller wanting to sell me something. My thumb poises over the screen, ready to decline the call, but for some reason I answer it on speaker.

A monotone, androgenous, computerized voice comes through the phone's speaker.

"Detective Douglas, your request has been received."

What the hell? I haven't been Detective Douglas for a while now.

"Your research project can be performed for five thousand dollars and is payable up front. Wiring instructions will be forwarded to your inbox. Once payment is made, the project will commence and should take approximately five days to complete."

Before I can ask a question, the call disconnects and my phone dings with a new email message. Of course, a hacker would know my employment history. They probably took the time to look me up before considering my request. I wonder if me no longer being a cop and therefore less of a danger to them factored into them taking the job.

"Was that?" Jack asks.

"It's not the Crow, it's the Raven," I reply, looking at the email instructions and signature.

"Five thousand seems awfully cheap, even if it is just a five-day job," Jack observes.

I dial Serena's number. "Hey, I just got a response from the researcher. They've accepted our request and say it will take five days and cost five-thousand dollars."

"That seems cheap," she says, echoing Jack's words. "Forward me the information and I'll take care of the payment."

"Are you sure?"

My question is meant to ask whether she wants to send that much money to an anonymous person who could be anyone, but she takes it differently.

"Yes. I can cover that amount just fine."

"I meant, are you sure you want to send that much to a complete stranger online?"

"Oh. I know I was hesitant, but after seeing the lengths these people are going to trying to find children so they can keep abusing them, I'm ready to take the gloves off. We asked for help, and they're offering it and will probably be able to find more hidden dirt than we can. Much quicker, too."

"All right, I just forwarded the information to you."

"Thank you. I'll let you know if anything happens afterward."

"Great. Good night, again, Serena."

"Good night, again, Vance," she replies, and I can tell she's smiling.

I disconnect the call and look up to see Jack grinning at me. "What?"

"Y'all seem to be getting close."

"Baby steps," I tell him. "She's been through a lot."

"You'll get there, if that's what you want. Now, let's hit the mat so I can get a workout in while I kick your ass."

Chapter 25

Isabel

It feels like we go into town to go shopping for something every other day. Emme's parents went to Norman last night to get some stuff from one of those bulk warehouse stores, but there were some things Miss Roni said we needed to get from the grocery store today.

Emme likes to go into town at any opportunity, but I'd rather stay at the ranch. I always feel safe behind the gates of the property, but out in public, I feel scared. Exposed. Especially when it's just the three of us.

When there's a sizeable group of us, I feel more secure, but I can see why Miss Roni might get tired of hauling a gaggle of kids around. That's what she calls us: a gaggle. It has something to do with some kind of bird, but I can't remember what kind. Ducks maybe. Or geese.

Miss Roni is pushing the cart while Emme flits around, stopping to look at things, then racing ahead. She reminds me of a dragonfly, zooming and stopping suddenly, then zooming off again.

"Oh, Isabel, I almost forgot," Miss Roni says. "I saw the look on your face when I was putting away groceries and you saw the crunchy peanut butter I got. Two aisles back is where the peanut butter is. Why don't you go grab a jar of creamy?"

I duck my head in a mixture of happiness and shame. Mom always had to get what was cheapest, and that was when she remembered to actually buy groceries. Part of me feels positively rich because I get to pick out peanut butter just for me, but part of me wonders if I'm being too difficult to deal with.

Emme rounds the corner into the aisle with her aunt in tow, just as I round the corner on the other end to go in search of creamy deliciousness. "Mom! Look who I found!" Emme says.

My hand automatically reaches for the cheap store brand, but I force it to detour to a name brand. A grin spreads across my face and over my entire body when I turn and crash into someone.

"Sorry," I say, falling on my butt as I bounce off the person and try to keep the jar from falling on the floor and breaking.

"That's all right, Isabel. I'm just glad we found you and can take you back to where you belong."

That voice. It sends terror surging through me like a wrecking ball. My sense of safety and security crumbles to pieces like a paper wall.

I crab walk away from him on all fours, fear stealing my voice. If I can get to the other end of the aisle, I can get away. Then a shadow blocks out the sunlight filtering in through the front windows.

I throw a glance over my shoulder and see another man. The look on his face tells me he'll be no help to anyone but his partner, who is stalking toward me. I'm blocked in.

"Apela!" I say, but it's a scream trapped in a whisper. "Apela!" I say again, louder this time, but it's not Spanish or even English. Emme has been teaching me words in Chickasaw, and that one comes to mind because she taught it to me last night. But how many people in this store will even know what I said?

An old man rounds the end of the aisle, leaning heavily on a cane. He has long silver hair in two braids hanging over his shoulders. He says something to me, but I don't understand.

"I don't... I only know a few words."

"What are you doing to this girl?" The old man barks with more authority and bite than I'd have thought he could muster.

"Get lost, old man. We're the cops and this girl has been kidnapped, so we're gonna take her back to her mom."

Looking back at me, the old man asks, "Is this true?"

Still on the ground, I look up at him and pour as much sincerity into my voice as I can. Shaking my head vehemently, I say, "No! They're the ones trying to kidnap me."

The old man puts a hand on the arm of the scrawny cop who once took my police report at the station, only to show up several days later to be allowed to abuse me. "Leave this child alone!"

Scrawny cop shoves the old man. Instead of falling as I expected him to, the old man brandishes his cane at the cop and says again, louder this time, "Leave this child alone!"

Finally, Emme's Aunt Heather enters the aisle, and with one glance, assesses the situation. "Likinta," she says to the old man and puts an arm on his shoulder. When the scrawny cop turns to hurry away, quick as a snake strike, Heather has him up against the shelves, an arm twisted behind his back.

"Let me go," he squeals. "I'm a cop!"

"I know exactly who you are, Officer Draper, and you're no cop in this jurisdiction."

He begins to struggle harder as a crowd gathers, some with their cell phones out to record. I never knew his name, but Draper jerks away, turns, and throws a fist at Heather's head. She ducks it easily, then in some move too fast for me to track, puts Draper on the ground. This time, she pulls both his hands behind his back and cuffs them.

The fat cop has disappeared. I'm so fascinated watching Heather that I don't even see Miss Roni come into the aisle. Emme races over to me.

"Get back, ebaiye tek," Heather barks. "You, too, Isabel."

I take Emme's offered hand and let her help me up and drag me back to where her mom is talking to the old mam. Before I can think about what I'm doing, I throw my arms around him in a hug. "Thank you for hearing me!"

He pats my back and I pull away, embarrassed by my actions.

"Are you okay?" Miss Roni asks.

I nod, still focused on Heather. She pulls out her radio. "Hey, Shay, this is Heather. I'm in Abbott's with a suspect detained in an attempted kidnapping. Will you please call over to the sheriff's office and have them send someone over to pick this guy up?"

The man on the ground starts to squirm again. "You ain't got no right to detain me!"

"Go," Heather says to Miss Roni. "Go pay for your groceries and get the girls out of here."

"Come on," Miss Roni says.

"Mo-o-om, I wanna stay and see what happens," Emme whines. It's the first time I've heard her take that tone with either one of her parents.

"I'm not going to argue with you."

While I'm focused on Em and her mom, I lose track of everything else and jump with a squeak when the old man taps on my arm. He holds out the jar of peanut butter I'd completely forgotten about. "Thank you," I say again.

He gives me a knowing smile and pats my arm again. On the way home, Miss Roni tosses a question into the air of the SUV. "I wonder how they knew where to find you."

I don't look away from the scenery passing by on the other side of the window. The same thing had been rolling around in my brain and there's only one likely answer. "They probably followed Maggie or Serena down here on Sunday."

She gasps. "I think you're right."

In a matter of hours, the peace I'd found has evaporated and I'm back to wondering if I'll ever feel safe again.

Chapter 26

Serena

I'm reading a student's paper for the third time, unsure if this is truly what he meant to turn in because it would seem that perhaps he was inebriated or high. When my phone rings, I'm thankful for the interruption and set the paper aside.

It's after six, so my first instinct is that it's Maggie, but the readout shows it's Veronica Nomee and a sliver of trepidation wiggles in my belly. "Roni, hello."

They said they'd keep the girls safe, but they don't really have any sort of connection to them other than through my brother to me. It was instigated by me knowing Demi who knows Sarah who is connected to the Nomee family. How committed could they possibly be?

That sliver of trepidation threatens to turn into fear, and my mind immediately assumes the worst. What has happened to the girls? My calm voice doesn't betray my unease when I answer the phone.

"Hi," Roni says. "Do you have a minute to talk?"

"I do. What's up?"

"Something happened today and I want to tell you about it. Everything is fine now, but you should be aware and I thought

I'd leave it to you to let Maggie know. I don't want to alarm her..."

"Hold on a second, Roni. Vance is working in the conference room next door to my office. Let me get him."

On Monday, Vance had called and asked about coming to the office in the evenings to continue to work through the cases I printed. "You'll be busy, but I won't be, so rather than lose an entire week, it just makes sense for me to keep working," he'd said.

I was hesitant, but it had nothing to do with his investigative skills. Spending so much time with him was letting him get past my defenses. I mean, I just broke up with Diondre a very short time ago and it was too soon to get involved with someone else.

Wasn't it?

Mostly, I think it's because I don't trust myself. Diondre played me for a fool for months and I had no clue. Now, Vance knows it, too, so I can't help but wonder if he thinks I might be easily fooled again.

For now, we'll focus on the research and only on the research. It doesn't matter if we've gone out for dinner together for the past few evenings. We both have to eat and by the time we leave, I'm too tired to go home and cook. It's simply a matter of convenience.

That's all. Nothing else.

It's convenient and efficient.

I step inside the conference room and close the door behind me. Vance looks up, surprised, and raises an eyebrow as I place the phone on the table near him as I take a seat. "Go ahead, Roni. I've got you on speaker and I'm with Vance."

She tells me about the day's events in the grocery store. Vance reaches out and takes my hand in his and it's only then I realize I'm shaking.

"Heather had the sheriff's office come pick up Draper, but the other one, the big guy, he must have left when Draper took a swing at her and she put him on the ground. The bad news is that the officer who came to get Draper is one that doesn't like Heather very much and when Draper told him it was all a misunderstanding, he let Draper go without booking him."

"What?" Vance barks, incredulous.

"Yeah. Heather is livid. She told her boss what happened and he and the Sheriff are up in arms. I don't know what the end result is going to be, but for us, all that matters is that Draper and his partner are on the streets again."

"How did they even find you?" I ask.

"Isabel thinks they must have followed Maggie or you when y'all came down on Sunday and I have to agree with her. I can't think of any other way they could have known she was here."

My eyes lock with Vance's and he's clearly thinking the same thing.

"Now that we know they know," she continues, "we will be more prepared. The kids won't have as many outings and Takoda has already decreed that we don't go anywhere without an escort from now on."

"Is Isabel all right? Can I speak with her?"

"Yes. Understandably, she was rattled, but it also seems as if getting saved, in part by a complete stranger, did her some good. She's outside with the rest of the kids. They went out to play after supper."

The background noise on her end shifts, then becomes muffled.

"Hi," Isabel says into the phone.

"Isabel, this is Serena. How are you?"

"I'm okay."

A vision of her shrugging comes to mind, and it makes me smile. She sounds surprisingly unaffected, almost upbeat.

"I heard you had an eventful day today."

"Yeah. Those cops found me. I went to get some peanut butter, and they were just there. One of the...um...men, I bumped into him and fell on the ground. When I tried to call for help, I could only think of the Chickasaw word Emme had taught me, and no one came. But then I said it again and this old Indian man...huh?"

Someone says something to her and I can tell she's not speaking to me when she says, "Yeah, sorry."

"This old indigenous man came into the same row. He had long silver hair in braids over his shoulders and used a cane, so I didn't think he'd be much help. But he told the cop to leave me alone. When the cop told him to get lost and pushed him, the man waved his can in the air like he was gonna use it like a baseball bat."

She takes a breath and I'm amazed that she seems almost excited about the story.

"Then Heather was there. The cop tried to hit her, but she ducked and took that guy down faster than I could blink. Boom! He was on the ground spitting and fussing like a mad cat."

"How are you feeling about all that?" I ask.

"It was scary at first. Miss Roni says I might not get to leave the ranch as often and when we do leave, we'll have to take one of the guys, or Heather, as a security guard."

"Does that bother you?"

"Nah. I don't like going into town all the time, anyway. I'd rather stay at the ranch. It's quiet here and nobody bothers me."

"Okay. I just wanted to check on you, but you can go back to playing. I'll see you on Sunday."

"Really? You're coming down again?"

"Yes, of course I am. It's what we agreed to, isn't it?"

"Yeah, but..." she starts, but seems to think better of what she was going to say. "I'll see you Sunday."

The phone disconnects. "Goodbye," I say to the screen.

Vance chuckles and squeezes the hand he's still holding. "Is it just me, or did she seem almost happy?" I ask him.

"She was rescued in the middle of a dangerous situation for probably the first time in her entire life. Not only was she rescued, but a complete stranger stepped in to help her. That's probably something that's never happened to her before, either.

It's a wondrous thing to realize there are still a few good people left in the world."

What must life have been like for Isabel? To what depths does her trauma go that the help of one stranger could make her feel so much lighter? Sure, the Nomee's are helping her, but she could view that as them doing a favor for me since my brother is part of their family.

"You're probably right," I reply with a nod. "Her own mother threw her away into the hands of evil men to serve her own addiction. I feel for her mother, too. She was completely taken advantage of, but when you become a parent..."

Chapter 27

Vance

I squeeze her hand again, ecstatic she's been holding onto me for comfort this long, but she pulls it away as if just realizing we're still connected. "I know what you mean. Come on, let's put everything away and get out of here. I doubt you're going to be able to concentrate until you talk to Maggie and let her know what's happened."

Rolling her lips inward while thinking the prospect over, after a moment, she concedes with a sigh. "You're right. I just have a few emails to return before I can leave, though."

"How about I grab us something and meet you at your house?"

"That sounds much better."

She helps me gather up the papers I'm working on, keeping them in their stacks. Over the past few evenings, I'm making decent progress and a pattern is emerging from his client list. In a few more days, we'll have the report from the hacker and, hopefully, enough to hand off to detectives to launch an official investigation.

I stop in the door to her office and look back. Part of me is hesitant to leave her here alone. If those assholes risked getting caught over an hour away from their jurisdiction only to fail, they may go after Serena to get her to back off and turn over the girls.

She looks up at me. "What?"

"I just...I'm worried they'll come after you next."

The look that crosses her face is so sweet I want to walk right over there, pull her into my arms and kiss her until she's breathless.

"It's been a long time since anyone has been worried about me," she says. "I appreciate it, but I'll be fine. It will just take me a few minutes and I'll be right behind you."

I nod. "All right. I'll see you in a few."

When I get to her house, she's already there, and relief washes through me. I know she can handle herself, but today's events changed things. It would be so easy for those guys to go after Serena to get to Maggie to use her to get to the girls.

I wonder if she'd be open to having a personal bodyguard until this is resolved. Probably not, but I'm going to ask her, anyway. Hers is a body I have a powerful need to protect. Call me a neanderthal, if you like, but it's an instinct I'm not inclined to ignore.

She lets me in, and I follow her back to the kitchen with our food. While she waited, she changed her professional work clothes for a pair of shorts and a loose tank. Damn, she's got great legs.

When she stops by the kitchen island, I almost run into her. She looks at me with a question on her face, then notices where my eyes had been focused and raises an eyebrow at me. Deciding it's time to stop playing it so safe, I say, "You've got great legs, baby."

Maggie comes into the kitchen, maybe to see who arrived or maybe she smelled the food. Her eyes are red like she's been crying, so I guess Serena had time to tell her about what happened with her cousin today.

"You okay?" I ask her.

She nods. "Yeah. Just shocked and worried. It doesn't help that this is a super stressful week for me and I'm already on edge. My last final is tomorrow, so I'm going to work on packing up my things so I can head down to the girls as soon as I finish."

"Good," I reply. "The sooner you're down there under their protection, the better."

Serena unpacks the food and hands it out, along with silverware. I pull one of the barstools around to the side so I can see their faces as we talk and eat. Wanting to divert her focus, I ask Maggie, "How are your finals going?"

"I think they're going well, but it will take some time to get my results back to know for sure. This semester, as long as I pass and don't have to repeat any courses, I'll be happy. Once all this is over, I'll be able to focus on my GPA."

Maggie finishes first, talking while she disposes of her takeout container. "Thank you for bringing me dinner, Vance. And thank you for all you're doing for my cousins and for watching over Serena. Knowing you're there has helped a lot."

"You're welcome on all counts."

"Please don't let anything happen to Serena. We need to keep people like her in the world."

"I am perfectly capable of taking care of myself, thank you very much," Serena grouses.

"Will do," I say to Maggie, ignoring Serena's protests. She is superwoman in so many ways, but she's not bulletproof.

Maggie nods and goes to her room after saying good night. Now that it's just the two of us, Serena seems on edge. I thought we were getting closer, but ever since Sunday and the confrontation with her ex, she seems to be withdrawing.

Maybe she was embarrassed by what I overheard. Or maybe it's something else.

"Well, you've had a long day, so I won't linger," I tell her. "See you tomorrow at the same time to continue working the cases?"

"Yes, that's fine."

"Are you okay?"

She sighs with her entire body. "Yes. I just...well, these girls, they've gotten under my skin. I've known Magdalena for a while because she's been a student. She's always impressed me because she's smart and hardworking and she just...gets it. Some students are going into law because they think it's lucrative. Others for some form of prestige. But Maggie, she's in it for the law, if that makes sense."

"Reminds you of yourself, huh?"

She smiles and looks away.

"I guess. Oh, wait, no, I won't be here tomorrow evening. I need to go have dinner at the Society."

My brows draw together. Why would she *need* to go have dinner there? "You *need* to?"

She gives herself away when her chin hitches a fraction of an inch. "Yes, I need to check in with Cait and Alicia to see if they have feedback from their significant others, the trustworthy law enforcement folks I told you about."

"You could just call them," I say. There's more to this story, and I'm not going to let her off the hook. Mostly because I'm curious, but partly because I want her to trust me with whatever it is she doesn't want to tell me.

Her lips thin as she scowls at me, and my curiosity doubles. I can tell the instant her willpower breaks.

Getting up from her seat, she goes to the sink and rinses her glass in which she'd had exactly one serving of wine. When I knew her in Atlanta, she wasn't so buttoned up. Not that I want her to be a lush or anything, but she was more easygoing.

I want to get beneath the surface to find that enthusiastic, passionate woman again.

Chapter 28

Serena

This tenacious man just isn't going to let it go. "I need to go there because there's something I can only do there."

He just keeps looking at me expectantly, and raises an eyebrow. My answer is going to make him think I've done gone and lost my damn mind.

"I need to go make a wish."

His entire body clenches, trying with all his might to hold back the disbelieving laughter. A single bark escapes when he opens his mouth to ask, "What?"

When he sees my glare, he works harder to get himself under control. "I'm sorry," he says. "But did you just say you need to go there to make a wish?"

"That's exactly what I said and you know it," I reply with ice in my voice. "Listen, I know it sounds strange, but there is empirical evidence that it works."

"That what works?" he asks, still shaking with suppressed laughter.

"Never mind," I say, turning away to wet the washcloth from the sink so I can wipe down the countertop where we ate. "I can't meet tomorrow night."

When I turn back around, he's there and I turn into his arms, which come around me gently, tenderly. I should really pull away, but my traitorous body refuses to cooperate with my logical mind.

"Hey," he says, cupping my jaw and turning my face up to his. "I didn't mean to offend you. Why don't you tell me about it?"

For a moment, I hesitate. The owner, Noémie, might not want people to know about that crazy box. However, the only ones with access to it are members and members have to be invited. As a Christian, I shouldn't be giving it a second thought, but in this situation, I'll take all the help I can get.

"Fine, but if you laugh again, I'm going to end the story. Got it?"

He nods, but doesn't let me go, and I still can't muster enough willpower to pull away. "You remember me telling you about the Belladonna Society?"

He nods again.

"In one room is one of those old mechanical fortune teller machines. If you make a wish and push a button, it will tell you if your wish will come true."

The skeptical look that takes up residence on his face is to be expected.

"I know. It sounds completely implausible, but it works. My friends have all made wishes and they've all come true. Although not always in the way they intended, but they *have* come true."

"Self-fulfilling prophecies?" he poses.

"I don't think so, particularly because of the unexpected aspects. Alicia just wanted an ex-boyfriend to leave her alone, and he did because he was killed robbing a bank. However, her cousin, over whom she was guardian, was killed at the same time."

He still looks unswayed.

I shrug, hitch my chin, and pull out of his arms. "You don't have to believe me, but I want to hedge my bets, so to speak."

"I'm not saying I don't believe you. If you feel the need to make a wish, then that's what you should do."

Although I don't need his permission, that's exactly what I do. I arrive at the Society a little early the next evening and hang out in the lounge until there's no one else around. Taking advantage of the lull in foot traffic, I move to the machine with purpose, not running, but not dilly dallying, either.

"All right Oracle Orenda, here we go."

The box houses a raven-haired beauty with tarot cards spread before her. On the top in gilt is her name and there is a large button on the front that says, *Make a Wish.* There is no slot for coins or bills, so it's not about money. I'd be very curious to know how this thing came to be.

I've been thinking about what to say and decided not to go too broad, like trying to wish for the demise of all pedophiles. However, I want to be sure that I don't leave anyone out. Taking a deep breath, I press the button marked *Make a Wish.*

"I wish that we would find enough evidence to put away the pedophiles and all their cohorts that hurt Isabel so that she and her sister can be safe and live full, happy lives and never have to look over their shoulders for them again."

The machine whirs.

"And quickly," I add. It might just be my imagination, but the machine seems to pause with my addendum.

Using a wish for others and not for one's self is something that might give some pause,

Before all is said and done, much will be required to keep little ones from evil's jaws.

I frown at the card. *What the hell is that supposed to mean?*

"Did you do it?"

I look up to see my friend Cait grinning over at me. "Yeah," I sigh. "But I have no idea what it means."

When I hold the card out to her, she takes it, frowning as she reads the message.

"I didn't either. You wished something for the girls Demi told me about?" I nod. "Seems to me like there may be a price to pay to keep the girls safe, but that they will be safe in the end."

"I hope so," I reply, taking back the card and tucking it into my purse.

She links her arm with mine. "Come on, let's go get some supper. I'm eager to hear what's gone on with the girls and give you an update about what Ford and Carlos have been up to."

I'd been hoping for...well, I don't know what I was hoping for from that infernal machine, but it certainly wasn't what I got. When I get home, Vance is going to want to know what it said and now I'm going to have to show him I've gone and made a fool of myself.

Again. Maybe I am losing my mind because I sure have been foolish a lot of late.

For once, all five of our orientation quint shows up for the Thursday evening meal. They all look so happy, so fulfilled. It's been almost a decade since I felt truly happy. Even longer since I felt fulfilled.

When we all came for orientation to the Belladonna Society - goodness, is it going on two years? – Cait suggested that we have a weekly dinner date. If I'm available, I will come. Sometimes it's only one or two of us, but on rare occasions, all five of us will show.

"Serena?"

"Huh?"

I look up to see our server waiting to take our orders. After I apologize and place my order, the group focuses on me. "Tell us what's happening with the girls," Demi says.

The table is silent as I tell them about the officers showing up on campus and the confrontation in the grocery store. Demi is curious about Isabel's reaction and agrees with Vance's assessment of it is plausible.

Cait's face is full of concern when I finish and her hand flutters to her throat. "I fear our giving the information to Ford and Carlos is what led to the attempted kidnapping. They reported Officers Draper and Pierce to their superiors, and the officers were suspended. That's why they could go down there on a weekday when they'd normally be working."

"It's not your fault," I tell her. "The fault is solely on the shoulders of those evil men."

"But aren't you afraid they'll grow suspicious of you?" Gabriella asks. "I mean, they have to know you know from the way you've hidden the girls away and facilitated their protection and keeping Maggie close, too."

"Maggie took her last exam this morning and made it to the ranch just fine. She'll be difficult to get to, as well."

"You need to be careful," Alicia says. "With the three of them under wraps, they could possibly target you or the girls' mother, especially if they suspect you're investigating them."

"Vance and I are making good progress going through the court cases," I tell them. "We are already seeing some patterns we want to dig deeper into."

"Vance, huh?" Demi says, a wicked gleam in her eye.

I swear, my neck gets hot like I'm some teenager caught necking under the bleachers at a high school football game.

"Yes," I reply. "He's an excellent investigator. His arrest and conviction rate in Atlanta was exemplary."

"So you knew each other there? Were you close?" Gabriella asks after sharing a knowing look with Demi.

"Wait, what happened to Diondre?" Cait asks.

Time to share my shame and let them know just how stupid I've been. When I tell them about our breakup, I tell them everything. Well, maybe not the part about him being too drunk to get it up, but they hear all about the events at the church and about his subsequent attempts to reconcile.

"What a dog," Gabriella growls. Her vehemence on my behalf warms me.

"Vance seems like a good guy, though," Demi says. "Jack can't say enough good things about him."

I lift my hand to stop the direction the conversation is taking. "It's good to know he's doing well at his job, but don't start reading things into our friendship. I've decided I must have a broken picker when it comes to men and I'm better off by myself."

"She made her wish tonight," Cait says, tattling on me.

The other women at the table look at each other and grin.

"I didn't wish for a man or even anything for myself," I say, as if I need to defend my actions.

"Neither did I," Demi says. "In fact, I didn't even officially make a wish."

"All right, all right, y'all need to stop trying to marry me off. I'm telling you, I'm happy on my own."

Yeah, I wouldn't believe me either, but it really is better this way.

Chapter 29

Vance

"How did the wishing go?" I ask when I step into Serena's office the next day.

Finals are over, but she still has grading and paperwork to do before her semester is complete, so I'll still be coming to her office to work on our files. Part of me wonders why we're still going through cases instead of just waiting to see what the hacker dredges up.

Their information is likely to be more thorough than anything we come up with. However, the bigger part of me knows that continuing to do this work allows me to spend every evening with Serena, so I keep my big mouth shut.

She looks up, her eyes narrowed. It seems she might still be a little tender about me pushing her to admit her plan to make a wish to a mysterious oracle on behalf of the girls. Holding onto an air of nonchalance, I slide into a chair on the visitor side of her desk.

She takes off her reading glasses and sets them aside, then reaches for her pocketbook. "It went well."

After a moment of fishing around inside her purse, she removes her hand and is holding a small card. It's about the size of a business card and the color of yellowed parchment. When I take it from her, it's thicker and heavier than I expected it to be.

The message is printed in black using a scripted font, but not overly fancy. My eyebrows raise when I read the words and I look up at her. "What did you wish?"

"I wished we would quickly find enough evidence to put away the threats to the girls so they can be safe and live full, happy lives and never have to look over their shoulders for them again."

I nod. "Good wish. The message implies that not many wishes are made for magnanimous reasons."

"Yes. That's how I took that, too."

"What do you think that 'much will be required' part means?" That phrase gives me a sense of foreboding. However, that's probably what the maker of the machine intended. A little bit of promise, a little bit of danger, and just enough mystery that however things turn out, the machine can be praised for its foresight.

"Your guess is as good as mine," she replies, taking the card when I hand it back and dropping it back into her purse. "I think that baby has already paid a high enough price, though."

"Agreed. How's grading going?"

"Slowly, as usual. Did you have a good day today?"

I tell her all about my day and installing two systems with Moses. It's not exciting, but it's also not very dangerous like it used to be when I was a cop. Every day, I'd toss up a prayer of thanks when I'd make it home alive.

I enjoy just sitting and talking with her. However, the longer I keep her talking, the longer it will take for her work to be done, so I excuse myself and take the stacks of paper to the room next door.

The stacks are getting more organized as we whittle them down, distilling and correlating the information we glean from them. Discarding what's useless is the most troublesome part of the process because it might seem of no consequence now, but it could have some bearing on something we haven't come across yet.

That's always the chance you take when trying to discern what evidence is relevant and which is not. Over time, you learn to trust your investigative abilities and your gut. Yet, I'm still covering my ass and noting the case numbers on paper as potential revisits.

I've only been at it for an hour when Serena comes into the room. "My eyes are crossing. Would it be horrible of me if I'm ready to call it a day?"

Without hesitation, I start gathering up the pages. "Nope. It's been a hectic week. Dinner?"

"I've got some chicken marinating at home," she says, sounding tired.

"Sounds perfect."

Once we've eaten, and she's getting comfortably relaxed with her glass of wine, we settle into her living room, both of us taking a seat on the sofa. As much as I'd love to sit next to her and pull her close, I don't. Baby steps.

"Tell me more about this Belladonna Society."

"At first, I thought it must be some kind of scam, but I did a little research and it seemed legit, so I joined. In a lot of ways, it's just like the old school gentlemen's clubs...and I don't mean strip joints."

That makes me chuckle. "Is there a lot of wheeling and dealing that goes on in the back room?"

"Nothing as overt as that, but the amount of money and power in that building on any given day is astounding. Women from the most influential families in the state belong. Brainpower is pooled. Careers are made. Charities are funded. You saw how all I needed to do was make a phone call and people came to help."

"Part of that was family."

"Yeah," she replies, snuggling deeper into her seat and toasting me with her wineglass. "Part of it was family."

"Tell me that story. I know what Dale told us, but there seems to be a lot more to that tale."

Starting from when her brother landed in the hospital with Sarah's brother, she tells me how he came to be in Oklahoma. She gives me an overview of his relationship with his wife and the trials they faced.

It's quite a story, but I'm glad she has seen such a powerful example of what people can overcome when they really want to be together. "They seem really well matched."

"They are. I'm not sure there is anything such as a perfect couple, but they come close."

The clock on her mantle and the drooping of her eyelids tell me it's getting late. Exhaustion is written all over her, and she still has a week of school left before she can dive into helping me with the investigation again.

"I tell you what," I say. "Why don't we take the day off tomorrow? We could go down to where the girls are, hang out with them, and come back after lunch on Sunday."

"What about the investigation?"

"The girls are safe. I know you want to see Isabel even though you know she's fine after what happened. It's just one day, then you'll be refreshed to get your school stuff done, then we can hit it hard. We'll also be close to getting the search results from, well, you know."

Her eyes are closed, but I know she's considering it.

"I'd really like that," she finally says.

That makes me smile. She's clearly ready for bed, so I get up and go to her. "Great! We should probably touch base with Roni and Takoda in the morning before we go barreling down there."

She nods, still not opening her eyes. "I'll call them in the morning and let you know."

"Perfect. You're ready for bed, so I'll call you in the morning and we'll work out a plan. Now, walk me out so you can turn in."

The corners of her mouth tilt up. She places her glass on the coffee table and takes my outstretched hands, letting me pull her up.

At the door, I take her in my arms and kiss her forehead. Her mouth is where I'd rather kiss her, but the way she tensed when I wrapped her up lets me know that probably wouldn't have gone over well.

After that initial tightening of her muscles, she relaxes and hugs me back. "Good night, Serena. I'll call you in the morning."

Chapter 30

Serena

"Which sister is this one?" Vance asks as I park the car. "She's the youngest of the four, an artist," I reply.

He looks up at the house through the windshield. "Must be a heck of an artist."

"She is," I chuckle. "But her husband is also a heck of a business wizard. Felicia, Dale's wife, works for him."

When I called Roni this morning, she told me she was bringing the kids up to her sister Lynzee's house to go swimming. Since she lives right outside Norman, we decided to just meet them there.

Dale caught wind of the plan and invited Vance and me over for dinner tonight, so we're still planning on going to Ada after the kids are waterlogged and ready to go home. Once I've gathered up my things, we head toward the front door. It opens before Vance has a chance to knock.

A boy who appears to be about seven with wavy brown hair and his mother's soft brown eyes is standing in the open doorway. "Oh, hello," he says.

"Hi there, Walker. You probably don't remember me; it's been a couple years since you saw me, but I'm your Uncle Dale's sister."

"Okay," he says with a shrug, walking away and leaving the door open.

"Walker, was there someone at the door?" A man's voice carries to us before Preston Kearney rounds the corner into the foyer to find us standing there.

He grins and shakes his head. "Sorry about that. That one has some issues with basic manners. He said he heard a car outside and just had to see if he was right. Apparently, being proved right was enough for him and he lost interest."

Preston takes the dish I'm carrying and leans in to kiss my cheek. "Serena, it's good to see you again. You didn't have to bring anything. We're just going to throw some burgers on the grill and toss a bag of chips to the horde a little later."

"I know," I reply with a grin. "That's what Roni said, but my southern mama would be aghast if I showed up at someone's house empty-handed. Preston, this is my friend Vance Douglas. Vance, this is Preston Kearney."

The men shake hands, and we're ushered into the cool house.

"I've heard about you," Preston tells Vance. "You're working with Jack and Jerald, right?"

"I am. It's nice to meet you and thanks for having us."

"You're welcome. Working with Jack and Jerald, you're practically family."

Vance chuckles. "You keep adding family at this rate and you're going to have to rent out a coliseum for family reunions."

Preston grins back. "I know, right?"

While the men continue to talk, I make my way through the house to the back door where the sounds of children filter through into the house. Before I even make it to the door, I hear Isabel. "Serena!"

Then she's there, wrapped around me like a boa constrictor. "Hi there," I reply, putting my arms around her.

The emotion evoked by this tiny human is overwhelming. We haven't spent much time together, but she has chosen me to bond with and it astounds me. I want to be worthy of her affection and bring her tormentors to justice.

As soon as she's there, she's gone. "Mister Vance!" she exclaims, then races off to him. She doesn't give him the same hug, but she takes him by the hand and pulls him toward me.

"Aren't you swimming?" he asks in reference to her fully clothed body.

I take a look at her, a good look. Not only is she not dressed for swimming, but she's completely covered. She's got on long pants and a shirt with long sleeves.

Oh, sweet baby girl.

"No. I don't like swimming," she replies with a shrug and a sidelong look outside where the other children are squealing and laughing.

She releases Vance's hand and takes mine again. "Come on," she says, dragging me toward the door.

When we're through the door, I see Roni and Lynzee seated on an outdoor sofa under the pergola. The space is beautiful and perfect for entertaining, with plenty of seating in comfortable groupings.

The women look up with smiles and wave me over. I take a seat and Isabel snuggles up against me. Maggie is in the pool with the kids and they are swarming her like flies to honey. She laughs and plays with them.

One tiny girl, who I think is Lynzee and Preston's youngest, is clinging to her like a spider monkey squealing with delight every time she gets splashed. When I notice Isabel watching the other children intently, I ask, "Are you sure you don't want to swim?"

"Yep." She says it with finality, then gets up and goes into the house.

Now that my eyes have been opened, I think back and realized that I've never seen the skin of her arms and legs. She's been covered from neck to ankle the entire time. Did those bastards mark her? Or is she simply afraid to show any more of her body than she absolutely has to?

Roni leans over toward me. "She didn't want to come at all, but then she heard you and Vance were going to be here, and she changed her mind."

Wondering if her experience with Isabel is different, I'm compelled to ask, "At your house, has she worn anything other than long pants and long sleeves?"

Roni's eyes go vacant for a moment as she thinks, then go round with surprise. "No." Her hand goes to her mouth. "No, I haven't. Oh no. No wonder she didn't want to swim. Do you think..."

I shake my head. "It just hit me when she got up. I don't know why she's staying covered, but there's a powerful reason for it to her."

We sit there in silence, watching the other kids playing. "If you don't mind watching my hooligans for a bit, I think I have an idea for Isabel," Lynzee says.

When we both agree, she rises and goes into the house. A few minutes later, she comes back out and crosses the patio toward a second building set back from the house. Roni smiles and just says, "Studio."

I've heard that art therapy can be extremely effective for traumatized children. Perhaps she will enjoy whatever Lynzee has planned for her. If so, I will be happy to facilitate her continuing to explore art.

Anything that gives her another avenue to express herself and work through the horrific things done to her would be fantastic. I will do whatever she needs to help her move toward healing.

I'm not sure how long Roni and I are sitting there alternating between talking and watching the kids before Preston and Vance come out of the house loaded down with a platter of burgers, hot dogs, and some other stuff I can't identify. Preston's grill has more cook surfaces than I've ever seen on a grill.

I was going to offer to help, but I think I'll just stay out of his way.

Once he's unburdened himself, Vance comes and sits next to me. "How are things going out here?"

"Great!" Roni answers and I smile in reinforcement of her statement.

I'm distracted by today's revelations and she's being gracious, covering for my spotty participation in conversation. Or maybe she's feeling the same way because I haven't noticed any awkwardness between us, just periods where we both go quiet, talking in starts and stops.

Vance carries the conversation with Roni while I drift back into my concerns for Isabel and what, if anything, I can do about it.

Chapter 31

Vance

After we eat lunch, Isabel goes back to the studio and the rest of the kids jump back in the pool. I'm not sure what happened while I was in the house with Preston, but Serena seems distracted.

The only time she was completely in the present and focused was when Isabel snuggled up next to her for a few minutes before returning to the studio with Lynzee. There's every sign that it has to do with Isabel, but I won't ask her about it until we're alone.

I like Preston. He seems like a good guy. Based on the size of the house, I was worried he'd be some uppity stuffed shirt, but he's extremely personable.

When the littlest girl comes to him dripping wet and holds her arms out, he wraps her up in a towel and pulls her onto his lap, completely unfazed by her getting him wet. Without missing a beat, he continues to talk as if there's nothing out of the ordinary.

She yawns and snuggles against him. "Come on, Cranberry, let's take you upstairs and rinse you off before you fall asleep. You won't like waking up all salty."

"No salty," she echoes.

"Excuse me," Preston says. "I'll be back once I get her rinsed, changed, and down for a nap."

Roni looks at her watch. "I think I'm going to round up all my rascals to get them started on rinsing and changing, too."

"Salty?" I ask.

"It's a saltwater pool. They converted to salt water when the middle child, Alex, had a reaction to the chemicals in the chlorine tablets," Roni answers, then turns her attention to the kids in the water. "All right, hooligans, it's time to get ready to go!"

She's met with groans of protest, but no one whines, which is surprising. Maggie gets out first along with another small girl, but this one is a little older than the one Preston took inside. I don't know all their names yet, but there are a lot of them, so it will take some time.

"I'm going to go find Isabel," Serena says when we're getting close to everyone being showered and changed into fresh clothes.

"My legs need some stretching, so I'll come with," I reply as I offer my hand up from her seat.

She smiles and takes it. "Thank you."

We follow the path to the secondary building and when we get closer, it's apparent that the building is Lynzee's studio. There are broad expanses of windows to let in lots of light. When we draw near, music carries out to us.

Rather than knocking, I push open the door to let Serena in and she walks through ahead of me. After I cross the threshold, the scene I take in is astounding. There is color everywhere in the form of canvases in various phases of completion.

Most of the paintings are abstract works, but there are a few that have some recognizable features. One canvas is enormous, like something you'd see in some fancy company's lobby.

"Wow," I breathe.

Lynzee looks up from where she's painting and smiles. "Hi. I thought I heard Roni rousting the kids out of the pool."

"You did," Serena says, smiling back. "This is amazing."

"Thank you." Lynzee rises from the stool she's been perched on and puts her brush into a large cup of liquid. The smell of turpentine lingers in the air, but it's not strong, so I doubt that's what's in the cup.

Serena crosses to where Isabel is hunched on a stool in front of a canvas perched on an easel. "May I see?" she asks the girl.

Isabel just shrugs so Serena moves to stand behind her, putting her hands on the girl's shoulders.

"Oh, Isabel," she says on a breath.

Lynzee's smile broadens. "She's got some natural talent, especially with color theory."

Isabel ducks her head, but pleasure at the compliment is written all over her slight frame.

"Can I see, Isabel?" I ask.

She nods, giving me permission.

If you'd asked me yesterday, I would have said that I didn't think painting was a personal thing. It's just some paint on canvas. However, when I see Isabel's painting, I realize it's very personal.

There are a few places where the colors have gone muddy, but overall, it's good. Black with bold slashes of red and purple dominate the color scheme, with glimpses of other colors showing through. Anyone looking at it could read the pain she poured out onto the surface.

"Come on," Lynzee says. "You'll need to wash up."

Isabel removes the apron she was wearing to cover her clothes and follows Lynzee to a large industrial sink where they lather up to get the paint off their hands and arms. Lynzee laughs when she scrubs a swath of paint from Isabel's cheek and the girl grins.

Washed and dried, she makes her way to Serena and I swear, she's almost bouncing like a typical carefree kid would do. I know Serena sees it too, because she's smiling when Isabel takes her hand.

"Did you have fun?"

"Yes!"

"Good," Serena replies.

Lynzee goes over to a bookcase on one wall, takes two books down and puts them into a tote bag. Then she moves to another set of shelves and pulls other items to put into the bag. When she returns to us, she holds the bag out to Isabel.

"Remember what I told you," she says. "I've had almost no formal training. But like I said, training isn't a bad thing, just don't get too hung up on needing it. If you take classes and enjoy it, then take them and take more. The best thing is that you practice your craft and develop your skills. These are a few things to get you started with drawing which with help you develop your visualization skills. That's essential for taking what's in our head and putting it on canvas."

Isabel's eyes go round with surprise. "Oh, Miss Lynzee, thank you." She takes the bag from Lynzee like it's precious cargo, which to her, I'm sure it is.

"Thank you, Lynzee," Serena says, then turns to Isabel. "All right, kiddo, I'm sure Miss Roni and the others are waiting for you. Are we taking your painting home?"

"No. Miss Lynzee says it needs to dry first or paint will get everywhere. She's going to bring it to lunch tomorrow if it's dry. If not, she'll bring it the next week."

We leave the studio and the closer we get to the horde of kids waiting under the pergola, the more Isabel's shoulders deflate. She looks up at Serena and says something too quiet for me to hear.

They go back and forth for a moment before Serena stops and asks me. "Do you mind if Isabel goes with us to Dale's tonight? I think she just needs a little bit longer break from the chaos."

Lynzee chuckles. When I look down at Isabel, I get the woe-begone look every child masters by age two. I chuckle, too. "Not at all."

Serena pulls out her phone.

"Hey Dale, can you do one more for dinner tonight?"

He must say yes because, after being quiet for a moment, she says, "Great, thank you."

Chapter 32

Serena

When I talked to Roni about Isabel wanting to come to dinner with us instead of going home with everyone else, I'm surprised when she's not offended.

She simply smiles at Isabel and says, "I understand. Felicia was the same way. Just give us a shout before you head out to the ranch from town, so we know to expect you."

"Will do."

In the car, Isabel pulls the books out of her bag and silently flips through them for the hour-long drive to Dale and Felicia's house. Vance glances at her in the rearview mirror, then looks over at me and smiles. With a look over my shoulder, I smile back.

It seems we've found something that interests Isabel. I've heard that art therapy can be effective for children suffering from trauma, so I think I'll look into it for her.

Talk therapy doesn't appear to be helping her simply because, based on reports from the therapist, she doesn't do any talking. However, art seems to have sparked something in her and I'd love to foster that spark turning into something more. Some means of self-expression and working through all those feelings roiling around inside her.

Vance and I talk quietly on the drive, but there are no topics of consequence. Not with big ears on a little body in the back seat. The time passes quickly and before I know it, we're coming into town and I direct him to the right location.

Isabel gathers up her things and puts them back into the bag Lynzee provided. She's intent on taking it inside with her and I don't balk, thinking it will keep her entertained during an otherwise boring evening with a bunch of grownups.

"Come in," Dale says when he opens the door with a hug for me and a grin for everyone else.

"It smells wonderful in here," Vance says as he shakes Dale's hand.

"That is mostly thanks to my beautiful wife. Hello again, Isabel."

She presses into my side and grips my hand tight, but says, "Hello, Mr. Dale."

Felicia appears next to him, wiping her hands on her apron. "Hello," she says without looking at any of us, as is her way. "What do you have there, Isabel?"

Her grip on my hand doesn't tighten with Felicia's question, so it's only men that make her nervous, which isn't surprising. "Art supplies your sister gave me."

"Well, that will come in handy," Felicia replies, surprising me. "You have something to keep you entertained while we finish preparing supper. Will you be comfortable in here or would you like somewhere less distracting?"

"I don't know."

Felicia holds out her hand to Isabel, which does surprises me again. Felicia isn't one to touch other people besides her husband and occasionally her sisters. "Let me show you your options."

Long minutes later, Felicia comes back alone, but I know where Isabel is and it is perfect for her. In one corner of her office, Felicia has an enormous beanbag that she likes to nap, read, and watch television in when she takes a break from her work on the computer.

Ever since she was attacked by a former boss, she has to take regular breaks from staring at the computer or she will get a migraine. The man beat her and kicked her in the head, coming very close to killing her. That she only has occasional headaches when she overdoes it on screen time is a miracle.

"You sold her on your beanbag, didn't you?" Dale asks.

Felicia hitches her chin and says matter-of-factly. "Of course. It is extremely comfortable."

"Yes, it is," he agrees. "Come on, let's get dinner prepped. Sister mine, how about you chop us up a salad?"

"I can certainly do that. Do you have any of that bottle of wine left from last time?"

One thing I love about coming here for dinner is that I get to take part in the preparation, another is that the food is always delicious. I wash my hands while Dale takes down a glass and pours some wine into it before placing it on the counter where vegetables have been washed and laid out for chopping.

Dale offers Vance a glass, but he declines, opting for a beer instead. Dale asks about our investigatory efforts, so in low voices that won't carry, we tell him about our slow progress through the information.

"Have you heard from the...um...?"

"Not the final information yet," Vance replies. "I did get a response, though. They said it would take five days, so that would be Monday or Tuesday."

"Wow. That's pretty fast. Was it pricey?"

"I thought it was fast, too," I say. "It was more than pocket change, but not nearly as much as I was thinking it would be."

Dale makes an indistinct humming noise just as Isabel comes into view. She sidles up to me and I give her a piece of carrot from the ones I've sliced. "Hungry?" I ask.

"Yes," she replies, taking the carrot and popping it into her mouth.

I upend the cutting board into the bowl and give the contents a quick toss. "Everything is just about ready. Why don't you help me set the table?"

"Sure," she agrees without complaint.

Today has been quite an eye opener for me with regard to Isabel. First there was the revelation about her clothing, then the way she responded to the artistic pursuits presented by Lynzee. Her entire demeanor seems lighter this evening and I send up a silent prayer of thanks for guiding me to avenues to help her heal.

Isabel eats everything on her plate and even takes part in the conversation quite a bit. When dessert is finished, she also helps with the cleanup without prompting. I wonder if that's usual for her. She was only at my house for a short time, so I guess I just assumed she'd be like a lot of children and grumble when asked to help with chores.

Once the dishes are washed, dried, and put away, she disappears back to the comfort of the beanbag in Felicia's office while the adults settle into the living room for more conversation. My brother and Vance seem to have an easy camaraderie thing going on and that makes me happy.

I watch them as they talk and realize they're similar in some ways. They're both quick to teach and smile easily. A generally laid-back demeanor is another likeness, as well as their ability to flip a switch and be assertive about protecting those they love.

It was probably difficult for Vance to move up here, away from his network of friends and co-workers, not knowing much of anyone but his mother and aunt. He knew me, of course, but our running into each other was pure chance. Maybe he and Dale can be friends. With me, that would make at least two friends for him here.

Isabel trudges in looking half asleep, which lets me know it's getting late. She sits next to me on the side away from Vance and snuggles into my side when I put my arm around her. "It looks like you're about ready for bed," I observe. She just nods and yawns.

"Well, that's our cue," Vance says, rising. "Thank you for having us for dinner. It was great and we'll have to do it again sometime."

He and Dale shake hands, then he turns to me and offers me a hand up. Dale gives me a hug and kisses the side of my head. "Always good to see you, sister mine."

"Good to see you, too. Felicia, thank you for a wonderful evening."

"You're welcome. Will we see you at lunch tomorrow?""Yes, of course."

When we're settled in the car, Isabel surprises me when she says, "I don't like my therapist."

Rather than react right away, I simply say, "Oh?"

"She reminds me of a teacher I used to have that was mean to me. Plus, she smells funny."

Vance turns a bark of laughter into a thinly veiled snort.

"Okay. We'll see about getting you a new one." I guess I'll need to research art therapy sooner rather than later.

"Thank you. Miss Felicia said a therapist I like will make a big difference."

"She did, did she?"

"Did you know she was hurt by a man she worked for?"

"I do. It was a terrible thing."

Isabel turns and looks out the window. "She told me about it when she took me to her office and asked if I was talking to someone. When I told her I didn't like my therapist, she said I needed to tell you."

"I'm glad you did. Thank you for that."

Vance reaches over and takes my hand in his, giving it a squeeze.

Chapter 33

Vance

We deliver Isabel out to the ranch and take a quick tour of the ranch manager's house, where the girls have moved with Maggie. Isabel seems pleased to be in a quieter space, but Sophie, not so much.

I'm just glad they're still on the ranch property behind the fences and where the entire property is monitored by security cameras. Even though the girls are safe, I still want to get this resolved as quickly as possible.

Once those bastards that hurt Isabel are behind bars, the girls can get on with living their lives. Serena, too, and hopefully I'll be able to be a part of her life in the future.

Truth be told, I wanted to pursue something with Serena back when we were both in Atlanta. If it hadn't been for my kids, I would have. However, they were at that crucial age where they were transitioning from children to teenagers.

My gut told me that if the divorce took place, my kids, especially my son, wouldn't handle it well. It was a tough decision to make, but looking back, I know it was the right one.

There was no animosity between my wife and me. However, there was no great love between us either. We were young when we got married and she had a difficult time with my job.

Roommates who also happened to be married was a good descriptor for our relationship when we separated and I started seeing Serena. But when we talked about how we should move forward and either divorce or not, the one thing we both agreed on was that we should do what was best for the kids.

Now it looks like Serena, and I might have a second chance. At least I hope so. Second chances don't come around very often, so I need to make the most of it.

When we get to the hotel, I can tell she's tired, so I don't push for more time with her. I wonder how much of it is caused by the stressful finish of the school year and how much from worry for the girls.

I walk her to the door to her room. "Well, you have an entire night with no interruptions and you can sleep in as late as you want tomorrow."

Her smile is wan. "I need it, too. Your idea of taking a day off was a great one. Would you be terribly put out if I didn't meet you for breakfast?"

"Nah. I know you're not a big breakfast person. Meet me downstairs in the lobby at eleven and we'll head over to the family lunch."

"That sounds perfect."

Just as I start to turn away to go down the hall to my room, I stop. She's halfway turned to unlock her door when I put a hand on her arm. With a question on her face, she looks up at me.

Of its own accord, my hand goes to her jaw, cupping it. When I speak, my voice comes out rougher than I intended. "Serena, I'd really like to kiss you."

She doesn't move, and she doesn't reply, just stands there looking up at me. Then her eyes close and I'm sure she's going to tell me no, but then her lashes rise and she gives me the barest of nods.

My other hand rises to cradle her face between my big mitts, trying to be as gentle as I can as I lower my mouth to hers. Although I'd love nothing more than to devour her, I keep it light, brushing my lips against hers, then I deepen it, just a bit.

She reaches up to wrap her fingers around my wrists and leans into me. I'm not going to pass up an opportunity like this, so I release her face and wrap my arms around her, pulling her close. Her palms smooth over my chest and stop to rest on my pecs.

She smells like cinnamon and vanilla and tastes of chocolate and wine. It's a heady combination. The last thing I want to do is stop, but that's exactly what I do.

Resting my forehead against hers, I say, "It's late. I'll see you in the morning."

Her lips tuck in at the corners in a tired smile. "Good night, Vance."

This time I let her go through her door and wait for it to snap shut before I go down the hall to my room.

Right on time, she meets me in the lobby carrying her bag. I take it from her and lead her out to the car. "Did you sleep well?"

"I did," she replies. "It was just what I needed."

"You ready to face the horde?"

She just chuckles in reply.

It's late in the afternoon when we head back toward Norman. While at the family lunch, we made use of the resting room to talk with Roni and Takoda, conveying Isabel's comments about her therapist.

Roni just smiles and says, "She does have a unique mixed aroma of rose water and those strong breath mints that come in a tin."

She also took it well when Serena said she wanted to look into a therapist that uses art therapy in some form. Serena has become so involved in these girls' lives that I wonder how she's going to handle it when it's time for them to go back to their mother.

It's been a while since she's said anything, so I ask, "What are you thinking about?"

"Everything and nothing."

"I get it," I reply, because I do. "There's a lot to think about. So much that it's a little overwhelming."

"I like the house where they put the girls. It seems like a better space for Isabel and gives her somewhere to escape to when there's too much activity. Sophie can go over to the big house whenever she's in need of more engagement."

"Yes, it's a great compromise."

The silence falls back over us as I drive us home. It's not uncomfortable, or restless, but we both seem to have settled into a relaxed mood. I reach over and take her hand in mine and she lets me, her lips tilting as I thread our fingers together.

Her gaze returns to watching the trees go by, interspersed with expanses of sprouting fields. When we reach the outskirts of Norman, I break the silence. "You up for dinner?"

"Yes, I was just thinking about that. There's nothing at the house. I haven't had a chance to get to the store, but I don't feel like going out because I am feeling so relaxed and want to hold on to it. So, are you okay with getting something and taking it home?"

"Sounds good."

We agree on a restaurant, Serena calls it in, and we swing by to pick it up. All day today, she's been fine with being close to me. When we sat, she sat right next to me. When we moved through the house, she didn't tense when I put my hand on the small of her back.

I guess finally kissing her broke the tension I felt between us. It was as if she wasn't really sure of where she stood with me. Or that she couldn't quite trust me. After seeing her asshole ex, I understand how she might have trust issues.

At her house, I carry in her bag and the food. She takes her bag while I unpack the food and get out dishware and silverware. I've been here enough that I've about figured out where everything is.

She returns quickly and has changed into some slinky black pants that look stretchy and comfortable, topped by a blue tank top. Those pants look phenomenal stretched over her round ass, and I'm fantasizing about pulling them off her when she clears her throat.

My head snaps up to see a bemused look on her face. "What was that?"

She waggles the wine bottle at me. "I asked if you wanted a glass of wine?"

"Sure," I reply, not at all embarrassed about being caught checking her out.

Chapter 34

Serena

Okay...Vance was checking out my butt. Part of me is amused. Another part of me thinks it's hot and wants to jump his bones. However, there's still that part of me that thinks I'm a damn fool for even considering it and need to stick with my plan of swearing off men forever.

I'm not going to run away screaming, but will remain cautiously optimistic. It's easy to tell he's interested by the way he's been slowly creeping forward through little touches and kindnesses. Then last night, he kissed me and what a kiss it was.

My lips were still tingling after I closed the door to my room and leaned back against it. If he hadn't stopped things, I'm not sure I would have been able to refuse if he asked to come into my room. Why am I such a pushover when it comes to men?

Maybe it really is the whole daddy thing. My withholding father set me up to seek a father figure in a man, someone to love me unconditionally like my father never did. Perhaps. But perhaps I'm just a needy idiot.

If you'd asked me when I was just starting college where I thought I'd be at this age, I would have said happily married to an adoring husband, with a couple of kids, and a career on the judge's bench. That fresh-faced, hopeful girl would have been so wrong because I have none of those things.

Gee, that's depressing. Speaking of depressing, I'm starting to realize that I've been mildly depressed ever since I left Atlanta and I'm about to get sick of it. There is safety in isolation, but it's time I allowed myself to find at least a little joy in the world instead of denying myself of it.

Maybe Vance will bring some. Maybe he won't. If not, I'll find it for myself as I have done for most things in my life. I kind of hope he does, though.

We settle in at the kitchen island to eat. "How long does it usually take for you to wrap up the end of a semester?" he asks.

"Usually a couple of weeks, but with the long days I've been putting in, I think I'll finish up tomorrow or Tuesday mid-day at the latest."

He nods. "That will be good timing. The...um...Raven...gosh that sounds stupid...said we should have results in five days. If that's five regular days, that's tomorrow. If it's five business days, that will be Wednesday."

"I doubt a hacker would be constrained by the regular business week, but you never know."

He points his fork at me. "True, but either way, it's good timing."

"Yes, it is. I'm very curious to see what they turn up or whether it was a waste of five grand."

Vance shrugs, then gets up to rinse his plate and put it in the dishwasher. "My gut is telling me it was an excellent decision to enlist their help."

"Well," I say, "I hope your gut is right."

"It usually is," he replies with a grin.

When I give him a skeptical look, his grin widens.

"I, for one, tend to trust the evidence," I retort.

He leans down and kisses my temple, which makes spider feet dance up and down my spine. With his lips near my ear, he says, "My gut is just as good as evidence. You'll see."

That draws a laugh out of me as I get up to rinse my plate. Vance has already put away our trash and leftovers. He's becoming quite comfortable in my home.

I like it and don't in equal measure. Coming out of hibernation can be a scary thing.

"I'll be right back," I say. Then, deciding to push the boundary of my comfort zone a little, I add, "Why don't you see if you can find something good on the television?"

He's sitting in the middle of the sofa when I return and instead of sitting to one end, I sit right next to him. When he raises his arm to put it around my shoulder, I scoot in closer and put my hand on his thigh, leaning into him. The little worry witch in the back of my mind is screaming.

Shut up.

She doesn't, but she does tone it down some.

By degrees, my body relaxes as we watch the comedy Vance chose. It feels good to laugh. It also feels good to have a man's arm around me again.

His fingers are tracing lazy circles on my upper arm. The feel of those fingers wrapped around my jaw while soft lips brushed mine stirs in my memory and heat blooms in my belly, settling between my legs as a throbbing ache. I wonder what those long, thick fingers would feel like to other places on my body.

My fingers tighten on his thigh as I shift in my seat. Vance looks down at me. "You okay?"

Embarrassed, I look up and realize just how much I want him. When our eyes meet, my breath catches and my lips suddenly feel dry. My tongue snakes out to wet them and his eyes drop to watch.

Just like he did last night, he leans down slowly, giving me time to make him stop or tell him no. I don't want to say no, though. His lips on mine are exactly what I want, so I turn into him, putting my hand on his ribcage, feeling the taut muscles flex under my hand as he shifts his position to pull me closer.

Within moments, we're necking like a couple of kids on the couch while my parents are out for the night with one ear cocked for the sound of the garage door, making the most of the moment. Our tongues dance. Our lips pucker and slide, and it's stirring all kinds of lustful feelings in me.

I never had this kind of experience when I was a teenager. It's probably a good thing because I don't know that I'd have had the strength of will to say no to a lot more if a boy had kissed me like this.

When Vance's hand strokes along the side of my breast, making my nipple pebble and strain at the fabric of my bra, I want him to tweak it between his fingers. I want him to touch me everywhere.

As if he's reading my mind, his thumb strokes over the hard peak and the tiniest of moans oozes up my throat. With that encouragement, his thumb returns and those luscious fingers cup the rounded flesh. Between thumb and index finger, he teases my nipple and I press into his touch.

Things are getting boiling hot between us and I'm ready to start pulling off clothes, but just as I grip the hem of his t-shirt, his phone goes off and about gives me a heart attack. Vance puts his forehead to mine, breathing hard, as he pulls out his phone and looks at the screen.

"Sorry, it's mom."

I nod and extricate myself from him. Distance between us is needed for me to get my addled brain under control. What is he doing to me?

During my lifetime, I have had lovers. But only a few and none of them were good men. I think Vance is a good man, but can I really tell? Those other men seemed like they were good, too, but they weren't.

My instincts when it comes to men are horrible. I want to trust Vance, but that worry witch in the back of my brain is telling me not to. That's what my mama used to call that nagging little voice in your ear, your worry witch. I've been listening to her for so long she's not that little anymore.

So, I stand and move away, pretending not to notice when he has to adjust himself in his jeans, while he talks on the phone to his mother. It sounds as if some mishap has occurred, which most likely means he's going to need to leave. That's probably a good thing.

In the kitchen, I dispose of the empty wine bottle and pull out a pad of paper to start making a grocery list as he paces back and forth in the living room. When he's wrapping up the call, he comes over to me.

"Okay, mom. I'll be there soon." He disconnects the call and puts his phone away. "I'm sorry, but..."

"You need to go," I complete for him. "It's all right. Your mother needs you."

"Yeah," he agrees with a sigh. "Sure comes at the worst moment, though."

I smile up at him. "It does."

He leans down and gives me a quick peck on the lips. "Good night, Serena."

"Good night."

Chapter 35

Vance

Serena waves good night from her front door. Damn. I love my mother, but she sure has some lousy timing.

When I walk into my auntie's house, the smell of char hangs in the air along with the overarching odor of ammonia from the extinguisher. In the kitchen, it's so strong I almost turn around and walk right out. But I don't.

"What's going on here, ladies?"

Auntie Dot gives me an abashed look over her shoulder from where she's cleaning off the counter. Apparently, she put something on the stove to cook, walked away and forgot about it along with the dishtowel she left a little too close to the skillet.

"She didn't need to call you," Dot says.

I go over and pull her into a side hug, wresting the sponge from her at the same time. "Why don't you ladies go take a rest and let me handle this for a while?"

"Yeah," Mom huffs, "show up when we're almost done, so you can do the last little bit and act like you did the whole thing."

I know she's teasing, trying to make Auntie Dot feel less embarrassed. "You know it," I reply with a grin. "I've always had great timing like that."

"Hope we didn't interrupt anything important," Dot says.

They did, but that's not what she needs to hear. "Nah. It's all good."

By the time I finish in the kitchen, they're both dozing in their recliners in front of the television. Thankfully, whoever thought to use the extinguisher did it soon enough to avoid any serious damage. Mostly it's superficial scorch marks. Some tile and paint will need to be redone, but that's it.

When I turn off the television, they both snort and wake. "Y'all need to get your butts to bed and get some of that beauty rest," I tease.

Auntie Dot harrumphs, but pats my arm when she passes by.

"Good night, son," Mom says, pausing to kiss my cheek.

I watch them go down the hall and wait for their doors to close before I go to my room and turn in for the night. Thoughts of Serena fill my head as I try to let sleep in.

She felt so good against my body and under my hands. I wonder how far we'd have gone if Mom hadn't called. Just thinking about her has my dick getting hard again.

With my eyes closed, I recall the feel of her full breast filling my hand and the hard peak of her nipple straining against her clothes. Her kisses were just as hungry as mine and I have no doubt she wants me just as much as I want her.

My hand goes to my cock, seeking the only kind of release I've had in a long time. I'm not one fuck around, much less to do it casually, so it's been self-service for longer than I care to admit. The woman I want is in my sights and I'm willing to wait for her.

Something tells me it won't be much longer. I lie there, tugging and stroking my cock until the orgasm builds in my balls. When I'm very close, I go to the bathroom and finish the job, squirting hot come into a wad of toilet paper.

God, I hope it's soon when I bury myself deep into Serena's sweet pussy. I want her so badly, but I can't decide if I want to taste her or be inside her first. Maybe inside her and then, when the edge is taken off, I'll take my time and taste her everywhere.

With a much needed, albeit mostly unsatisfying, release taken care of, I go back to bed, sleep coming easier this time. Tomorrow is another day and I need my brain cells fresh to help Moses with three installs. He's bound and determined to make a techie out of me, but I don't know if it's gonna take.

Just as Moses and I are finishing up our last install, my phone pings, letting me know I've gotten a message. I'm up to my elbows in wiring and if I stop to check the message, I'll lose track of where I'm at.

Hopefully, it's nothing important like Mom and Auntie Dorothy trying to burn down the house again. Although I'm eager to have my own space again, part of me wonders if me leaving them alone to create even more havoc is a good idea.

An hour later, we're finished, and on our way back to the office when I remember my phone.

There is a text message but there's no number tied to the message, it's just there. I'm hesitant to open it, but knowing today is the first of the possible five-day deadlines for the hacker, I tap to open it.

Check your email, Detective Douglas.

I'm tempted, but want to wait to open it with Serena because it's her message, too. Adrenaline surges through me in anticipation of the results, making me antsy. As soon as Moses parks the SUV, I'm out the door and in the offices, looking for one of the Carver brothers.

I find Jack first, training with Moses. "Jack, sorry to interrupt, but we got the results."

He cocks his head quizzically, then understanding blooms across his features. "What did it say?"

"Don't know yet. I wanted to wait until I was with Serena to open it."

"Well, what are we waiting for? Let's go."

Rather than question his desire to go with me, I turn back toward the front door, intent on getting to Serena as quickly as possible. We startle her when we burst into her office at the college, both of us talking at once.

"Wait. What? You got it?" she asks.

I grin at her. "Yes."

With wide eyes, she asks, "What did it say?"

I shrug. "I haven't opened it yet. Wanted to wait and open it with you."

She gives me a pleased smile. "Send it to me and we'll open it on the big screen in the conference room next door."

Within a heartbeat, I have my phone out and forward the message to her. She unplugs her laptop and all three of us go to the other room. It only takes a minute or two for her to get set up, but it feels like it takes eons.

She logs in, opens her email and hesitates before clicking the attachment. I can't say that I blame her. The person who sent the file is less than scrupulous, after all.

She opens the file and reveals hundreds of documents. "There," Jack says, pointing. "Open that one that says summary."

I scan over the first page twice before it dawns on me what I'm seeing. This document is a chronological statement of facts, with reference notes to the names of the supporting documentation included in the file.

"Holy shit," I breathe.

The initial date in the chronology was almost twenty years ago. There are over a dozen victim's names and several of them, I recognize from the case information Serena and I have been going through.

"Holy shit is right," Jack agrees. "Look, there are even the names of men the victims got pimped out to, along with the payments."

He moves to the screen and points. "There's that fucker Draper and it looks like there were other cops getting pay offs prior to that. This asshole better get locked up or..." He doesn't finish the statement, but we all know what he means.

"I don't think we can take this at face value," Serena says. "We have to see if there's anything we can verify to prove the information's veracity."

For a moment, I'm taken aback, but then I think about it from a cop's perspective. An electronic file of information from an unknown source, some of it obviously acquired illegally. If someone brought it to me like that, I don't know that I'd trust it.

"You're right," I finally say into the silence that had fallen in the room. "Some of this stuff can only be duplicated by the police through the service of a warrant, like the bank records and such, but this will at least tell them where to look."

"If we could somehow talk to some of the victims, perhaps the older ones that are still alive. We wouldn't necessarily have to ask them direct questions, but if we phrase our questions well, we might be able to corroborate the information we were sent. At least enough to make it believable for the cops."

It's alarming just how many of the victims are dead and most of them by their own hand. Isabel could have been one of those statistics. And those bastards didn't care, just wanted her mom to hand over her other daughter to be abused.

Thank God, Maggie stepped in when she did. A lot of women her age with minimal income, no home, and tied to the demands of law school could have easily ignored the call for help. I'm so proud of her for stepping up to help her cousins.

No matter what it takes, I'm going to do everything I can to make sure things turn out all right for all three of those girls. They deserve some good in their lives after what they've been through.

"That's what I was thinking," Serena replies.

How could we possibly approach these women? They've been through a lot and are probably closed off. And the last thing we want to do is cause them more trauma.

"We'll have to be very careful," I say.

"Yes."

"Well," Jack says, "if you need anything from Carver Security, let me know and we'll make it happen."

"Do you want me to take you back to the office?" I ask him.

"Nah, I'll hoof it. My girlfriend delayed my departure this morning, so I didn't get my run in."

I give him my hand and he pulls me in for a bro hug with a slap on the back. "All right. See you tomorrow."

We watch him leave, then Serena closes out of the files and shuts down her computer. "If you'd like to come over for dinner, we can talk about our approach and decide which of the women who were victimized would be the best to approach."

She says it so nonchalantly, but I can tell she had debated with herself whether she wanted to ask me over again. I'm learning to read her and I can see the tension in her body even though she's trying to act casual.

Maybe she's afraid. Or maybe she's excited. Which remains to be seen.

"That would be great. I'm going to run home to shower and change and then I'll head your way. Do you want me to bring anything?"

"Not unless you want to bring some of that beer you like. I wasn't sure of the brand when I went to the grocery store last night, so I didn't get any."

Just outside the doorway to her office, I lean over and kiss her temple. "See you soon."

Chapter 36

Serena

Maybe I should have kept my damn mouth shut, but I couldn't. I enjoy having Vance at my home. With him there, it's not such a lonely place, but is that selfish of me?

There's a chance that we'll pick up where we left off last night. That makes my pulse kick up a notch. I'm probably a fool for even thinking about entertaining a man in my bedroom again, but maybe I'm going to be the one just getting what I need this time.

That's what men do, isn't it? It seems they only want to get what they need or want, then go about their business without regard for the other person. I'm more than a little sick of it.

More than once I've thought that maybe I should just get a vibrator and be done with men altogether. Heaven knows I seem to have the world's worst picker. Mama would probably turn over in her grave if I ever walked into one of those adult stores.

I wouldn't even have a clue what I'd like. Shoot, I haven't even been able to bring myself to look at those kinds of things online. However, if one more relationship goes south because the man turns out to be a dog, I'll have to figure it out.

The doorbell rings, but before I can rinse my hands and go to the door, Vance calls out, "It's just me."

"Just you, huh?" I tease.

He comes over and puts a hand on my hip before leaning in to kiss my cheek. I like it when he does that. Other than last night, he's not handsy. Even then, he wasn't pushy. He gave me plenty of time to say no if I wasn't comfortable.

Maybe he'll surprise me and turn out to be the good man I've been thinking he might be.

"Mmm... Something smells good," he says, putting a six-pack of beer into the refrigerator.

"Salmon, garlic parmesan green beans, and buttered new potatoes."

"You and Dale's Sunday family lunches are dangerous to my girlish figure."

"You'll have to start running from place to place like Jack does," I tease.

"Maybe," he says, going to the sink to wash his hands. "Is there anything I can help with?"

With the tongs I'm using to put the green beans into a bowl, I point to the cabinet. "If you wouldn't mind, take down a couple of place settings. Food wise, everything is done except for pulling the fish out of the oven in a minute or two."

Perfectly comfortable with the request, he goes straight to the cabinet where I keep the dishes and the exact drawer where I store the silverware. He seems right at home here. I'm not sure why that hits me and it seems my mind can't decide if it's a good thing or not.

Stop it. Just go with it as long as it suits you and keep your stupid, silly heart out of it.

Easier said...or thought...than done.

"So," he says once we sit down to eat. "Have you thought about an approach we can take for talking to previous victims?"

I give him some side eye. "We just had that conversation a little over an hour ago."

He points his fork at me. "Yeah, but I know how your big brain works. You've probably already got everything figured out while I'm still trying to wrap my head around the enormity of it. Every time I think about it, I get pissed off all over again and want to go out and do something I shouldn't."

His praise flatters me, but I don't let it show. "Believe me," I reply, "I'm tempted to let Jack do his thing on this one. Knowing the law constrains me, but I also know how inept the law can be, even when you do everything right."

"So you have a plan, then," he says smugly.

I smile and shake my head. "Well, I was thinking that we could pose as individuals organizing a non-profit to work with people who have gone through the foster care system trying to identify gaps where we could most be of help. Of course, we need to review the records to see who was actually in foster care before we go knocking on doors."

"And because we're organizing it, we don't need a paper trail or social evidence that it exists. That's brilliant."

My insides go all mushy at his words, which is even more evidence that I can't trust myself. A few sweet words and I'm ready to roll over like a puppy for a belly rub. Metaphorically, a *belly rub* might be kind of nice, though.

"I should be finished with the last of the paperwork to close out the semester tomorrow morning," I tell him.

"Excellent. Do you think you'll be ready to go through the data and choose our prospects tomorrow afternoon?"

With a nod, I say, "Yes. Then we could start making contact as soon as possible."

"This has me all worked up like I used to get when I was on a case."

"That's not surprising. You were an excellent detective. To be honest, I was surprised when you said you'd given it up because you were so good at it."

He shrugs. "I may have been good at it, but it wasn't good for me."

His comment is relatable to me. That's how I was feeling in those last days when I was sitting on the bench. Mrs. Jackson's suicide was just the straw that broke the camel's back, because I'd already been thinking about seeing what else might be out there.

Wanting to move us away from the sad memories of the past, I ask him about his mother. He tells me of their kitchen mishap and, although it could have been a terrible situation, he has me laughing by the end of the story.

"They're quite the pair," he says. "Mom's mind is sharp as a tack, but her body is frail. Auntie Dorothy's body is sturdy, but her memory is failing her more often."

We finish eating at the same time and work together to clean up and put the leftovers away. I'm rinsing dishes and turn to put a plate into the dishwasher, but Vance is there, much closer than I expected him to be.

I'm not startled, though; his nearness makes me smile up at him. He takes the plate from me, the last of the dishes, and puts it into the dishwasher, closing the door after it. He cups my jaw like he did last night.

It seems as if he enjoys doing that. I know I enjoy him doing it. It makes me feel special, treasured, even.

We stand there in the middle of the kitchen kissing for several long moments and I decide I'm ready to get my belly rub. I step into him, sliding my arms around his waist and my palms flat against the planes of muscle in his back.

He strokes his hands down my throat, taking his time and making me shiver. One arm goes around me, pulling me close. But his other hand stays on my shoulder, his thumb resting on my pulse point.

It feels incredibly intimate, this connection with the thrumming of my heart and the way I can feel the strong tattoo of his through my palms on his back. Two bodies, alive and virile, filled with desire.

His desire is evident with his need pressing against my abdomen. My own need is throbbing between my legs where I'm hot and slick with it.

He smells so good. His cologne is earthy, with hints of cinnamon. I love it when a man smells nice. One good hug and you can carry his scent with you all day long.

I want this...want him. As a grown ass woman, there's nothing wrong with indulging my libido, no matter what the preacher says. I mean, look who the preacher has for a best friend...a lying, cheating, scum sucking...

Stop it.

Putting away the negativity that threatens to rob me of all these tantalizing sensations I'm feeling, I take Vance by the hand and lead him to my bedroom. When I stop in the middle of the room to face him, he cups my face again.

Looking down at me, his eyes searching mine, he asks, "Are you sure?"

I nod my head and stretch up to kiss him. That's all the invitation he needs, and his mouth falls on mine. With that simple gesture, he looses his desire and seems intent on devouring me.

Because I've wanted to get my hands on him practically since I first met him all those years ago, I pull at his shirt. He breaks the frantic kiss and pulls it off over his head, leaving me speechless and frozen, taking in the sight of him.

I suck in a breath before I pass out and reach out a tentative hand, stroking it across the hard planes of muscle in front of me.

As soon as I make contact, it's like a bomb goes off in my brain and everything is incinerated except the wanting of him.

My own clothes are coming off so quickly I might have actually torn something, but then I'm down to my underwear and I stop, insecurity creeping in. He is beautiful in every way, his body, his spirit, his heart.

Beautiful is not something I've ever been called by a man who wasn't using the word as a tool of manipulation. Before the fear has a chance to take hold, he's there. His arms go around me, pulling me close.

A tender kiss is planted on my temple, then his lips brush my ear. "You are perfection," he says, his voice low and dripping with lust. Another kiss is pressed to my neck just below my ear, and spider feet tickle up my spine, making me tremble.

He backs me up until the backs of my thighs hit the side of the bed, then moves to the other side and repeats the motions. This time he says, "Every curve of your body is flawless and lush."

Well, now. A woman could get used to hearing that kind of talk.

All tension eases out of me as I give in to the desire again and banish the doubt. He unhooks my bra, and I let him pull it off me. When I'm bared above the waist, he leans back and takes me in.

One meaty hand reaches out to cup my heavy breast, and he drags a nail across the nipple, making it pebble in response. His mouth lifts on one side, pleased at the result. Leaning down, he wraps his lips around the peak and sucks it as his other hand reaches up to knead and reshape my other breast.

The pleasure is so acute that I have to put my hands on his shoulders to keep my balance. When I do, he wraps an arm around my waist and lowers me onto the bed and adjusts me so my butt is hanging halfway off, then resumes his good work.

His mouth left my nipple wet and aching, but instead of returning to it, he turns to the other, giving it similar attention. We're not even naked yet and my panties are dripping.

As if he could read my thoughts, with both hands on my breasts, he begins kissing his way down my stomach and lowering his body until he's kneeling before me. Once he's on his knees, he hooks his fingers in my panties and pulls them down, denuding me completely.

He presses my legs apart, leaving me exposed to his view. This gives me a little spark of trepidation because I've never had anything like this happen.

Yes, there was foreplay, but oral only happened under the cover of darkness and only rarely because I didn't find it particularly enjoyable. Diondre was more than happy to skip it.

When Vance moves between my legs, taking in the sight of me, I fist my hands in the comforter. I feel so unsure, so...so...*naked*.

He runs his nose through the thatch of curls at the apex of my thighs, breathing my scent in. When the flat of his tongue strokes over my labia, I flinch a little. After he shoulders my legs wider, he gets a firm grip on my hips and puts his mouth to my most intimate flesh.

I'm about to tell him he doesn't have to do this when he does some kind of swirly thing with his tongue that makes me let out a little squeak. Which is weird because I don't know that I've ever squeaked like that in my life. A dark chuckle drifts up from between my legs.

Fingers slide easily into me in my well-lubricated state; first one, then two. After a few preliminary strokes, it's as if he unleashes the full power of his cunnilingus arsenal.

His tongue is licking and flicking and swirling. Lips are sucking and kissing. And those fingers, oh, my God, those fingers are fucking me better than I've ever been fucked in my life. If he's this good with his fingers, what's it going to be like when he puts his dick in there?

The onslaught of his arsenal batters down all the walls of my insecurities and inhibitions. One perfect strike of his weapons of wantonness, his fingers hitting a spot inside of me I didn't know I possessed combined with his lips wrapped around my clitoris has me crying out and trembling as an orgasm detonates inside me.

Never have I felt anything so powerful. This man, this wizard of pussy magic, has just rocked my world in a way I didn't know was possible.

I've barely regained my senses when he kisses me on the mouth and I can taste myself. This is another new thing for me and although I had thought I'd be repulsed by it, I find it strangely erotic, so I kiss him back. Hungrily and thoroughly.

When he pulls away, he rasps, "Condom?"

That's when I notice his hips are wedged between my thighs, my legs still hanging off the bed. There's another moment of panic when I realize he intends to have sex with me like this.

I've never done anything but the missionary position and again, only in the dark. The only thing Diondre ever wanted to do with the lights on was me giving him a blow job. He enjoyed watching.

Shut up. I tell the panic. So far this is fucking fantastic, so I'm on board for more new things. And yes, Mama, I used a curse word...in my mind...and I'm not going to apologize.

I watch unabashedly as Vance retrieves a condom and rolls it down his length. His very thick, very long length which is crisscrossed with ropey veins. The sight of it makes me swallow.

When I look up, I see Vance watching me, watching him.

"You okay?"

A smile spreads across my face and I reply, "Yes, definitely."

He grins back at me. Now that he's fully sheathed, he moves closer and notches the head of his cock at my opening. "It's been a while for me, so I apologize in advance if this doesn't last as long as I'd like."

Before I can reply, he slides inside me, taking his time and stretching me tight. When he is buried to the hilt and begins to move, I let my head fall back onto the bed because it feels so good.

I look up to see him watching where we're joined. His lips are pressed together like he's concentrating awfully hard. It's my turn to ask, "Are you okay?"

His eyes snap up to mine. "You feel too good. I'm not going to last long."

Wrapping my legs around his hips, I sit up and kiss him, loving that he's so turned on by me, by us together like this. When I change position, in response to the increased connection and friction, my clitoris wakes up again.

Only rarely have I ever had one orgasm from sex, much less two. I didn't think it was possible. Reaching around him, I cup his ass, loving the feel of his flexing muscles as he thrusts into me over and over.

He breaks our kiss. "Baby, if you keep that up..."

I kiss him again. The pressure is building in me again, so I flex my fingers and press my nails into his skin.

Poised on the edge of the precipice, I pull my mouth away from his and gasp, "Vance."

When the orgasm bursts and flows over me, I put my forehead to his shoulder, clutching at him with legs and hands. After a few brief moments, he groans and loses himself inside of me.

We stay there like that, wrapped in each other's arms, for I'm not sure how long. I finally have the strength to raise my head from his shoulder and look at his face to find him smiling at me. "Hey," he says.

I duck my head and smile. "Hey."

He kisses my forehead. "Baby, you are incredible."

Chapter 37

Vance

Monday was a turning point for Serena and me. When she took me to her bed, I felt like the luckiest man in the world. Not only was the sex incredible, that she let down her walls and opened up to me like that was amazing.

Afterward, as we lay in bed cuddling, she told me that some of it was new for her. I didn't expect that she was a virgin, and she wasn't but she is inexperienced in a lot of ways.

It's going to be my absolute pleasure to try new things with her as she discovers what she likes beyond just the basic mechanics. Basic mechanics seem to be the bulk of what she's experienced so far.

We've been together every day since, just being together, living and loving. Sometimes she seems uncertain, but when I ask her about it, she tells me everything is fine. I hope it is because everything is more than fine with me.

I met her at noon on Tuesday and we went through the victim lists. Out of the dozen or so victims, almost half of them are dead, the majority by suicide. One of the young women just went missing and was never heard from again, so we put her with the ones that are no longer with us.

We decide on a list of four women. All of them are adults now, which was key to us. Questioning minors with their parents there would be difficult and we'd never, ever consider questioning them alone.

We spoke with two of the women yesterday and have two appointments today. I was shocked when all of them responded so quickly and seemed eager to talk. The first two didn't come right out and confirm anything, but with our carefully worded questions, there was enough information to infer that they likely experienced something similar to Isabel.

Our first appointment this morning was a no-show. We rang the bell, knocked on the door, and even waited around for a while. At a half hour, we tried again, even though we hadn't seen anyone coming or going from the apartment.

She was one of the most recent victims. So, understanding how a traumatized young woman might be skittish about talking to strangers about her experiences growing up, we left.

The last appointment is late in the afternoon with a woman who was one of the earliest victims. By all appearances, she's turned her life around.

She lives in a middle-class neighborhood and, based on the kids' toys in the front yard, she has a family. However, I know better than most how appearances can be deceiving.

The front door opens as soon as we set foot on the porch. Maria Stephens is in her mid-thirties based on the information we have. She's pretty with dark hair and big brown eyes.

Those eyes are sharp, scrutinizing both of us from head to toe as she says, "Y'all the nonprofit folks?"

After meeting the two women yesterday, and this woman today, if I were to line them up alongside Isabel, it's clear that the attorneys have a type. Although they're different ethnicities, Latina, Native American, or mixed, they all have light to medium brown skin and large dark eyes.

"Yes." Serena confirms.

"Come on in out of the heat," she says, stepping back and inviting us inside. "Y'all want something to drink? I've got water, tea, or a couple different kinds of pop."

Both of us decline as we sit on the sofa where Maria indicates. There are more toys strewn throughout the house and smiling family photos showing Maria with a man, who I assume is her husband, and three children – two girls and a boy. In every picture, the children are smiling or laughing.

Serena takes the lead, as we agreed was the best approach, and introduces us by our fake names. She starts off with the general questions, easing the discussion into Maria's past.

After the fourth question, Maria holds up a hand. "Wanting to help kids in foster care is all well and good, but you want to know what those kids really need? They need someone who will listen to them and believe them."

Serena writes it down on the pad of paper clipped to a clipboard. "That's good," she says. "That's exactly the kind of thing we're looking for. It's clear you feel strongly about the subject. Can you tell us why that is?"

Maria's face turns dark. "I was just fine until some asshole got my mama hooked on drugs. She drained her bank account, lost her job, and started hooking to support her habit. He agreed to represent her in court, but she had no money. It had all gone up her veins or into the crack pipe."

She rises from her seat, clearly agitated. There are a few moments when she paces as she continues speaking. "He agreed to take the fees out in trade."

Serena leans forward and I'm about to start pacing myself. This is more than we could have hoped for. Direct correlation that the evidence we have is solid.

"Oh?" Serena asks when Maria stops and stares out the back door that looks out onto another manicured lawn and one of those colorful plastic swing sets.

"I was bartered to pay her bill," Maria says, her voice barely more than a breath.

"I'm so..." Serena starts.

Maria waves a hand. "It was a long time ago, but when I tried to tell, it fell on deaf ears. Even when I told the cops. Of course, when I got too old for the perverts, Mom went to jail, and I was put into foster care. Stupid me, I had the thought that I was safe. But no, I was still fighting only now it was my foster daddy I was fighting off. I told the social worker about all of it and she did nothing. In fact, the next time I saw her, she was driving a new car."

"Maria..."

She waves her hand again, cutting Serena off. "I don't want your pity or your sympathy. But if you really want to make things better, have someone, a counselor or something, talk to those kids without their parents around. Someone who will believe them and take action."

Her fingers dash across her cheeks. Without looking at us, she says, "Now, y'all gotta go. My babies will be getting home soon and I don't want them asking questions about your visit."

"Thank you Mrs. Stephens," Serena says. "We appreciate your time and will take your comments to heart."

We see ourselves out when Maria doesn't move from staring out the back door. Neither one of us speaks until we're down the block and stopped at an intersection.

"Wow." Serena says, breaking the silence.

"I know. She was one of the first, so that confirms their predatory scheme had already started back then."

Serena nods as she pulls out her phone. She finds the contact she wants and presses the call button, putting it on speaker so I can listen in.

"Pickering," a gruff voice answers. The familiar sounds of a precinct office filter through the phone, giving me a pang of nostalgia for a moment.

"Ford, hello. This is Cait's friend Serena Chilton. I have you on speaker, and I'm with another friend of mine, Vance Douglas."

"Hey Serena, what can I do for you?"

"We have some information we would like to give to you and Carlos."

"What's this about?" His voice has taken on the wary tone of an officer well trained in following protocol.

"I'd like to tell you that in person, but it has to do with the girls I recently took in. Did Cait tell you about them?"

"Yeah. Just broad strokes, but she did mention it."

"What you do with this information is up to you, but I want to ensure it is put into the hand of law enforcement, and even more importantly into hands I know can be trusted to not sweep it under the rug because that's what's happened before."

"Before?" Now his wariness is superseded by his detective's inquisitiveness.

"Yes. Could we come by today?"

"Hang on. I'm at the station. Let me see if Carlos is around."

We wait while the noise on his end fades and renews as he moves through the building. "He's here, but it looks like he's about to head out," Ford says. "Let me see what he's got cookin."

The rumble of low male voices goes on for a moment, then Ford comes back on the line. "He's going out on a call, but we're both free on Monday morning. Why don't you come around ten?"

She looks over at me and I nod in response to her unasked question.

"Perfect," she says. "We'll see you then."

I reach over and put my hand on her thigh, giving it a squeeze. "This has come together much quicker than I thought it would."

"If it hadn't been for the information we were able to get from the Raven, we'd still be slogging through case information. My legal brain might squawk about it, but my practical brain says it was money well spent."

"Why don't you let me take you out tonight? Not really to celebrate, discovering a decades long trail of abuse isn't something to be happy about, but to toast to the fact that the perpetrators will be behind bars soon and the abuse stopped."

She hesitates. My inclination is to fill the silence that has fallen between us and soothe her concerns, but she's going to have to decide what she wants from this relationship.

If she just wants more of me coming to her house to hang out, eat, and have sex... Well, I wouldn't exactly be happy with it, but I'd be willing to keep going that route for a short time to see if something more developed.

I don't want some ongoing casual hook-up thing. If that's what she wants, I'll be shocked, but after the last guy, maybe she's not ready.

"Sure," she finally says. "What did you have in mind?"

"Oh, just something laid back. Dinner and something else."

"What else?"

I smirk at her and tease. "You'll just have to say yes to find out."

Moses had mentioned taking a date on a river cruise up in the City where it's adults only because they serve drinks. It sounded like fun, and if you take the later one, you get to watch the sunset, which sounds romantic. I just hope they have tickets available.

Chapter 38

Serena

Vance takes me home after I agree to go out with him tonight. Why on earth I did that, I don't know. I'm only supposed to be getting metaphorical belly rubs, nothing more serious.

My stupid heart keeps overriding my good sense, though. It's telling me it's a good thing to hope for something more. To hope for love.

Stupid heart.

So, I agreed to go out with him. To be honest, I was surprised he asked me out. With every other man I've been with, they've taken me out on dates until I agreed to sex and then it was mostly them coming over for me to cook a meal and sex after.

That's why I'm so surprised by Vance. After all, he's already getting what he wants. We've had sex almost every night since that first time and sometimes more than once in a night. The only night we haven't been together is last night when I went to dinner at the Society.

It's been incredible. I've had more orgasms in a few days than I'd had in my entire life previously. Probably three or four times more.

I change clothes several times before settling on an outfit. He said laid back, so I finally settle on a pair of stretchy black pants that could almost be considered leggings, a black camisole, a sheer filmy colorful top, and comfortable flat sandals in case we do any walking.

When the doorbell rings, a million butterflies take wing in my stomach. Why am I so nervous? For goodness' sake, we've been together almost every day for weeks and have seen each other naked several times; there's not a lot of mystery left.

But this is a date. Not just a casual get together. Not just me cooking for him in my home, my place of power. This is a date. A serious date that could mean something more.

I open the door to find him standing there with flowers and have to blink to make sure I'm not hallucinating. He holds the colorful bouquet out to me. "I wasn't sure what you liked, so I got something with a variety."

"Thank you. They're beautiful," I say, taking them from him. "Let me put them in water real quick and grab my bag."

All a fluster, I turn and walk back toward the kitchen. When I take down a vase from the cabinet and turn toward the sink, I almost drop it because he's there, a wall of man flesh that looks delicious enough to eat.

He's got on dark wash jeans and a stylish copper colored tee that pops against his dark skin. It also shows off the body underneath.

He takes the vase from me and places it on the counter next to where I placed the flowers, then steps to me. One hand goes to my jaw. He either really enjoys doing that or realizes that I really like him doing it because he does it a lot.

His other arm goes around my waist and pulls me close. The kiss is soft and tender and when it starts to get heated, he pulls away and puts his forehead to mine. Looking into my eyes from an inch away, he says. "Hi. You look beautiful."

I swallow, my traitorous heart melting and my lips curving into a shy smile. "Hi. Thank you, you do, too."

He lets me go and I quickly tend to the flowers. I'll take more time arranging them when I get home. Or maybe tomorrow if we get up to other things tonight. I hope we get up to other things tonight.

When I have my bag, he lets me lead the way to the door, then waits on the porch while I lock up. As always, he opens my car door for me and waits for me to settle before closing me in.

I'm surprised when he heads toward the City. "Do you like Cajun food?" he asks when we're nearing downtown.

"I did grow up in Louisiana," I chuckle.

"I'd forgotten that," he replies. "Guess because we knew each other in Atlanta, my mind defaulted to Georgia."

"Also, my daddy was half creole. My brother Dale's mama was Cajun, and he's always loved to cook, so I've been eating crawfish, jambalaya, and gumbo since I was a baby."

"Cayenne pepper in your blood, eh?" he teases in a Louisiana patois.

"You know it," I reply with a grin.

The restaurant in Bricktown isn't fancy, but it's nice and I appreciate Vance's version of laid back. Our food is not as good as home, but does stir a feeling of nostalgia in me. I haven't been back to Louisiana since Daddy died and I went off to college.

My half-brother Dale goes home occasionally and has even taken Felicia down there several times, but he has his mama's family there. My other two full brothers never did have any time for me and haven't reached out since I left.

Good riddance to bad trash is how I feel about them. Mean trash, too. I don't even know if they're married, have children, or even still alive. It's odd to think I might have nieces and nephews out there in the world I haven't met.

"You ready?" Dale asks, pulling me out of my ruminations.

"Yes."

"What were you thinking so hard about?"

"Home, mostly. I haven't been back since I left for school," I admit to him.

"Do you miss it?"

"Not really," I reply with a shake of my head. "I do miss the food, though."

He chuckles and rises from his chair, offering me his hand. We make our way through the restaurant, his hand on the small of my back. All of this feels way too good.

I keep a firm grip on Vance's hand when I'm stepping onto the boat for the cruise he has planned as our something else for tonight. Although I know it's perfectly safe, this is another new experience for me.

He steps on board, not letting go of my hand. "You okay?" he asks, probably in response to the way I'm crushing his hand.

"Yes. I've just never been on a boat before." He looks at me sideways. "Really?"

I nod and lick my lips, nervous. "Yes, really. And you'd better not tease me or I'll get right back off."

A chuckle rumbles out of him, but he doesn't say anything. He also keeps letting me squeeze the crap out of his hand, so I'm fine for the moment.

Once I acclimate for a few minutes, I'm much more relaxed. The boat isn't large like a cruise ship, but carries a few dozen people. There is an enclosed cabin where the bar is, as well as seating on the deck.

We go inside and get drinks, taking a seat inside while we're still docked and other passengers arrive. It's too hot outside to stand out there in the sun.

Vance is sticking very close to me. It seems he has a need to be touching me, always. This is another thing that's different for me, but I'm not hating it.

I find myself wanting to lean into those touches and lean into him. For so long, I've been this single entity out there without anyone to lean into or lean on. Dale and I are close, but he was in the military and outside the US for much of his career. Other than him, there's been no one.

I've never been able to make friends easily either. As an attorney, I was so focused on work that there wasn't time to build friendly relationships. When I reached the bench, there was a need to guard my personal life.

It was amazing how many people would attempt to sidle up next to me on a personal level for one reason or another. Either they wanted to be able to say they were friends with a judge, or they were trying to use me as a tool to manipulate the system.

My parents were very closed off and closed minded, so a general spirit of distrust is something that was ingrained in me from an early age. Things you learn as a child are difficult to shake off. However, my experience with Vance so far has me wanting to try harder.

It took over a year of being a member of the Belladonna Society to start participating with the five women from my orientation group. They've all been wonderful and although their friendships are much further along, they're so warm and welcoming that I've never felt left out.

The cruise gets underway and we chat with the other passengers some, but mostly with each other. Vance is much more outgoing than I am and seems to enjoy talking with others, but he keeps turning his full focus back to me.

When the sky begins to light up with color, we go outside. With the boat moving, it's much cooler outside. Everyone else seems to have the same idea.

Vance takes up a position where he is leaning back against the cabin and pulls me against him, my back to his front, and wraps his arms around me. I hook my hands on his arms and relax against his solid body.

When he nuzzles my neck, I smile and tilt my head to the side to give him better access. As the boat pulls up to dock, I'm a little sad the cruise is over. It was nice once I got over being silly.

"That was nice," I say, telling Vance my thoughts as we walk through the parking lot arm in arm. "Thank you for taking me. The whole evening has been great."

"The first of many, I hope," he replies, smiling down at me.

I stop us and lean up to kiss him, then resume our journey to the car.

He's just turning onto my street and I'm hoping he'll want to come in when the car's electronics tell him he's getting a call from his Aunt Dorothy. "Sorry, I'd better take this."

"Of course," I say as he pushes the button to accept.

"Auntie Dot," he says into the air. "What's up?"

"Your mama has gone and fallen. The folks in the ambulance think she may have broken her hip."

He looks over at me, and I reach out to put my hand on his arm. "Where are they taking her?" he asks.

His aunt rattles off the hospital information and says she's going to leave to follow it as soon as she hangs up with him. He assures her he will be there as quickly as he can.

When he puts the car in park, I get out, not wanting to delay him. Headlights wash over me as I round the front of the car and walk straight into his arms.

"I'm sorry," he says. "I envisioned a very different ending to this evening."

"Don't be silly," I say, putting a palm to his cheek. "It's your mother. You *have* to go."

He leans down and kisses me. "Good night, baby."

With a smile, I say, "Good night. Be safe."

Then he's gone and I'm left watching after him, concerned for his mother.

Chapter 39

Serena

I'm in the hospital's gift shop, standing in the short line to pay for a card to go with the flowers I purchased when I see Vance walk by and my heart soars at being so lucky to run into him. My hand rises to wave to see if I can get his attention, but then I see the woman walking along beside him and all those good feelings disappear.

I make my purchase and step into the hall. Instead of going toward the elevators to take the flowers to his mother's room, I turn in the direction he was going with the woman. They're strolling along slowly, caught up in their conversation.

I should turn around and go to his mother's room. That's what I should do, but I can't force myself to do it. It's like a car accident that you can't look away from, but instead of tragedy playing out in front of me, the crash and burn is happening inside my chest.

Her arm is tucked in his just like mine was last night, and it's clear they know each other well. She turns her head and looks up at him adoringly, laughter pouring out of her. There's a carefree bounce in her step and she looks so full of life.

She's young and pretty and nothing like me.

I stop in the hallway as they push through the doors into the cafeteria. My breath is coming in short, quick pants and I put a hand on the wall to keep from losing my balance when I become light-headed.

"Why don't you just go in there and say hello? Vance is a good man, a trustworthy man," whispers the angel on my right shoulder.

Diondre's lips are right next to my skin when he whispers into my left ear, "You thought the same thing about me and look how that turned out."

I spin around, expecting to see Diondre standing there, but no one is there in the hallway but me. When I'm sure I can put one foot in front of the other, that's what I do. I turn around and head to the elevators.

Vance's mother is sleeping in her bed and another woman who looks very much like her is dozing in the chair next to the bed. Rather than wake them, I place the flower arrangement on the windowsill with the others, but I don't leave the card. It's better if no one knows I was here.

I keep it together until I get to my car. Once I'm behind the wheel, I let the heartbreak sneak in, but I don't cry. I will not cry for a man ever again.

The next morning, I wake to a text from Vance asking me to give his apologies for not showing for lunch because he needs to stick close to his mom in the hospital. I confirm I will, relieved that I won't have to see him today.

When I do have to see him again, it's going to be tough, but I'm tough, too. I'll just need to shut down whatever it was growing between us. Squash it for good so he can get on with his life with whoever that woman is and I can get on with mine.

This time the lesson has been learned.

I need to find a new church. If I was still attending, I'd have that to occupy my morning. However, since everything that went down with Diondre, I've been reluctant to go again.

This sitting around all morning waiting for it to be time to go south for lunch so I can see the girls is enough to set my teeth on edge. There's too much time to think, and I already do too much of that.

I'm barely out of the car at the ranch when Sophie is there, wrapping her arms around me. "Hi! Where's Mr. Vance?"

"He couldn't come today," I tell her, hugging her back. "His mama fell and is in the hospital, so he stayed there with her."

"Oh no! Is she gonna be okay?"

"She'll be fine. I promise."

"Good!" she says and goes bouncing back to the group of kids.

Taking a deep breath, I plaster on a smile, greeting people and making nice even though I don't feel an ounce of the happiness I'm showing on my face. This is familiar, though, so it comes easily. Most of my life has been spent playing a role, acting out a make believe life so no one would see what was under the surface.

First, it was so everyone would think we were a big, happy family, for Mama's sake, and that my dad wasn't a horrible person. Then it was so my brothers wouldn't think I was a threat. On and on it went. Even when I was on the bench, I was forced to keep a calm façade and let criminals go when I wanted to throw the book at them.

So, today is easy. Or at least I thought it would be, but the person who saw behind my mask was not who I expected. If anyone was going to be able to call me out, I would have thought it would be Dale.

Isabel slides in next to me on the glider where I've been sitting in the shade drinking tea and watching the children playing after lunch. All around me, people are talking, but I've ignored it, focusing on the laughing faces of the kids as they race around, playing some convoluted game of tag.

She leans against me, and I lift my arm so she can snuggle underneath. "Why are you so sad today?" she asks as she takes my hand in hers.

"I'm not sad."

"Liar." With that word, she almost undoes me.

"You don't need to be worrying about me."

"Need doesn't have anything to do with it when we care about people."

I squeeze her against my side and lean down to kiss the top of her head, Then I plaster the smile back onto my face. My eyes snag on my brother's. He's watching from his seat in the shade next to Felicia. He raises an eyebrow at me and my smile falters.

His eyes narrow and he flicks his gaze to the house, the message clear. Apparently, I'm not the only one paying attention because Isabel moves away from me. "Go tell Mr. Dale what's bothering you. You'll feel better if you do."

"You are too smart for me," I say with a chuckle as I rise from my seat, meeting my brother on our way to the house.

Neither of us says a word until he closes us into the resting room, the room people use when they need a break from the chaos. "Spill it," he says.

"It's nothing. I'm fine."

"Liar."

I huff out a laugh. "That's what Isabel said."

"She's a smart girl."

Before I can stop it, my mouth takes over. "I saw Vance with another woman."

"Were they having sex?"

"No!" I glare at him.

"Were they kissing?"

"No."

"Tell me what you saw."

His voice is tender, cajoling, so I tell him about the hospital.

"Did you ask him about it?" I look away. "No."

"Sounds like you two need to have a conversation."

I shake my head. "Why? He'll just give me some bullshit story; they always do. I have concluded that I have a horrible picker when it comes to men and I'm tired of being lied to.

Romance just isn't meant for me, because every time I try, I end up with more broken bits inside."

He pulls me into a hug. "You're a grown woman and Lord knows I've never been able to tell you what to do, but I think you're wrong about Vance. You need to talk to him and sort this out."

I put my arms around him and rest my head on his chest, taking in the comfort he is offering. "That's your answer for everything, isn't it?"

"Yes, because it works."

Chapter 40

Vance

The blaring of my alarm drags me out of sleep and right into a foul mood. Maybe it's the worry over Mom or the burning the candle at both ends. Or maybe it's too many days without seeing, or even talking to, Serena.

If that's the case, that will be remedied today when we meet at the police station to hand over our evidence to Ford and Carlos, the detectives Serena knows. After spending time with her almost every day, I miss her.

After a quick stop at the hospital to check on Mom, I pull up to the station. Of course, she's already here. That woman is always two steps ahead of me. Just the thought of it makes me smile.

She's waiting there in the lobby, dressed to impress in a professional outfit. Her eyes flick up, but she doesn't return my smile. Something's wrong.

I lean down to kiss her, but she turns her head and my kiss lands on her cheek. Something is seriously wrong. What could have happened since Friday? I thought we were good....great, even.

Just as I'm about to lean over and ask her what's wrong, a man walks into the lobby. For him, she smiles. "Carlos," she says, as she stands, "it's so good to see you again."

He hugs her and kisses her on the cheek. If I didn't know he was already with someone, I'd be a little jealous. Why does he get her smiles? What the fuck is wrong?

"Carlos, this is my friend Vance Douglas. He was a detective with the Atlanta PD for many years and took part in gathering the information we're going to show you."

Friend? The way she said it is so distant and cold. My bad mood from this morning is simmering under my skin and her calling me a friend turned up the heat.

"Carlos Gutierrez," the detective says as he extends his hand to me. I shake it and give him a nod. "Come on, Ford's waiting in a conference room and you know how he loves to wait."

Serena chuckles.

As I follow them through the station, my mind is whirring, trying to figure out what's going on. She and I need to have a talk because for the life of me, I have no clue.

We step inside a small conference room where another man is sitting on the other side of the table, texting on his phone. He looks up and smiles at Serena. She smiles at him, too, as if she doesn't have a care in the world.

"Hey Serena! Cait says hi."

She lets him touch her just like the other guy and he kisses her cheek.

"Tell her hi back from me." When she turns her head to accept his kiss, she's grinning.

She turns to introduce me, and her smile falters, but she covers it. "Ford Pickering, this is Vance Douglas, an old friend of mine. He recently moved from Atlanta, where he did the same job you and Carlos do. He's now working with Carver Security."

"Good to meet you," I say, as I shake the man's hand.

Those of us who entered take seats at the small conference table and Serena pulls a folder out of the bag she's carrying and sets it on the table between us. First she tells them Isabel's story and how that started our quest for information.

We talked about what we should say about the hacker and decided to leave Raven out of it. The information he provided proved that Officers Draper and Pierce, along with other law enforcement personnel, were being paid off by the attorneys.

We will tell them our suspicions about the payoffs, but without a warrant to acquire the information, it's inadmissible in court. Serena is to the part where Isabel tried to report the abuse to an officer, which we now know was Draper, and how he showed up and was allowed to abuse her as well.

Carlos swears under his breath. Ford's face is stone.

"After that, she tried to commit suicide, and that's when her cousin was pulled in by the girl's mother."

She quickly tells about Maggie coming to her and how they moved the girls down to the ranch owned by members of her brother's family. "From there, we started gathering information, going through case logs and eventually talking to potential victims and their families."

"What?" Carlos' head snaps up. "You could have…"

Serena puts up a hand to interrupt him. "I'm a former judge. I know what's admissible and what's not. Our approach was that we worked for a non-profit and were gathering information about their experience with the foster care system."

Page by page, she goes through the information in the folder. Ford and Carlos lean over the table, scrutinizing every bit of information. "We think both the partners in the law firm are involved, but Graham was the instigator and he's been at it a long time, almost twenty years. At least that's what the data implies."

That's what we know, but we can't tell them that without revealing our source, which would taint everything.

"We found several companies in which he is a partner and you'll find a list of properties owned by them," I say and pull out a map and tap a finger on it. "This one was identified by Isabel as the house where Graham took her and kept her. She said he had recording equipment and other…things."

"Son of a bitch," Ford breathes. "Can you leave this folder with us?"

"Yes," Serena replies. "These are all duplicates."

"Okay. We'll take it up the chain."

"Be careful," I say. "We have a feeling there are more cops getting paid off than just Draper and Pierce."

"I understand," Ford replies. "We'll take it from here."

Serena nods. "Thank you, Ford, and you Carlos. I knew we could trust you."

She hugs each of the men again.

"Cait is talking about doing another barbeque at the house, but she wants to wait until the fall after Demi and Kellen get married," Ford says.

"Just let me know when, and I'll be there."

Carlos escorts us back out of the building and we exit to the parking lot. "Well, I think that went well," I say, trying to break the ice between us even though I don't know how it got there in the first place.

"I agree," she says as she opens her car door. Before she can get inside and close me out again, I step into the gap. I don't crowd her, just keep her from closing the door.

"Serena, baby, what's wrong? You've been giving me the cold shoulder ever since I walked through the door."

She sighs, but she doesn't look at me when she says, "I think what happened between us was a mistake. In the heat of the moment, I was excited about what we'd been able to achieve, but I never should have instigated sex with you."

My bad mood comes flooding back to the surface.

Chapter 41

Serena

Vance scowls at me. "What?"

"You heard me." Steeling my spine, I look up at him.

This needs to be finished so I can get out of here and away from him. Being this close to him is weakening my resolve.

"I don't play games, Serena, so if this is your idea of a joke, it's not funny."

"I'm not playing games, Vance. It was great, but I made a mistake."

He's quiet, just standing there scowling at me, then a strange look I can't identify crosses his face. "Oh, I get it. I got too close, and you got scared."

His voice is tender, and he reaches for me. Tears prickle. If he touches me, I'll cave, so I need to end this now. "Vance, I'm not scared; I just came to my senses and decided to stop fooling myself. Trust me, it's better this way."

He steps back and relief washes through me. "All that misplaced guilt you're carrying is going to eat you alive, Serena. You've sentenced yourself to prison for something that wasn't your fault. The door's not locked, but you're acting like it is."

That's it. I can't take anymore, so I slide into my car and close the door. He stands there for a moment, then shakes his head, puts on his sunglasses and walks away.

I let out the breath I'd been holding since closing the door and start the car. Instead of going home to an empty house, I go to my office. As soon as finals were over and the grades posted, I jumped into the information we got from the hacker with both feet so my office is still in finals week disarray.

Once I'm inside, I turn on some music as a distraction and start arranging the papers strewn everywhere on my desk. A knock on my door startles me.

"Hey Prof," Tom Harvey of campus security says.

"Hi Tom. It's been a while since our paths crossed. How's the family doing?"

He grins. Tom loves to talk about his family. He's been married for almost twenty years and has three children. He works nights and his wife works days, so someone is always home for the kids.

If he's on duty, it's later than I thought. When he catches me looking at the clock, he says, "I'm a little early on shift tonight because one of the other guards needed to cut out early."

Then he goes back to telling me about his son's baseball team and his daughter, who has recently started dating. He has me laughing at his reactions to her dates showing up at the door.

"Anyway, I'd better get back to my rounds. I'll swing back around on the regular because the campus is pretty deserted during the break until summer session starts up."

"Thanks, Tom, I appreciate it. Have a quiet night."

"Here's hoping," he says with a grin, then continues working his way through the building, checking doors.

Sometime later, I sit back in my chair and rub my eyes. They're gritty from staring at the computer for so long. With a pinch to the bridge of my nose, I try to stave off the headache I feel blooming behind there. I roll my shoulders, trying to release the ache.

Silly me, I decided to clean out my email folders that haven't been scrubbed for a few years. It seemed like a good idea at the time.

Anything to keep from going home alone to my empty house. Maybe I'll drive down to the ranch tomorrow to hang out with the girls. Or maybe I need to find a project to occupy my summer.

There's no help for it now. Time to go home. I shut down my computer and gather my things, not bothered by the darkness as I make my way through the empty building.

The air outside is thick and muggy. Off to the southwest, flashes of lightning illuminate the clouds. Looks like we're going to get some rain tonight.

When I was a little girl and lightning would streak across the sky, Mama would say, "Smile, Serena! God's taking your picture." I'd grin up at the clouds, sure in the knowledge that God wanted to put my photograph into a frame on his mantle.

I'm thinking about whether I want to get something for supper or just go home and go to bed when a shoe scrapes on the sidewalk behind me. My car is just a few feet away, so I pick up my pace, elongating my step.

Then a shape emerges. Draper unfolds from where he was crouched behind my car. "You have been busy, professor. A smart person would have figured it out sooner, but we're here to send a message to keep your nose out of other people's business."

It's probably going to antagonize him, but I can't stop the laughter that bubbles out of me because they clearly don't know we've already been to see the police. "You think this is funny?" Pierce snarls behind me.

Suddenly, I'm propelled forward. My guess is I'm shoved by a foot to my backside. Although I'm wearing heels, I stumble but stay on my feet. I laugh again because the image of his fat ass getting a foot that high is amusing.

You really need to calm the hell down. They're here to hurt you and you're just making it worse.

Logic has no place in my brain right now apparently because I bend over, still laughing. No matter what they do to me, their days of walking around as free men are limited.

They're going to have fun in the prison showers every day for the rest of their miserable lives. Child molesters and cops don't fare well in prison, and these two are both.

Pierce shoves me again and this time I go down, tiny rocks biting into my palms and knees as I hit the pavement next to my car. My laughter turns to a cry of pain.

"Not laughing anymore, are you, bitch?" Pierce hisses, his upper lip curled with disgust.

My laughter is gone. Now I'm just pissed. With a firm grip on my purse, I get my feet under me, then swing the bag up and around at Pierce and connect with his groin. He folds like a deck of cards, hands clutching at his balls.

In my moment of triumph, I lost track of Draper. His fist slams into the side of my head and my legs go wobbly and I sink back down to my knees.

"Let's take her so I can fuck her black ass," Pierce says, his voice still breathy and pained. "She needs to learn her place."

"Hey!" A shout rings out from across the lawn. "You there! Campus Security!"

God bless you, Tom.

My head is aching from the blow and the pain is driving me to get the upper hand so they know they haven't won. I want to tell these fatheads that it's too late. They're already screwed, but I don't want to show them our cards. They might try to run.

Draper squeezes my head between his hands and leans in close, his vile breath crawling up my nostrils when he speaks. "Remember, bitch," he hisses, spittle peppering my face. "Keep your nose out of other people's business or we'll be back."

He jerks my head forward, then slams it back against my car door and everything goes black.

Chapter 42

Vance

My bad mood quadruples when I walk away from Serena and follows me all the way to the office. When I go inside, Jack calls me in to get an update. He knew we were going to see the cops this morning and wants to know what happened.

"Can we spar while I tell you? I need to blow off some steam."

"It went that badly?"

"No. Everything with the cops went great."

"Then what?"

"I do not understand women."

He looks at me for a long moment but doesn't say another word, just rises from his chair and follows me to the locker room to change. As we put on workout clothes, I tell him about the visit and how ticked off Carlos and Ford were.

We step onto the mats and face off. "You want to talk about the rest of it?" Jack asks.

"Nope. I just really want to hit something right now."

He grins at me. "Well, you can try anyway."

I let the anger take root and go for a throat strike. He doesn't lose that shit-eating grin as he dodges and counters. The fight is on for real and I get lost in the dance of trying to kill each other.

When we finally step back, both of us sweating and breathing hard, I see we've attracted a crowd. Jack bumps knuckles with me. "Good workout today; it was actually a challenge to keep up with you, so feel free to hit me up anytime you're pissed off. You want to talk about it?"

"Still no, but thanks."

"I want to be you when I grow up," Moses says as I pass by him on my way to the locker room to shower off the sweat. "I can't imagine going toe-to-toe with Jack for real. Heck, even his girlfriend can kick my ass."

Feeling looser and more in control than I have all day, I chuckle back at him. "That's many years of training, Moe, courtesy of Uncle Sam. All those years you spent growing your brain cells, I spent twice as many learning how not to get killed in combat. But now you know how I feel when you're trying to teach me about wiring schematics."

Moe grins back at me just before I duck into the locker room. In the shower, as the water sluices over my shoulders, my mind returns to the conversation with Serena. I'm still mystified as to what happened between Friday and today.

I thought we were on the same page, and she was finally starting to open up to me. It seemed like everything was coming together. We were coming together and things looked so promising. And the sex...the sex was incredible.

She said *she* made a mistake. That she'd been fooling herself. Fooling herself about what?

We need to have another conversation now that I've had time to absorb what she said and am not in the heat of the moment being blindsided. When I'm not already in a pissed off mood and coming off a weekend spent going back and forth from the hospital worried about Mom.

The other side of the conversation may still end up with us going our separate ways, but I want an honest explanation. No evading. No blowing me off.

I thought we were getting close, but I could have mistaken the situation. Maybe the sex wasn't as good for her as it was for me. It sure seemed like it was, but I could be wrong.

Maybe I did something that pissed her off. If that's the case, she needs to step up and have it out with me, not run away.

Yes, Miss Chilton and I are going to talk whether she wants to or not.

The rest of the day goes by in a haze as I walk through installing a system with Moe. He tells me I'm getting the hang of it, but it still seems like a bunch of Greek to me. In the late afternoon, Jack talks to me about Mom and a protection client coming to town in a few weeks.

When we've finished with the conversation and worked out a preliminary schedule for the client, he says, "Get out of here. Go see your mom and I'll see you tomorrow."

"Thanks man," I say as I stand. "I appreciate the leeway you're giving me."

He shrugs. "It's a temporary situation and family comes first."

Once I'm in the car, I call my Auntie Dorothy to see if she wants me to bring her anything for supper. Mom says she wants a chocolate milkshake, and that makes me laugh.

I'm glad her appetite is coming back. Her surgery was early Saturday morning, but she was so nauseated from the anesthesia that she wasn't eating. She probably could have already gone home if she'd been taking in more nourishment.

Her request for a chocolate shake means she's rounding the bend. Not for the first time, I'm glad she's living here with her sister.

If it hadn't been for Auntie, who knows how long Mom would have been laying there on the floor? And once she goes home, Auntie will be there at home with her while I'm at work and I'll never be able to express how thankful I am for that.

If she'd still been living in Atlanta, it could have been days before anyone found her. I tried to go by as often as I could, but when I was in the middle of a case, I didn't get by as often as I'd have liked.

We eat dinner together, then Auntie goes home. She's been at the hospital all day keeping Mom company, and I'm sure she's exhausted. I clean up the trash from our food and take it down the hall to throw it away so it's not smelling up Mom's room, then return and settle into the chair for an evening of watching television.

When Mom is sitting in bed dozing off, I turn off the television. I lean over and kiss her on the forehead and tuck the remote back in next to her on the bed.

It's almost ten, but I know Serena will be up, so I dial her number. I want this talk to happen sooner rather than later. Her voicemail picks up. That's weird. She always answers her phone.

Except that with the magic of caller ID, she knows it's me calling and probably isn't inclined to take my call. The phone beeps in my ear, "Hey baby... Sorry, I know you probably don't want me to call you that. I'm sorry I snapped at you this morning, but you caught me off guard. We need to talk, so please call me back."

I want to keep talking, but another beep sounds letting me know I've left all the message I can leave. Rather than calling back to leave another message to say what I want to say, I will hold on to it until we see each other in person.

When I next check my phone, it's still an hour before my alarm is set to go off. There's no way I'm going back to sleep, so I get up, figuring I'll go for a run since I have some time to kill. Even with the exercise, I'm still arriving at the hospital earlier than usual, so I swing by the café to get some coffee.

There's a familiar figure in line. Familiar, but far from home. "Dale?"

He turns to face me, and he looks tired. "Oh, hey, Vance."

"What are you doing up here?"

"Serena was attacked last night."

There must be something wrong with my hearing. "What?"

"Let me get some coffee and I'll tell you all about it."

He orders coffee and I step up to order mine, paying for both. We take them to a table in the back, away from everyone. Once I slide into a chair, I say, "I'm sorry, but it sounded like you said Serena was attacked last night."

Dale scrubs a hand over his face. "I did. A security guard said she must have been leaving her office. He'd seen her there earlier, then was making his way back around to see if she was still there and saw two men kicking and punching her by her car. They ran off before he could get a good look at them or their car. All he could say was one was bigger and heavyset and the other was average height and slim."

"Draper and Pierce," I growl. That sounds just like those assholes, two men ganging up on a woman and beating her. Cowards.

"The hospital kept her overnight because she had a concussion and couldn't be left alone, but they're going to release her in a few hours."

"Is she going home?"

He shakes his head. "No. Well, she wants to, but I'm trying to convince her to come home with me. She's being more than a little stubborn."

"Yeah, I've noticed she has a tendency to do that."

He's quiet for a few minutes, drinking his coffee. Just when I think he's about to get up and leave, he sets his cup down.

"I like you, Vance."

"I like you, too," I reply, confused by the change of subject.

"Good. Because I like you, and think you're good for my sister, I'm going to tell you some things. If Serena finds out I've told you, she'll skin me alive, so if you let on that you know these things, I'm going to deny telling you."

I chuckle. "Copy that. You didn't say a word."

He nods and scrubs his hand over his face again. "I'm not sure how much you know about our upbringing, but Serena didn't have it easy. While her mother was alive, things weren't so bad, but once she died, our father told Serena every single day how much of a disappointment she was."

An elderly couple comes and sits at a table nearby, so Dale leans forward and lowers his voice.

"I was the bastard son he got on his secretary. I didn't go live with him until I was ten after my mom died and my mom had told me how he was, so I mostly ignored the evil he spewed at me. But Serena...she had no defense against him."

He stares into his coffee cup for long moments, as if reliving the memories of his childhood.

"She wasn't allowed to date at all, but then Dad got sick when Serena was a senior in high school. A young guy who worked in accounting at the family's company took a liking to her. When Dad died and the guy found out Serena only inherited just a little more than she needed to put herself through school, he dropped her like a hot potato. He knew how much Dad was worth and thought she'd have a payday coming. Turns out he was engaged to another woman the entire time and was just after Serena for the money."

I'm following his story, but I'm not sure what it has to do with me.

"In law school, there was a guy who got close to her so she would help him with the classes he was struggling with. After graduation, he broke it off. Then she met you and you went back to your wife."

I lean forward to protest, but he holds up a hand.

"Don't get me wrong, I understand your situation and don't blame you. I'm just establishing a pattern. She didn't date again until last year when she got involved with Diondre, who was also separated from his wife. He came on strong with her and swept her off her feet, then promptly got back with his wife and didn't bother to tell Serena."

I'm frowning now. "But what does that have to do with me?"

"She saw you with another woman."

"What? When? I'm crazy about her and there's been no one else. Hell, if it hadn't been for my kids, I would have pursued something with her back in Atlanta."

"She came up here Saturday morning to bring flowers to your mom and saw you walking down the hall with another woman. The two of you were laughing and walking arm in arm and touching in a familiar way. That's how she put it...familiar. So now she's convinced herself that you're with someone else and that woman is better for you because she's younger and you seemed so happy with her."

I sit back in my chair and shake my head. "Why didn't she just come up and say hello?"

"She believes she's too broken to be with anyone and always assumes the worst. That woman comes off as all kinds of confident, but it's all a front. I think she's falling in love with you and it's scaring the shit out of her, so she has to push you away."

"If she wasn't hurt, I'd turn her over my knee and spank her, but then she'd probably like that too much." I can't help but grin at that thought.

He groans. "I do not need to hear that kind of shit."

I wondered where those flowers came from. When I'd gotten back to Mom's room, they were just sitting there on the windowsill with no card, so I didn't know where they'd come from and the nurses didn't know, either.

"Thanks for letting me know. What room is she in?"

"I'm headed back up there now if you want to tag along."

Chapter 43

Serena

My head hurts. My hands hurt. Everything hurts.

I have a concussion and my left eye is swollen to a slit. Good thing Tom came along when he did, or it could have been much worse. At least I managed to get one good blow in.

As soon as I'm better, I'm going to get some self-defense training because I will never be hit by someone again without giving back as good as I get. If they want to target me, I'm not going to make it any easier for them.

That feeling of utter helplessness is not something I ever want to feel again.

I've heard Demi talk about taking classes in Krav Maga several times, so maybe I'll start doing that with her. Or without her. She just found out she's pregnant, so I doubt she'll be taking martial arts classes anytime soon.

The door to my room whooshes open and I look up, hopeful that it's the doctor telling me I can go home. When Dale walks in, I smile anyway, happy to see my brother returning from his coffee run. I also feel guilty for him getting called out in the middle of the night to come all the way up here.

He was here for me when I needed him, and that makes me all kinds of grateful. Especially since it's not an experience I'm used to.

I've been standing on my own two feet for a long time and I'm not used to needing to lean on someone, so I'm beyond thankful that when I had no other choice, someone showed up for me.

Then I look behind him and see Vance. I roll onto my side, giving my back to the two men coming through the door. Maybe I can convince them I'm still asleep.

What the hell is he doing here?

"Give it up," Dale says, sounding amused. "I know you're awake and your head is probably swimming and hurting from rolling over so fast."

It is, but I'll never admit it.

"But I know you'll never admit it because you're proud and stubborn like that. I ran into Vance downstairs while I was getting coffee."

I turn back over taking my time because he's right, that first roll hurt like hell. "Coffee?"

"You can't have any yet."

I try to scowl at him, but he just laughs. When I flick my eyes to Vance, he's just staring at my face. I look away, unable to stand his scrutiny.

Dale hasn't let me look into a mirror yet, but if it looks one iota as bad as it feels, it must be ghastly. The door whooshes again and I hope he's gone, unable to stand the sight of me.

Why did he even come up here? He doesn't owe me anything. In fact, he shouldn't be here. We're not together anymore. Not that we ever were.

Maybe he just wanted to gawk, like a passerby rubbernecking to get a look at a gruesome accident. When I look back toward the door, he's not gone. He's still here, but Dale has gone. Not only is he still here, but he's moved closer.

"I'm so sorry," he breathes. "I should have been there."

When I shake my head, I wince at the pain that lances through my skull. "No. This isn't your fault. You had no reason to be there, remember? We aren't together anymore."

"And why is that, Serena? Why aren't we together anymore?" His voice isn't hard or angry. It's just quiet and questioning and it almost undoes me.

"I told you, it was a mistake."

"Bullshit. Something happened between Friday and Monday that caused you to go running scared, and I want you to tell me what it was."

Damn observant man. He sees too much. Chewing on the inside of my bottom lip, I'm mulling over what I should tell him and how to say it, so it doesn't make me sound like a coward.

"I saw you." I say, hitching my chin. My aim was to appear strong, but my voice comes out weak and I hate it.

He sits on the side of the bed and takes my hand in his. I try to pull away, but he holds tight and even that much effort hurts, so I relax my hand in his grip.

"When did you see me?"

Fine, if he wants to know, I'll tell him and let him know he's been caught.

"Saturday morning, here at the hospital. You were with another woman, and I am sick to death of being a man's second choice. I know we weren't really together officially..."

Tears prickle in my eyes and it pisses me off, so I stop talking and turn my attention to the sky outside the window because I do not want to cry in front of him. If I wasn't in pain, I would be better at holding my emotions at bay.

With a deep breath, I get myself under control before I speak again, my words bouncing off the window. My eyes stay glued to the clouds outside because I can't bear to look at him.

"She was making you laugh. You looked so happy together and you deserve to be with someone who makes you laugh like that."

"Hey," he says, his voice quiet. "Serena, look at me, baby."

He squeezes my thigh and gives me time. I turn to face him, and he cups my jaw gently, his eyes dancing back and forth between mine.

"You were never a second pick for me. Since the moment I saw you again, you've been the only woman I've been interested in. In fact, if it hadn't been for my kids, I would have made you my pick all those years ago in Atlanta. That woman you saw me with, she's my cousin and was here visiting Mom. We were just going to get some breakfast when you saw us."

Embarrassment floods through me. I hate this insecurity. When I try to look away, he doesn't let me.

"I wish you'd said hello," he continues. "My cousin would have loved to meet you, and my Mom, she loved the flowers you snuck in and left."

My eyes snap up to his. "How did you?"

The doctor chooses that moment to stroll into the room.

"Miss Chilton, how are we feeling?"

I try to pull my hand away again, but Vance still isn't having it. That phrase always mystifies me. I feel like I've been run over by a truck, but I have no clue how he's feeling.

"I'm good," I lie. "Hoping to go home."

He shines a light in my eyes, talking all the while. "The nurses tell me your overnight was good and your responses were all spot on when they woke you. You'll need to take it easy, though. How is your pain level? I can prescribe something if it's too much."

"It's fine. If I need something stronger than over-the-counter pain relievers, I'll contact you."

"Perfect. You'll need to focus on reducing stress. Rest is the best treatment, and although I'm not prescribing any pain meds, avoid caffeine and alcohol for a few days. If you get a headache, go to a dark room and put a cold cloth on your forehead. If there are recurring headaches, I want you to come back in. The swelling in your eye is mostly residual from the blow to the side of your head. It should go down on its own, but again, if it doesn't improve, come back in and we'll take another look. Do you have questions?"

"No, sir."

"Well, as far as I'm concerned, I don't see any reason for you to stay any longer. I'll have the nurses get to work on your discharge paperwork."

"Excellent. Thank you, doctor."

Dale stays in the room after the doctor leaves. When the door clicks shut, he says, "I'll take you by your house so you can pack a bag."

"Dale…"

"This isn't an argument you'll win, Serena. You're not going to stay at home alone. Those bastards are getting desperate and they don't even know that you've already gone to the cops. When they find out, it's too much of a risk that they'll come back."

"I'm not going to stay in your house and I'd rather the girls didn't see me like this. Inside my home, I'll be perfectly safe. They can only get in if I open the door."

"You could stay at Sarah's house."

I can't help the laugh that barks out of me. "Sarah's house? I'd still be alone, and it's not nearly as secure as my house is."

"What if she stays at her house, but she's not alone?" Vance asks.

"What?" my brother and I say together, our eyes locked on him.

"I could stay at your house with you. You'd be alone during the day, but it's unlikely they'd try anything in daylight. Then I'd be there after work and could take care of whatever you need, like groceries and errands, until you're ready to go out again and go with you once you are like your own personal bodyguard." He grins at me. "It'll be good practice for my new job."

I blink at him. Well, one eye blinks at him, the other is in a temporarily constant blink. Then I try to scowl.

He's still grinning at me, not fazed at all. "I'll even sleep in the guestroom or on the couch or whatever. But your brother is right, you shouldn't be alone."

These damn men. Give them an inch...not even an inch. Give them a millimeter and they take ten miles. Overbearing doesn't even begin to cover it.

I sigh and sink back into my pillows as they talk back and forth, hammering out the details of my near future as if I'm not in the room. They're worried about me and want to take care of me. How could that be a bad thing?

It's not. But it still pisses me off that they're not bothering to include me in the conversation.

However, one thing is for sure, I don't want to be alone if those guys come calling again. I underestimated them and their capacity for violence.

My own home would be the most comfortable. I also still stand by the fact that I don't want the girls to see me like this, so going down south with Dale is out of the question, no matter where they would plant me.

Maybe by Sunday the swelling will have gone down enough that it won't look so horrendous. If not, I may have to skip lunch no matter how much I'll miss seeing them. I just don't want to add to their fear.

Staying at home means I have to be willing to give a little. I've about made up my mind to agree to let Vance stay with me. Would that really be so horrible? I mean, apparently I jumped to all the wrong conclusions when I saw him Saturday, and it seems like he is willing to forgive me.

"If you'll let Vance keep an eye on you, I won't push you to come down south," Dale finally says, as if he saw the direction my thoughts were going.

Damn men. As if he is the boss of me and I need his permission to stay in my own home. I can't get too mad at him, though. After all, I'm getting what I want.

"Fine," I grumble. "Vance can stay with me."

Oh, sweet Jesus... Vance is going to be staying with me. He lifts my hand to his mouth and kisses the back of it.

Thankfully, it's not shaking with the jangle of nerves prickling through my body at the thought of Vance sharing my space.

He's been to my house many times and even shared my bed, but he's never stayed overnight. I had hoped Friday night would be the first time, but that plan was set aside so he could care for his mother.

"What about your mom?" I ask, feeling terrible that I totally forgot about her broken hip.

"They did a hip replacement. The surgery went well, but she's struggling a bit in physical therapy. They're thinking she'll be ready to go home tomorrow, but even when she goes home, Auntie Dot will be there to keep an eye on her."

"The last thing you need is to be surrounded by helpless women. You need to focus on your mom. She's your priority, as she should be, and I'll be fine by myself."

Chapter 44

Vance

Just when I thought we were making progress, she tries to get all hard-headed on me again. "Listen here. I know you're not used to leaning on anyone, and I know you're a strong woman. But this is one time you need to take the hand of help that's being offered to you."

Dale had been staying back by the door, letting us work it out, but steps up to the bed. "He's right. You'll either go home with me and we'll set you up in our spare bedroom, at Sarah's, or the ranch, or you go to your house and let Vance stay with you. Those are your options."

She sets her jaw in a stubborn line. "Fine. Vance can stay with me."

"And don't think that means you can get away with closing me out once you're inside," I say with a grin.

Her good eye snaps to me and I know that's exactly what she'd been thinking.

I lean close and look her in the eye. "Picking locks is something I've been doing for a very long time."

She tries to scowl at me, and it's fucking adorable. I close the distance and kiss her forehead. "Dale, if you can get her home,

I'm going to stop by Mom's room to check on her before I go to work. Serena, text a grocery list to me and I'll run by the store on my way home."

"Sounds like a plan," Dale says, offering me his hand and when Serena harrumphs, we both give her a loving look.

I return to her and brush a gentle kiss across her split lip. "If you need me for anything today, let me know, okay?"

She looks down and away, that stubborn streak still scratching against the surface. With a curled finger under her chin, I raise her face and say again, "Okay?"

She gives me the tiniest of nods. "Thank you, baby," I say, and kiss her again before I leave the room and go to find my mom.

It's almost noon before my phone buzzes with a text from Serena letting me know she's at home.

Me: *That's good, baby. How are you feeling?*

Serena: *Wonderful.*

Me: *Somehow I don't believe you.*

Serena: *Okay, I feel horrible. Going to take a nap. When I get up, I'll go through the cupboards and send a grocery list.*

Me: *Perfect. Rest well, baby.*

She's quiet the rest of the day and I hope that means she's taking it easy. I stop by the hospital first and confirm that Mom's likely to go home tomorrow. When I tell Auntie Dot to let me know when they're ready to release her, she balks, telling me she'll take care of it.

I swear, I think the good Lord surrounded me with hard-headed women to teach me patience. When I shut that down, she begrudgingly agrees to notify me as soon as they are ready to release her. Maybe I need to get an enormous house to put them all in so it will be easier to keep an eye on them.

"Where are you running off to so soon?" Mom asks when I start saying my goodbyes.

"You remember me telling you about the college professor?"

"The one you knew in Atlanta that's up here now?"

"That's the one. She was hurt last night by some men that are upset about us looking into their evil deeds."

"Then why are you still here with us old hens? Go look out for her."

"That's where I'm headed," I say, grinning at her as I lean down to kiss her cheek. "Love you Mom. Love you Auntie. I'll see y'all tomorrow."

I swing by the house and pack a bag with enough clothes for a few days, then go to the store to pick up the items on Serena's list. The door is locked when I arrive. It would have pissed me off if it hadn't been.

After I press a finger to the bell, it takes a moment, but her voice floats out of the speaker by the camera. "On my way."

"Take your time, sweetheart."

The door opens sooner than I thought it would. She's wearing loose, oversized clothes, but her face is pinched with pain. "Honey, you look like you're hurting. When is the last time you took something for pain?"

"I'm due," she replies.

"All right. Take a seat and let me set everything down and I'll get you something."

"Normally, I'd tell you to hush and that I'd get it myself, but I think I'll let you be the boss of me just this once."

I chuckle as I go to the kitchen and set the grocery bags on the counter. Then I go to her spare bedroom and set my bag on the bed. Once I unzip it, I reach in and take out the pill bottle I brought with me, open it, and shake out a pill.

Another stop by the kitchen for some water and I find her just settling onto the sofa. Once she's situated, I hold out my hands to her, one with the pill, the other with the glass of water.

She eyes the pill. "What's that?"

"Eight hundred milligram ibuprofen. I tweaked my knee last year, and this is what they gave me. It's a little stronger than what you can get over the counter, and you probably need something a little stronger for a day or two. You're sore today, but the worst of it is going to hit tomorrow."

"It's going to get worse?"

"Yeah, sorry, baby. I've been beaten up enough times to know."

She takes the pill and pops it into her mouth. Then she takes the water and swallows it down. "You've been beaten up?"

"Yeah. Basic training is a daily exercise in getting the shit beat out of you in one way or another every day. Special forces training is a lot like that, too."

She nods and drinks the rest of the glass of water. Staying hydrated will be important for her healing, so I need to dig through her cabinets to see if she has a water bottle or something larger. Then I can fill it with water so she doesn't have to get up every time she needs a drink.

"Now stay put," I tell her. "I'll put the groceries away, but it was getting late, so I brought you something home."

"Perfect," she says, settling back into the sofa with a sigh.

I bring her another glass of water and a plate of food. She frowns when she sees the glass of water. "Sorry," I say. "No wine, remember?"

"Yeah. I was hoping you would have forgotten that."

I chuckle and get some food, then join her in the living room. She has the television tuned into some true crime show, which is surprising. I didn't expect her to be watching Hallmark or anything, but probably HGTV or something like that.

"How's your mom?" she asks.

I tell her all about my visits to the hospital today and what I did at work. Then she drops a bombshell on me.

"Two police officers came to see me today, but I didn't let them in right away. When I told them why and told them the only way I'd open the door is if they were vetted by someone, it turns out one of them used to be partners with Carlos years ago, before moving to Norman. He got Carlos on the phone and once I had his assurance, I opened the door."

She stretches out a finger. "Their cards are on the table by the door. Campus security made a report about the assault, so they wanted to take my statement. I identified Draper and Pierce to them, but only gave broad strokes as to why I thought they targeted me. Said they'd been by the house and then to campus looking for a missing child."

"That's good. We should probably let Ford and Carlos know about the attack, too."

"Carlos called me. Apparently, he called the officer. I'm sorry, I don't remember his name; my head is all fuzzy. Anyway, they talked after the pair left, then Carlos called me, concerned about my safety. I told him you were watching over me and he said not to hesitate to call if we needed anything."

Talking must have tired her out. Soon after she tells me about the visit, she sets her half-eaten plate of food on the side table. Soon she starts dozing off.

I'm ready to help her off the sofa and put her to bed when my phone rings. "Hey, Dale," I answer when I see the caller ID.

"There was some activity out at the ranch today. They don't know for sure whether it was related to the girls, but I wanted to let you know."

"What happened?"

"First, a guy came to the gate and said he was a horse owner and was thinking about bringing his stock there. When the hand on the gate said they were full up, he insisted on talking to the owner and got rather forceful about it. Takoda went out and told him the same thing the hand did. Says the guy was surprised to see him instead of Roni, and questioned him about being the actual owner a few times."

"Like you said, it might not be related, but I have a feeling it is."

"Yeah, and that's not all of it. Around dusk, the horses in the fields were getting antsy and wouldn't settle. A couple of hands went out on an ATV and saw a drone flying in a grid pattern over the ranch. They shot it down. When they went to get it, the guy was a little too spot on with his shot and the thing was destroyed."

I tell him about the visit Serena had today from the Norman police department. "At a minimum, Draper and Pierce are probably aware their days of freedom are numbered. The higher-ups are likely scared about them flipping, and rightfully so. They're probably going to get very desperate and either run or come hard and heavy to tie up loose ends."

"You're right. Keep her safe."

"I intend to."

With that, we disconnect, and I relay the conversation to Serena. She still looks like she's about to fall asleep where she sits, so it's time to get her settled for the night.

"Come on, baby," I say, standing in front of her and offering her my hands. "Let's get you to bed where you'll be more comfortable. Your body needs plenty of rest while you're healing."

She mumbles something, but takes my hands and lets me help her up. Once I get her settled in bed, I go back, straighten up the living room, clean the kitchen, then go to the spare room to shower and change.

Although I told her I'd be willing to sleep in the guest room, it was a lie. Oh, if she tells me to go sleep in there, I will, but until she tells me to, my place is right by her side.

I climb into bed with her and scoot close, putting a hand on her hip. She surprises me when she reaches up and pulls my hand down so my arm is around her, which makes me have to move closer.

She sighs when I kiss her shoulder and in a few moments, her breathing deepens as sleep overtakes her.

Chapter 45

Serena

The next few days are a blur. I sleep and eat and take pain pills. Vance is right there with me, caring for me, feeding me, and sleeping with me. Other than Vance's comings and goings, the house has been quiet.

So when the doorbell rings on Friday afternoon, I nearly jump out of my skin. Which sends a throb of pain through the side of my head. Other than lingering stiffness and a twinge if I move too fast, the pain is mostly gone, even though I still look horrible.

I reach for my phone on the side table to check the doorbell camera, but then I hear the familiar rumble of Vance's car. Through the camera, I see him step onto the porch with Ford and Carlos. Vance uses the key I gave him after the first night and lets them in. I'm not fit for visitors, but there's nothing I can do about that now.

I'm pushing myself up when they enter the living room. "Don't get up, honey." Vance says.

This is another time I'm more than happy to do what he says, so I settle back onto the sofa and mute the television with the remote that was sitting next to my thigh. "What's going on?" I ask.

Vance sits next to me, taking my hand in his, and Carlos and Ford take chairs on each side of the sofa.

"We called Vance so he could hear this at the same time. I'm afraid we have some bad news," Ford says, getting right down to business. "We went by Mrs. Baker's house to talk to her. When we got there, a unit was already on sight because they'd been called by a neighbor. No one had seen her for a few days, which wasn't unusual, but there was a smell..."

My hand goes to my mouth.

"Mrs. Baker?" Vance asks.

"That's the girls' mother's name," I breathe.

"Aw, no," Vance breathes.

"The preliminary estimation is that she's been dead since Monday," Carlos adds. "She was in terrible shape, beaten black and blue."

Vance looks at me. "Sounds like they paid her a visit before they came to see you."

Hot tears slide down my face. How are we going to break it to those babies? Isabel has been through so much already.

Something like this could finally break her. Vance hands me a handkerchief from his pocket. It's such an old-fashioned thing. I didn't think men carried them anymore and I just stare at it in my hand.

"Chances are that her body's depleted condition from drug use contributed to the fatality of the beating, but I still think you're very lucky that campus security officer came along when he did," Ford says.

"Pierce wanted to take me with them so he could rape me," I say, my voice so quiet even I barely hear it.

Vance curses under his breath.

"Based on your identification," Carlos continues, "it took a few days, but we've put out warrants for both Draper and Pierce. They're still on administrative leave and as soon as we leave here, we're going to their homes to see if we can serve them and get them in cuffs."

Ford shifts in his seat and pulls out a phone. Once it's free of his clothing, I can hear it buzzing. "Excuse me," he says and steps back toward the front door. He answers with his last name and that's the last thing I hear as he lowers his voice.

"We need to go tell the girls," I say, still staring at the hand-kerchief.

"We can do it tomorrow," Vance says.

I'm about to protest when Ford steps back into the room. "Pierce is dead," he says without ceremony. "A report of a gun-shot was called in by a neighbor and when they went in, he was sitting in a chair in the middle of his living room. It's unclear whether it was self-inflicted."

"Loose ends," I say. "We need to warn the ranch. Who knows what they're desperate enough to do?" I say.

"You don't know that it wasn't suicide," Vance coaxes.

"But I don't know that it was, either. Not tomorrow," I say firmly. "Tonight. They need to be told before they see it on television."

"Baby, you're not in any condition..."

I look up at him, and he stops speaking. "I'll be fine. They can't find out from someone else."

"All right," he concedes. "If we're going, let's go so I can get you back at a decent hour. You can call the ranch on the way."

Ford and Carlos stand.

"I hate to say it because those girls have been through enough, but I agree with Serena," Carlos says. "The ranch needs to be put on lockdown, and once the press gets wind of a couple of murders, they'll be all over them."

"We should get back to the City and see if we can track down Draper," Ford says.

While Vance shows the other men out, I debate changing clothes but decide that it would be silly to take off one loose, comfortable outfit just to put on another. When Vance asks for my keys, I hand them over without question.

As soon as we're on the road, I call Roni and tell her what's happened and that we're on our way down there to tell the girls. I also inform her about my own injuries, so she's prepared. She responds that she'll bring all three of the girls to the big house and they'll be waiting when we arrive.

My next call is to Dale simply because he's my brother and I want him to know what's going on. He's also former military and therefore better equipped to handle anything that might arise. I have to stifle a hysterical laugh when I realize that anything that might arise could very well be an armed assault on the ranch.

Surely they wouldn't go to those lengths.

I guess he was thinking along the same lines. When I'm finished talking to Dale, Vance has me call Jack and put him on speaker so they can talk while I listen in.

"The ranch is about as secure as it can be," Jack says. "Because of the value of some of the horses they breed, there are cameras everywhere and they're monitored twenty-four-seven. My only suggestions are that they should have the girls bunk in the big house instead of the manager's cottage. Depending upon how many hands they have right now, armed patrols might be a good idea."

"Copy," Vance says. "Those were my thoughts, too. I know they already have someone on the gate, but if they have the personnel, more might be called for."

"If you need me, let me know," Jack says.

"I seriously doubt they'd try to take on the entire ranch. More than likely, they'll bide their time and try to catch Isabel at an opportune moment. She's the one they'll think is the primary threat because she is a recent victim who can testify against them," Vance says.

"Yep. Isabel and Serena are the most vulnerable and in need of protection."

"Agreed," Vance replies before I can mouth off. "We're almost at the ranch. I'll update you if anything changes."

"Roger that."

The call disconnects. I'm about to give Vance a tongue lashing at saying I'm vulnerable and need protecting, but in light of my current state, I just can't muster the righteous indignity to do it. Vance reaches over, takes my hand in his, and pulls it up to his lips for a kiss.

Although it goes against everything in me, I let him past the walls I've built to keep everyone out. "I'm scared for those girls."

"Me, too," he says. "But they're not alone. They've got us."

They've got us. He didn't say that they've got me, but that they've got us and it almost brings me to tears again. I squeeze his hand and he squeezes back.

We're stopped at the gate when we pull up to the ranch, but an armed man lets us in when we identify ourselves. I try to draw on the dispassionate cloak I used to wear when I was practicing, but I can't.

These girls are too close to my heart and I'm about to give them news that will break theirs. "Do you want me to do it?" Vance asks. "I have experience breaking tough news like this."

I shake my head. "No. I think it would be best coming from me."

When Vance opens my car door and offers me his hand, taking it slow, I scoot out of the car. Although the pain has abated significantly, if I move too quickly, particularly getting up or down, I may get dizzy or maybe an ice pick of pain driven through my temple.

Most of my injuries are healing nicely. They're still ghastly, but healing. My left eye even opens now.

We creep across the distance from the car to the steps up to the porch. Just as I'm about to set foot on the first step, the back door opens and Dale steps out. I should have known he'd come here if he knew I was coming.

He goes to my other side, balancing me as I climb up the stairs. As soon as I step inside the back door, Sophie wriggles down from the stool where she'd been sitting and races toward me.

Vance quickly intervenes and scoops her up into his arms. With a frown of confusion, she looks at me and immediately bursts into tears. "What happened?" she wails.

Drawn by her cries, Isabel comes toward us and freezes when she sees me. Without taking my eyes from Isabel, I answer Sophie. "We'll get to that. Why don't we go to the parlor and have a seat?"

She tucks her head against Vance's shoulder, her little body still shaking with tears. Isabel comes over and takes the hand that Vance had been holding and walks slowly with me to the parlor. Dale helps me lower onto their sofa and Isabel takes her place next to me with Vance sitting next to her, still holding Sophie.

Maggie sits in one chair while Takoda and Roni take their places in others. Emme slides off her stool, but a sharp word from Takoda in a language I don't understand has her climbing back onto her seat. She's scowling, but obeys.

I draw in a deep breath and begin by telling them about all the information we turned over to the police. Maggie breathes a sigh of relief. Although I don't go into graphic detail, when I tell what happened to me, Sophie, who has quieted to hiccupping sniffles, begins to cry in earnest again.

Now for the hard part. "Apparently, before they came to see me, they went to see your mom. Because her body was so damaged from her addiction..."

"She's dead, isn't she?" Isabel interrupts.

"Yes, she is," I answer.

Sophie's cries turn to wails as she clings to Vance, who holds her tight. He pats her back and whispers soothing words to her. Sometimes I forget he is a father and must have comforted his own daughter like this, maybe for a skinned knee or someone being mean to her.

Isabel hasn't moved or reacted or shed a tear. I'm not sure how to comfort her or if she needs comfort because her face is stone, completely still, and stoic.

Dale and Takoda talk about the stepped up security on the ranch with Vance. They voice a hope that with the information we've given to the police, that the perpetrators will be put behind bars quickly.

Vance explains that even if they get locked up, there's still a possibility they could get bail and be right back on the streets in a day or two. As they talk, Isabel leans her head against my shoulder but hasn't loosed her tight grip on my hand.

Sophie quiets and eventually falls asleep, but Vance doesn't let her go. "I think for now, we keep things much the same," Takoda says. "None of the children leave the ranch and we have some very high value horses on site, so we had already stepped up security. If Roni or Miss Beth go into town, they go with a trusted hand to watch over them."

Maggie looks at him, but before she can speak, he says, "We've talked about this. The best place for you is here."

She presses her lips together, but nods.

"Have you all eaten?" Roni asks. "We were just fixing supper when you called. You're welcome to eat with us."

"That sounds great," Vance answers for us.

Roni, Takoda, Maggie, and Dale rise from their seats.

"I'm going to head home to my wife," Dale says. He leans down and kisses my cheek, then gives Vance a pat on the shoulder. "Keep her safe."

"Intend to," he replies.

The others go to the kitchen, leaving Vance and me alone with the girls or really just alone with Isabel since Sophie is still limp against Vance's chest. "What happened to you?" Isabel asks quietly.

For a moment, I start to sugarcoat it, but she deserves to hear the truth. Not the gory truth, but the truth. She might only be twelve, but she's lived more life in her short time than most.

"Well, I got hit...a lot. You can see my face, and my head was hit pretty bad. I had to stay the night in the hospital because of it. Also, one man kicked me in the back and made me fall. It strained a lot of muscles in my back and neck so I'm pretty stiff, which makes moving around difficult."

"It was those cops that came to your house, wasn't it?"

"Yes. One of them was also found dead today."

"Good." The word pops out of her mouth so quickly it appears to shock her. Her large brown eyes shift up to my face, but she'll find no judgment there. I had the same thought when I heard he'd been found.

Still looking at me, she breathes, "Am I a bad person if I'm glad she's dead, too?"

"No, baby," I tell her honestly.

I'm sure the prospect of being given back to her mother was a difficult thing to reconcile herself to. The love for her mother contrasted with the idea that the person who gave her life would so easily hand her over to predators.

"Do you want to talk about it?"

She shakes her head but asks, "What's going to happen to us?"

"Don't worry about that. Let's focus on making sure those evil men go to prison. Once you're safe, we'll talk about next steps."

"They say we have to stay in the big house for a while."

Vance, the authority on the topic, says, "It will be much easier to keep you safe if you're here instead of out at the place you've been staying."

She sighs. I know it was easier for her when they moved to the other house because she was out of the noise and chaos that stems from simply having several children in one place.

"Who's going to keep you safe?" she asks me.

"Don't worry about me; Mr. Vance is keeping an eye on me. You know that's what he does as his job, right?"

"Can't I stay with you, just for a couple of nights? If Mr. Vance is there the whole time, he could watch me, too. You could bring me back Sunday when you come for lunch."

Yeah, I stepped right into that one. I look over her head at Vance. Today is Friday. so Vance would be with us the entire time.

He simply shrugs one shoulder, so I deflect. "Let's go have supper. We'll think about it while we're eating, then talk about it afterward."

"That means no," she huffs and releases my hand, slipping off the sofa and going to the kitchen. The movement wakes Sophie who, after a yawn and a stretch, wriggles to get down. Vance sets her on her feet and she heads toward the kitchen, too.

"What do you think?" I ask Vance.

"I don't like it..."

"But? I sense there's a but in there."

"Although Sophie was the one to react to the news, Isabel was probably hit the hardest, and she's conflicted. Her mom was murdered, but the woman was also her pimp. It will be difficult for her to process under the best of circumstances. In this environment, which isn't one she's super comfortable in…it could be particularly difficult for her."

"That's what I was thinking, too."

"If we can keep the fact that she's with us under wraps, no one would have to know she's not here behind fences, cameras, and armed guards. She'd have to stay inside, but I don't think that would bother her. She's not the go outside and play type."

He's right, but the last thing I'd ever want to do is jeopardize her safety. But is it worth the risk to give her some peace where she can have a day to deal with the shock?

"Let's do what I said," I say. "Let's think it over while we eat, then we'll revisit the subject."

"Okay."

He rises and holds out his hands to me, helping me up from the sofa. The damnable thing is soft and comfortable, the kind where you sink down into it, so it takes all my effort to lever my butt up off the cushions. I can't stop the grunt of pain when I do.

Chapter 46

Vance

When we head back to Norman, we've got Isabel with us. As much as I know she'd be safer at the ranch, Serena made the point that her mental wellbeing is just as important as her physical safety. I couldn't dispute it, so we packed a few things in her backpack and brought her with us.

Because I was sure no one followed us from the ranch, I decided to stop in and check on Mom. It was early enough, and if I checked on her today, I'd be able to stay at Serena's through the weekend without worrying about her too much.

"Y'all should come in with me rather than sitting alone out here in the car."

I get out and go around the car, offering a hand out to Serena while scanning the area. As soon as Serena's on her feet, Isabel scrambles out of the back seat and moves to Serena's other side, holding her hand.

"Hey Mom," I say as I enter the door. "I've got company with me, so I hope y'all are decent."

"We're never decent," Auntie Dot says, then cackles at her own joke.

"Who you brought with you?" Mom asks. We step into the living room where Mom and Auntie Dot are in their recliners watching television. "Well, hello there," she says to Serena as soon as she sees her. "You must be Serena. Vance has told me all about you."

"It's nice to meet you finally, Mrs. Douglas," Serena replies.

"Who's this little one?" Auntie Dot asks, spotting Isabel hiding halfway behind Serena while keeping a death grip on her hand.

"This is Isabel," I say.

"Come on out here and let me get a look at you," Mom says. Serena looks down at Isabel and smiles warmly, and the girl creeps out from her hiding place. "Well, there you are," Mom says. "My son says you're quite the artist."

"Mr. Vance is your son?"

"That's right."

"My mom got killed," Isabel blurts.

Mom's eyes flick up to mine, and I nod in confirmation. "Oh, baby girl, I'm so sorry."

Isabel shrugs and says, "She wasn't a very good mom." Then she turns into Serena, looking like she's ready to drop from the emotional overwhelm.

I need to get this visit taken care of. Serena's exhaustion is showing after the busy evening. I'm sure sitting confined in the car for so long didn't do her any favors.

And if Isabel breaks, I'd rather it be somewhere she can lose it however she needs to without the added audience of my elders.

"I wanted to come by and check on you because I'm going to need to stick close to these two until we take Isabel back to where she's staying on Sunday."

"You go take care of that baby," Auntie Dot says. "We're grown and know how to call if we need you, but once your mama's bionic hip is healed, you need to bring them back so we can have a proper visit."

I lean down and kiss Dot on the cheek. "Love you." Then do the same to Mom. "Love you."

"Love you, too, son. You take care of them girls."

"Will do."

On the short drive to Serena's house, both of them fall asleep, but Serena wakes up as soon as I turn the car off. I help her out first and she goes to unlock the door. My first instinct is to pick Isabel up and carry her in.

That's what I'd do if she were my daughter, but she's not. She is a traumatized girl and if she were to wake up in my arms, it would probably cause her more harm. Putting a hand to her shoulder, I shake her gently.

"Isabel, honey, wake up. It's time to go inside."

She snorts and sits up straight, looking around. "Okay," she says, still half asleep, and stumbles out of the car. When she's past me, I grab her backpack, close the car door, and follow her into the house all the way to the spare bedroom.

I hand her the backpack, then leave the room to check on Serena. She's in her bathroom washing her face. Good, they'll both be in bed soon and getting the rest they need.

Stepping up behind Serena, I put my hands on her hips. When she bends over, her lovely round ass presses against the bulge growing in my pants. It's been a week since I've had her and my dick isn't happy about it.

However, as long as she's in pain, it'll just have to get used to being deprived. I kiss her shoulder when she straightens. "You okay?"

"Yeah, just tired.""I imagine. That was your first big outing. I'm going to sleep on the couch tonight."

She looks at me in the mirror. "You don't have to."

"I know, baby, but with Isabel here, I'm probably going to be restless, which means I'll be up and down. So rather than disturb you by getting up and down at all hours, I'll just sleep out there."

She makes a humming noise in her throat, but doesn't say anything more. Leaving her to her ablutions, I go into the bedroom and change into shorts and a tee. Although I'd originally put my things in the spare bedroom, when she didn't kick me out of her bed, I moved them.

I make my way around the house, checking the locks on the doors and windows even though I know they're secure. If I didn't, I'd be second-guessing myself all night.

Once I've made the rounds, I return to Serena's room to find her getting into bed. She looks up and smiles tiredly. "Will you stay with me until I fall asleep?"

"Of course, baby."

I hold the comforter up and offer her my hand. She takes it and settles into bed. "I am so sick of being an invalid."

"It'll start working its way out soon. You've just got to keep moving and healing. Hydrating and resting are key."

"Yeah, yeah."

She settles and I go around to slide in behind her. When I wrap my arm around her, she sighs.

"What am I doing? Sophie will be fine, I think. Every thought she has comes right out of her mouth. If she's suffering, she'll say it. But Isabel, I don't know how to help her."

"Baby, you are helping her. She's been through a lot, but you're giving her what she needs. You gave her some quiet when she asked for it. If she's telling you what she needs, that's a good thing. Between that and the therapy you've got her in, you're giving her the tools she needs. It doesn't guarantee she'll be fine, but it certainly gives her every opportunity to heal."

She yawns. "I'll bet you are a great dad," she mumbles.

As soon as her breathing evens out, I move to the side of the bed, trying not to jostle her. When I step through the door, I pull it most of the way closed and stop. There was something...

I cock my head, hold my breath, and listen. There it is. The tiniest of noises filters through the air.

I follow it to Isabel's door and recognize it. She's crying. After a quiet knock, I crack open the door and speak quietly. "Isabel, if you want to talk, I'm awake."

So that she doesn't feel pressured, I don't wait for a response, just pull the door closed again and continue on my way down the hall to the living room. I make the rounds again, checking everything, watch out the back door for several minutes, then move to the front door to do the same.

With that done, I take a seat on the sofa and turn the television on, keeping the volume low. I'm dozing in the way you learn in the military, sleeping but alert.

"I thought you said you were awake."

My eyes snap open. Isabel is in a chair wrapped in the comforter from her bed. "I am."

She half snorts, half giggles. "You were snoring. I don't think you do that when you're awake."

"I was not snoring," I tease. "You must be hearing things."

"Yes, you were. What are you watching?"

"Well, nothing, according to you."

She giggles again, and it sounds like music.

"Can't sleep?" I ask.

"No."

"That's fine. You can hang out here with me until you get sleepy."

"K."

Because I'd been dozing, I hadn't really paid attention to what was on the television. Thankfully, it's some silly comedy, so I turn the volume up a notch or two but still keep it fairly quiet so we don't bother Serena.

"Are you two going to get married?" Isabel asks.

I look over at her and give her an honest answer. "I don't know. Would it bother you if we did?"

She shrugs. "Doesn't matter what I think. I prolly won't be around, anyway."

Although she's trying to be nonchalant, the vulnerability in her voice oozes through. Not knowing what comes next for her and Sophie has her worried.

"Are you worried that once this is all over, Miss Serena is just going to walk away from you and Sophie?"

She shrugs again.

"Listen, Iz, I can't predict the future, but I think I'm starting to know Miss Serena pretty well and I think she's going to be part of your lives for a very long time."

Isabel doesn't reply. She snuggles deeper into the comforter and tucks it around her, so I return my attention to the television. I must doze off again because my eyes snap open sometime later and she's no longer in the chair.

Chapter 47

Serena

The next morning, I shuffle into the kitchen to find Vance cooking while Isabel stands on a stepstool and watches on. When I sidle up next to him, I see they're making pancakes. He's given her the spatula and tells her when to flip them while he tends to a skillet of bacon.

"Y'all have been busy," I observe.

Vance puts his arm around my waist and pulls me close. I'm surprised when it doesn't hurt as bad as I expect it to. It seems moving around last night, even just that small amount, helped. When I kiss his cheek, he looks at me sideways with one side of his mouth tucked up.

I realize that's the first time I've kissed him since we sorted ourselves out. Or I sorted myself out. He's been the one instigating kisses and little touches.

Somewhere in the last few days of him watching over me, I decided to trust him. If I'm really going to give myself over to trying to build a relationship with him, I need to put in some effort, too.

"I hope you made enough for me because I'm feeling famished this morning," I say.

"We have enough for an army, I think," Vance says. "Isabel is catching on quickly."

"That's great. I love cooking, too."

Cooking with Mom was one of my favorite things when I was growing up, but considering Isabel's loss, I don't say that. A vision fills my mind of me and the girls working in the kitchen together and it makes my heart do a stutter step.

I snake my arm around Vance's waist and poke a finger in Isabel's ribs. She giggles and leans away from me, wrapping her hand around my finger and pushing it away. It's such a beautiful sound that it almost brings me to tears.

Bringing her here was the right thing to do. It seems I'm not the only one feeling a little better this morning. With another kiss to Vance's cheek, I move away so he can focus on the food.

I pull down plates, silverware, and a glass. "Isabel, juice or milk?"

"Milk please."

Vance already has a cup of coffee, so once I pour a glass of milk for Isabel and put it by her plate where she usually sits, I fix a cup of coffee for myself. As I let the caffeine wake up my brain cells, I go to the fridge to take out syrup and butter, putting them on the island.

This all feels very homey and I love it. After living alone for so long, I would have thought it would feel like an invasion of my privacy, but it hasn't. When I opened the door to Maggie that first night, it's like my spirit opened right along with it and welcomed them in.

Honestly, I don't know what I'll do when this is all over if I have to go back to living alone. Thoughts have been prickling at the edges of my senses and I'm still too bound up with fear and doubt to indulge them.

Thoughts like bringing the girls home with me and us making our own family. There's more involved than just what I want, though. It will depend upon what the girls want, too. Then there's Vance to figure into everything.

He's already raised a family and might not be on board for continuing in a relationship with me if I bring the girls into my home. I wouldn't want to be put into the position of having to choose between them.

Then the thought hits me. Most of my life has been spent making decisions based on other people's opinions and expectations. For once, I need to choose for myself. Choose what I want and what I think is best for me.

If I decide I want to open my home permanently to the girls, it will be up to Vance to choose whether that's something he wants to be a part of. And if he says it's not, then I'll be just fine. This thing of letting down my walls but knowing full well that someone I care about might walk away is scary.

But I've survived being hurt before and I'll survive it again if it happens. I'm sick of hiding away, and putting the shoulda, woulda, couldas of my past in the driver's seat of my life.

Vance is helping Isabel stack cakes onto a plate when there's a boom of thunder outside. I hadn't checked the weather, but it was so muggy last night that a thunderstorm rolling through doesn't surprise me. A day snuggled up watching movies while it storms outside sounds downright glorious to me.

Normally, after almost a week of sitting around doing not much of anything, I'd be itching to get out and about. All of it was done alone, though. Having Vance and Isabel here changes things.

Maybe I have everything I need to make some cookies this afternoon.

After breakfast, we work together to clean up, and just as I start the dishwasher, Vance's phone rings.

He answers with, "Ford, what's up?" then moves down the hall. When I hear the name, I wonder why Ford is calling Vance instead of me. Then I remember my phone is still in the bedroom. He may have tried to call, and I didn't hear it.

"Come on," I tell Isabel. "Let's find a movie to watch."

"Okay," she replies, going into the living room with me.

We settle onto the sofa and start scrolling through the options. When Vance returns, we're debating between something funny and something adventurous. He sits next to me and puts his arm around my shoulder, pulling me close.

"Everything okay?" I ask.

"Better than okay. Draper was arrested this morning after causing a ruckus at a bank in Ardmore. Seems he was headed south and stopped to withdraw a bunch of money from his bank."

"He was running." I say.

"Probably. When he couldn't get what he wanted from the ATM, he went inside and tried to close his account. They told him it would take two business days to close the account and issue the funds, and he lost it. Cursed out the teller. The cops were called, and they found the arrest warrant when they ran his ID."

"Excellent." Isabel says, without looking at Vance.

"Excellent indeed," he replies, and reaches over to give a gentle tug to a strand of hair. She shrinks away, but she grins as she does it. "Funny thing is, the bank told the cops that the account had already been mostly closed. Only a few hundred dollars were in there."

"You would think he would have stashed his money somewhere besides a bank."

"He must have. When he was arrested, he had thirty-thousand dollars in a duffel bag under some clothes. Ford's guessing the money in the bank was his legit earnings from the department."

"Hmm," I say, and lean my head back against Vance's shoulder.

Chapter 48

Vance

The next day, we take Isabel back down south for family lunch and to return her to the ranch. Although things are looking promising with Draper's arrest, it could still take a lot of time for the two attorneys, and anyone else that gets caught in the net, to face trial and potentially be put behind bars.

Things don't happen fast like they do on television. Once there is an arrest made, it can still take a year for them to face trial, and that's only if they can't make bail and stay locked up. If they make bail, it can take even longer.

Lady Justice's wheels of due process grind along slowly.

We're on the way home when Serena squeezes my hand and says, "I think I'm going to apply to adopt the girls."

She says it like it should be some kind of surprise. Watching her with those girls and how she put their welfare above all else, I knew that's likely what would happen. Spending yesterday with her and Isabel just made me more certain.

She's as bonded with Isabel as Isabel is with her. When Sophie let me hold her and comfort her the other night, her little hand wrapped around my heart and embedded itself there. These girls are going to need just the right parents, and I think Serena is the best mother they could hope for.

When she looks over to see me grinning, she frowns. "What?"

"Baby, it's not a surprise."

"And yet you're still here."

"And yet I'm still here," I agree. "Honey, I love kids. I love being a dad. You having two daughters you've adopted isn't any different than it would be if you had given birth to them and I was dating you as an already single mom. We'll just keep moving forward and when you're ready, I'll pop the question and we'll get married. Then I'll get to be a dad all over again."

"When I'm ready?"

"Yep."

"So what if I said I was ready now?"

I know she's just being ornery, so I decide to be ornery right back. "You're not. But you're getting closer."

She huffs and tries to pull her hand out of mine, but I hold it tight. "I love you, Serena. You don't have to say it back, but I want you to know where I stand on the matter."

She stops trying to pull away, her hand relaxing in mine, so I lace our fingers together. When she doesn't speak again, I know she's thinking. Hell, I can practically hear the wheels spinning in her head.

In typical Serena fashion, when she has her thoughts organized, she tells me. "I think I'm going to sell the house and get something that would be more appropriate for a family. My house has been fine for me, but with only two bedrooms... I just think the girls each need their own room. They're so different that it would be good for each of them to have their own space."

Silence falls again and we're almost at her house when she lets the next volley fly.

"I think I need to go see Sophie's father in prison. Isabel's father was gone before she was old enough to remember him and I don't know if her mother even knew who the father was. But Sophie's father needs to know what happened to his wife and my intentions. First, though, I need to ask the girls if they even want to be adopted."

The next week, while we're at family lunch, we take the girls and Maggie to the resting room and close the door. We also asked Roni to join us because Serena felt she needed to be there in case there's any kind of delayed emotional fallout she'll be left to deal with.

Serena had already pulled Roni aside and told her of her intentions. Roni just smiled and said, "Takoda and I talked about possibly taking them in after we found out about their mother. I prayed about it, too, but as much as I love those girls, I knew they weren't mine. It makes me so happy that they're yours, and I think you're going to be a wonderful mother to them."

When she told me Roni's response, she got all teary-eyed on me and had to take a break on the porch before we sat down to talk to the girls.

"I wanted to talk to you all, particularly to Isabel and Sophie. However, it affects you, too, Maggie, so I wanted you to be here. After spending time with you, and knowing your circumstances..."

She stops and takes a breath and I can see her hands shaking with nerves. Folding them together in her lap, she continues.

"Well, you'll still need to stay down here for a while until those evil men are arrested, but I was wondering if maybe you'd like to come live with me once that happens. We could arrange for me to be your foster mom and then, if you like it there, we could see about making things more permanent."

"Yes," Isabel says without hesitation and that makes Serena smile. I figured she'd have that reaction. Isabel and Serena have become attached through this whole ordeal.

"What if I wanna stay here?" Sophie asks.

Serena gives her a tender smile. "This has been your temporary home to keep you safe, but once the danger is over, we'll need to find you a permanent home. I'd love it if you'd give me a try, but if you don't want to live with me, we'll look for another family."

She frowns and doesn't say anything more, but surprisingly, she gets up off the floor where she'd been sitting and comes to me, crawling into my lap.

"You don't got any other kids to play with," Sophie says to my chest.

"Well, I was thinking about that," Serena says gently. "When I bought my house, it was just me living there, so I didn't really think about kids in the neighborhood. Also, although it's big enough for all three of us, it's not really set up to be comfortable for all of us, so I thought that I'd sell it and buy something that would work better and would be in a neighborhood with other kids around so you would have people to play with."

"Really?" Sophie asks, sitting up straighter.

The smile that spreads across Serena's face makes me want to lean in and kiss her. "Really."

"Okay," says Sophie. "I'll try it."

"Thank you, baby girl. I appreciate you being willing to give me a chance."

With her two cents pitched in, Sophie leaves the room to go play. "Maggie, when school starts again, you'll be welcome to stay with me. Hopefully, by that time, certain people will be in custody or being monitored and we'll all be in a position to get back to a normal life."

"Thank you," Maggie says. "I appreciate that, and I agree with wanting to get back to a sense of normalcy."

The meeting officially breaks up and we hang out for a few more hours, much later than usual, before saying our goodbyes. Isabel has been locked to Serena's side and doesn't seem to want to let her go, but I totally get it. She probably doesn't remember the last time someone made her a priority like Serena has.

When we get into the car, Serena stares out the window at the passing scenery. "You okay, baby?" I ask.

Her voice is rough when she answers and my suspicions are confirmed about her being just as broken up about saying goodbye as Isabel was. "I just want this to be over."

"Yeah, I know. Every day brings us closer to a resolution."

She nods and we're quiet for the rest of the way home. For the rest of the evening, she remains quiet, contemplative.

We're getting ready to get into bed when I pull her into my arms. "If you want to talk something out, I make a great sounding board."

She sighs, but returns the embrace, resting her forehead against my shoulder. "I'm all right. It's just difficult to be on the outside of things after being in the know about everything. As much as I would love to put Ford and Carlos on speed dial for hourly updates, that's not realistic."

"Yeah. I know the feeling. But they're good cops and they'll get the job done as quickly as it can be."

She cups my face in her palms and looks me in the eye, the corners of her mouth tucked up in a small smile. "You're right. I know you're right."

Then she leans up and kisses me. I pull her closer, wrapping her in my arms, and she deepens the kiss. My hands slide down to cup her beautiful round ass, to pull her hips to mine, letting her feel how hard she makes me.

When she rolls her hips, grinding into me, she takes me completely by surprise. It would seem I'm not the only one missing the intimacy we shared. We haven't been together for almost two weeks and my body is keenly aware.

"I've missed you," I tell her honestly.

Her hands stroke my neck and shoulders. "I've missed you, too."

She pulls away from me and grips the hem of the tank, which is exactly like the ones she's been wearing to bed all week, and whisks it off, leaving her naked from the waist up. After tossing it aside, she pushes off her pants and panties, giving me an amazing view of her tantalizing curves.

When she pulls back the bedding, she lies down on her side, her head propped on her fist and beckons me like a goddess summoning a worshipper. She is incredibly sexy and I am more than happy to bow at her feet.

Standing before her, I remove my clothes while she watches. Her gaze strokes over my body, taking me in from head to toe. When I push off my shorts, letting my cock spring free, her stare turns hungry.

I join her in bed, filling my hands and mouth with her full breasts. When I stroke between her thighs, she's dripping wet with arousal. "Baby," I croon.

She spreads her legs to give me better access, and I sink two fingers into her slick, velvety heat. I press a thumb to her swollen clit and she whimpers as I begin to finger fuck her pussy and worry her clit.

Her hips grind in time with my fingers and I watch her as she loses herself in the sensations. "Vance," she gasps as her hand grips the wrist of the hand pumping between her legs. "Vance," she says again, then cries out with the orgasm rolling through her.

I hold her close, kissing and nuzzling her neck until she finds herself again and kisses me back. With my arms tight around her, I roll us until she's on top. She looks down at me with a confused look on her face.

"What's wrong, baby?" I ask.

"I don't…"

Understanding dawns. "You've never been on top?"

She bites her lip and shakes her head. With some simple guidance, she maneuvers into position and slides my cock into her pussy as she lowers herself. After a hair's breadth of time to adjust to the position, she begins to move.

When a roll of her hips presses her clit into my body, her eyes pop open and she smiles. I lick the pad of my thumb and slide it between us, creating a consistent contact point for her magical bundle of nerves.

With a little "Oh!" of sound, she throws back her head and finds her rhythm, undulating on top of me. It doesn't take her long before she comes again, her already sensitive clit reaching the pinnacle quickly and dragging her over the cliff of pleasure.

I roll us again so I'm on top and pump my hips, thrusting my cock into her over and over. After over a week, it doesn't take long before I feel the pressure building in my balls and explode into her, but not before she grips my hips, pulling me down hard and loses herself again, too.

Chapter 49

Serena

I am officially tired of being sequestered to my house. Now that I'm no longer sore, I'm ready to get some fresh air and sunshine. My face has healed enough that a little strategically placed concealer will cover the colorful splotches that always come with healing contusions.

I roll out of bed and go to the bathroom where Vance is shaving. He's already been up a while, gone for a run, had breakfast, and showered. Not necessarily in that order, though. I was asleep, so I have no clue.

Casually, as I put paste on my toothbrush, I say, "Today I plan on running a few errands. Just to get some groceries and such."

His hand stops dragging the razor over his skin, but he doesn't say anything. Meeting his gaze in the mirror, I go on.

"All public places with plenty of people in them. The grocery store, and I need to drop some dry cleaning off. Which, by the way, if you have anything you'd like to add to my pile of clothes, let me know. I even plan to take my stun gun if that makes you feel better."

He resumes shaving. "You have a stun gun?"

"Yes. I used to carry one all the time when I was in Atlanta because of all the...um...*interesting* people I was around. It got lost in the move, so I got a new one and used to carry it on campus, but everything was so uneventful that I stopped. It's locked up in my safe. I'll need to recharge it, but that only takes a few hours and I don't plan on going out until this afternoon. This morning, I want to see if I can locate Sophie's father and set up a time to see him."

He doesn't seem inclined to reply right away, so I brush my teeth. When I'm finished, he kisses me on the cheek, leaving residual shaving cream in his wake, and says, "Take the gun and only public places. Text me before you leave and when you get back."

"Yes, sir," I say with a grin.

With a wink, he goes to the bedroom to get dressed. We haven't talked about it, but our temporary protection situation of living together is feeling very permanent and I'm not mad about that.

That's actually something I can thank Diondre for. When I was with him, I'd already had it in my mind that living with someone wouldn't be so terrible. Of course, I was hoping that marriage would follow in short order, but we all know how that went.

Vance has already said he sees us together forever. At the time, his statement startled me, but after him being here for the last week, well, forever seems like it's a foregone conclusion. It's so comfortable with him.

He's patient with me and, just like this morning, doesn't have to act like the overbearing alpha man. I made my case, and he was fine with my logic. Yet, I know that if it came right down to it, he'd have no problem flexing his deadlier skills if it came to keeping someone he loves safe.

While I wait for the gun to charge, I have other things to take care of. First, I contact a former student who, in her first year of law school, decided it wasn't for her and transitioned into social work.

She's now in a leadership position at the Department of Human Services, the state agency that oversees foster care in the state. I tell her the situation with the girls and ask for her guidance.

Next, I look up Sophie's father and check for the prison's next visitation date and request a time to see him. I'm unsure if anyone in the police department has notified him of his wife's passing. If not, he deserves to know, and I want to talk to him about Sophie.

With those things taken care of, I finish getting ready for the day.

I'm on my way to the grocery store when I remember I need to stop by my office. There's a book I borrowed from the library that has been sitting on my desk unread, which needs to be returned or rechecked out.

The thought of going in there alone after what happened makes me hesitate. It's silly because I wasn't hurt in the building. I was hurt in the parking lot, but I told Vance I wouldn't go anywhere there weren't a lot of people and this time of year there aren't many people on campus.

Feeling self-conscious, I go to the campus security office. An officer I have met, but don't know very well, is on duty. "Hi Jose," I say when I step into the frigid office.

"Hey professor. Glad to see you're doing well."I guess the news of my attack has made its rounds among the security team. With an embarrassed smile, I say, "Yes, thank you. Actually, that's kind of why I'm here. I need to retrieve something from my office and was wondering if an officer could meet me there and stand guard until I come out just to make sure no one else goes into the building."

He nods. "Absolutely. Frank is on rounds. I'll give him a shout and send him your way. Just wait until he gets there."

"I know Frank. Thank you so much, Jose."

"No problem."

Frank shows up about ten minutes after I park. I get out of my car and meet him on the sidewalk. "I was sure sorry to hear what happened to you," he says.

"Thank you, Frank. I'm doing much better now."

"Looks like, and I'm glad to see it."

When we reach the doors, I use my key card and open the door. "I just need to get a book from my office and I'll be right back out. Shouldn't take long."

"Take your time. I'll be here until you're through."

My hands begin to shake and my nerves want me to hurry through the building and race back out with the book, but I force myself to take it slow. Frank is just outside the door, so no one can come in. Yes, there are other doors, but they are also locked.

It takes me a few tries to get the key into the lock on my office door. Then the book isn't where I remembered it being. In my cleaning exercise the other night, I must have put it somewhere I'd remember to find it.

Funnily enough, I don't remember where that was. After looking everywhere, of course, it's on one of my bookshelves. Grabbing it, I hurry to leave the building because I hadn't intended to keep Frank from his regular duties for so long.

When I step into the open library and study room at the front of the building, there is a man sitting at one of the tables, leaning back in the chair, two legs lifted off the floor. I slip my hand into my purse and grip the stun gun, my thumb on the power switch.

"Serena Chilton," he says, his voice pitched low and sonorous. But his tone is casual, not threatening in any way. At least not yet.

"I'm afraid you have me at a disadvantage, Mister..."

He waves a hand. "My name isn't important. The only name that is important is that of my employer. He says you took something from him and he'd like it back."

"Thing?" I say, incredulous that he'd relegate a human being, a child, to being called a thing. "Did he tell you what I have of his?"

"Makes no difference to me."

I can't stop the way my lip curls in disgust. It's probably not smart to clue someone in that you find them repulsive, but the feeling is too strong to hide.

"A child, that's the *thing* I took. A twelve-year-old girl that he'd been raping for two years. He'd traumatized her so badly she tried to commit suicide."

If I hadn't been watching closely, I'd have missed the look that flittered across his face. No, he hadn't known and now that he did; he was disgusted, too, even if just a little.

Hedging my bets, I go on. "He gave her mama drugs. The woman had been sober for years, then he ensured she got busted. Of course, out of the kindness of his heart, he agreed to represent her, but when she couldn't pay the bill, he took her ten-year-old daughter in trade. And just so you know, he's been doing it for almost twenty years."

The chair legs thump to the floor. He rises from the chair and puts it back in perfect formation against the table, leaving it as if it had never been disturbed. That's when I notice the latex gloves he's wearing and suck in a breath.

So he leaves no prints.

Now that my indignation has been vented, the fear seeps back in. My heart is racing as he walks toward me. I tighten my grip on the gun, ready if he gets too near.

Instead of coming close, he gives a wide berth as he disappears into the building, moving toward one of the other exits. Once I'm sure he's not going to do me any harm, I continue toward the front door.

I half expected to see Frank slumped on the ground with a bump on the head, or worse, but he's still standing nearby under the shade of a tree. "Sorry, Frank, I put it somewhere I'd be sure to find it."

He chuckles. "I go around the house looking for my glasses when they're on top of my head. My wife thinks it's hilarious."

"Well, I've got it now. Thanks again for coming to stand watch."

"No worries, professor. Enjoy the rest of your day."

"You, too, Frank."

I didn't tell him about the man in the building. Anyone who can bypass the school's security so easily is likely someone on par with Vance or Jack and more than campus security could handle.

Besides, he just talked to me and if I'm reading his reaction correctly, he might just be on his way to have a *talk* with his employer. I'd love to be a fly on the wall for that conversation.

As soon as I'm in the car with the air conditioner on and the doors locked, I call Vance.

"Hey, baby, what's up?"

I tell him everything that has happened in the last thirty minutes or so. He's quiet for a long time before he finally says, "I'm glad you're all right. That could have gone very differently."

"Yeah. I was so scared I about peed my pants."

He chuckles.

"I'm serious!" I say with indignation.

"Sorry, baby, I know you are," he says, but there's still laughter in his voice.

"Anyway, I'm off to the grocery store and then I'm headed home."

"All right. See you in a little while."

I'm sitting across the table from Sophie's father. David Baker was handsome before the drugs. But now he's another casualty of George Graham's perverse drives.

The man in front of me looks nothing like he did in the photographs Vance and I were allowed to take from the apartment where the girls used to live. There wasn't much worth taking, so we focused on family photos and anything that looked as if it might be a memento for them.

The handsome man's addiction has reduced him to a skeleton with skin on. He also has few teeth left, which made him look macabre when he smiled hearing me say I was here on Sophie's behalf.

Currently, he's sitting in his seat with tears running down his face. I've just told him about his wife and what happened to Isabel. In other circumstances, I'd give the man a hug, but in this place, I can't even take his hand in mine.

He recovers his equilibrium when I tell him about Maggie's involvement and how she's with them in a place where all three of them can be safe. With a sober look, he asks, "What's going to happen to the girls?"

"Well, that's part of why I wanted to see you today. It's my intention to take the girls into my home as a foster parent at first. However, I've bonded with them over the last few weeks and intend to adopt Isabel."

"What about Sophie?" he snaps, as if offended I wouldn't automatically include her in my plans.

"Mr. Baker, I'm not sure Sophie can be adopted because one of her parents is still alive."

He looks chagrined. "Sorry. Yeah, I get that."

For long moments he doesn't say anything else and I can tell he's thinking, so I let him sort out his thoughts.

"Ten minutes," a guard bellows from his position near the exit door.

"I doubt she even remembers me," David Baker says. "She was only four when I went in and her mama never brought her to see me. You said you're a college professor, right?"

I nod. "Yes." That's all I told him. While I wanted to inform him of what's going on in his daughter's life, I didn't feel the need to hand over a lot of personal information to him.

"She could have a real life with you. Better than anything I could have done for her."

Since we started this vein of conversation, he's been antsy, his leg bouncing ninety miles a minute under the table. Now he's chewing on fingernails already bitten down to nubs.

"Have the papers drawn up and I'll give her up. I'll probably never come out of here alive, so the best thing I can do is not hold her back. If I let her go, she has a chance."

"You don't have to decide right now. I can have the papers drawn up and bring them back next week after you've had some time to think about it..."

"Time to wrap up," the guard bellows again.

"I'll turn the pictures over to the clerk at the front so they can give them to you."

I'd taken some photos of the girls with my cell phone when we were at family lunches and printed them out for him after blurring out anyone else in the pictures.

"K. Thanks," he says, rising from his chair and moving to get in the line of inmates at the door, waiting to be escorted out.

When I'm back in the car, Vance asks, "How did it go?"

He thought it would be best that he not go in with me, but when I suggested going, there was no way he was going to let me go alone. So, he's been sitting out here in the car for the two hours I've been inside.

"I'm not sure how I feel about it," I reply, then tell him about the meeting.

"The ball is in his court when it comes to Sophie, but he deserved to know what's going on. You've done what you can and I think it was the right thing to do, baby."

I hope he's right because I still feel very conflicted about it.

Chapter 50

Serena

While I'm thinking about it, I log onto the Department of Corrections site to set up another meeting with David Baker for next week. I search for his name like I did last time, but nothing comes up.

Pulling the notepad out of my purse that I carry with me, I flip to the page with his prisoner ID number. There are no results for that, either, but there is a note that gives a phone number to call.

After being rerouted several times, I'm more than a little frustrated. Why give a number to call if the people who answer it don't have any answers? Finally, I get a woman named Penny on the line and she seems to know what she's doing.

"Are you a family member or his attorney?" she asks.

Fudging just a little, I say, "His wife passed recently and I am the temporary guardian for their daughter. I never acted in court on his behalf, but I am an attorney."

"Oh, no," Penny says. "All right, um, wait, what did you say your name is?"

"Serena Chilton."

"Ah, yes. Mrs. Chilton, I'm sorry to inform you that Mr. Baker is no longer with us."

I suck in a breath. The information is so startling that I don't correct her about my marital status. It doesn't matter. "What?"

"Yes, he was found deceased last night. An autopsy has not been performed yet to determine cause of death, but there's a note here in the computer that a letter addressed to you was found among his belongings."

I'm too shocked to respond for a half dozen heartbeats.

"Mrs. Chilton, are you there?"

"Yes. Sorry. I just spoke to him the other day, so his passing comes as a bit of a shock."

"The letter was addressed, stamped and ready to mail, so once it's reviewed by the department, it will be mailed to you. Would you like the rest of his belongings sent to you as well?"

"Sure." Penny puts my address into the system so whatever belongings he leaves behind will be sent to me and then we say our goodbyes.

I'm not sure having Sophie's dad's things sent to me was the right thing to do. However, with me being the first visitor he'd had since being incarcerated, it would seem there's no other family besides Sophie.

Once I get whatever there is to get, Vance and I can go through it. There's no telling what is considered a personal belonging in prison. For all I know, they might be sending his hairbrush.

I wish Vance was home so I could talk this over with him. Telling Sophie of her father's passing is something we need to do, but should we do it right away? She just found out her mother was gone. Will waiting a few weeks to tell her about the death of a father she doesn't remember do more harm than good?

As if my thoughts conjured him, my phone rings in my hand, startling me so badly I almost drop it. Then Vance's face appears on the screen. "Hi honey."

"Hey baby. Just wanted to give you a head's up. Graham is on the run, so stay inside and make sure everything's buttoned up and the alarm is set. There's no telling what he's going to do."

"On the run? How do you know?"

"He snatched a girl and an Amber alert has been issued. Other than a description of the girl, him and his car, we don't have any other details, but Jack and I think it's another client's child."

The prospect of that pervert taking another child and destroying her innocence has me putting a hand on the counter for balance.

"Oh no! That poor baby!"

"I know. There's nothing more I'd like than to track him down myself, but we have to trust law enforcement."

"You're right. It's just difficult to do when we know what's in store for that child if she's not found."

As much as I want to talk to him about Sophie's father, I won't do that now. He'll be home in a few hours and we can talk then.

"I'm right there with you, baby. Jack's calling me, so I'd better go. Love you."

"See you when you get home."

He's been making his declaration of love regularly, mostly when we're saying goodbye on the phone or he's leaving in the morning. I think he doesn't do it all the time because he doesn't want me to feel pressured to say it back.

My feelings are growing and if I'm honest, I'm already there. Those feelings are potent and they are deep. But this is unfamiliar territory for me and it is more than a little scary.

I make my rounds through the house, checking the windows and doors, just to be sure. They certainly haven't unlocked themselves, but double checking makes me feel better. I'm certainly not doing it because Vance told me to. It's just the practical thing to do.

As I move around the house, I pray for the child who has been taken by an evil man. My petition to the Almighty is that she is found before that deviant does anything to hurt her.

Feeling impressed to do so, my prayers continue when I return to the kitchen and begin to prepare for supper. The burden doesn't abate, so I put everything back into the refrigerator and go to my bedroom. Falling to my knees, I bow my head and fall into the arms of the Father.

When Vance comes home, he finds me still on the floor in the bedroom. My need to pray was exhausted, but I'd been so physically drained that I'd just laid down and closed my eyes.

"You okay, baby?" Vance asks when he comes into the room.

"Yes. Just had a need to pray."

"I understand. That must be why I had a powerful feeling that I needed to pick up some food on the way home. Are you hungry?"

"Starving. Thank you for doing that."

I hold out my hand to him and let him pull me to my feet. Once I'm standing, he pulls me into his arms and kisses me.

While we eat, I tell him about what I'd discovered about Sophie's father. We talk over my question of whether to tell Sophie right away.

After thinking it over for a few minutes, Vance says, "You're probably right about her not remembering him. She was only three or four when he went in. There's probably a vague idea of him in her mind, but I'd be surprised if there are any genuine memories."

"I was thinking we'd wait the few weeks it will take to get his belongings. That way, if there's anything in there she might want, we can give it to her then."

He nods. "Sounds like a good plan."

Vance's phone chimes with an incoming message. A frown creases his brow when he looks at the message. "What the?"

"What is it?"

He shows the screen to me. There is a message, but there's no number attached to it. Not even the obligatory Unknown Number identifier. It tells him where he can find a lost bird and gives an address on the outskirts of town.

"I'm coming with you," I say.

"Baby…"

He must see something in my face when I stare him down because he sighs. "Fine, but you'll stay in the car until I'm sure it's safe."

I make a noise in my throat like Mama used to make when she was agreeing, but not really.

We don't hesitate to even put our dishes away. However, I am overwhelmed by the need to grab a bag from my shopping errands earlier and take it with us. Once we're in the car, Vance calls Jack and relays the message and address.

"He's still at the office, so he may be there before us," Vance tells me.

The address leads us to an under-used warehouse area that has no traffic. There were some cars parked at one building, but most of the structures appear to be deserted. When we draw near the address, a Carver Security SUV comes into view.

My hand reaches to the door handle, but Vance gives me a look. "Stay put, baby. Please."

I'm not happy about it, but I settle back in my seat. Jack and another man, who is slightly older, shorter, and broader, are viewing the car from a few feet away. Based on their facial features and coloring, it's probably Jerald, Jack's brother.

My guess is they're trying to avoid disturbing any evidence around the car parked in the shade with the windows cracked. Before Vance reaches them, Jack is talking, but I can't tell what they're saying. Vance pulls out his phone and makes a call, walking back to the car.

Just as his butt comes to rest on the driver's seat, Ford answers the phone.

"Pickering."

"Ford, it's Vance. We've found the missing girl."

He tells Ford about the text and about coming to the location. "Other members of Carver Security are here, too. There's no sign of the suspect, but the girl is sleeping in the back seat. The car's in the shade, but she's probably pretty warm. Movement is minimal, but not stirring, though, so maybe drugged. We stayed at about a five-foot perimeter, so didn't get a close look inside. Don't know if the car is locked, or if there are keys."

There's some back and forth and Ford asks us to stay and keep watch until local law enforcement arrives. He's already made the call.

As soon as the sirens come into earshot, they're cut by the crying of the girl, who is now awake. After Jack and Vance made a circuit of the area to be sure we were reasonably safe, Vance let me get out of the car.

A red, tear-strewn face with sweaty strands of hair sticking to her forehead rises to peer out the window. Her eyes lock on mine, and she flings open the door and races to me. I squat down and catch her.

Once she's in my arms, the smell of urine overpowers my sinuses. Poor baby has soiled herself. I can't say as I blame her; she was probably terrified.

Two police cars arrive, followed closely by an ambulance. Unfortunately, the EMTs are both men and when they try to take her from me, her arms tighten around my neck and she lets out ear-piercing screams.

"How about I get in the back with her? We need to get her out of these clothes," I tell the EMT. "Vance, honey, will you please grab that bag I brought from the house, along with the wet wipes from my purse?"

He gives me a hand into the back of the ambulance and sets the bag on the bench beside me. After a stern discussion with the EMT, they allow Vance to hold up a blanket while I help the girl change.

When I went out this morning, stopping to shop hadn't been on my list of things to do. But when I saw the shop next door to my dry cleaner was having a sale on some of the most adorable girls' clothes, I stopped in and bought a few things for Isabel and Sophie. I guess the Lord knew I was going to need them.

"Here, sweetheart, let's get you out of those clothes. I'm sorry, but I don't have any panties for you."

There's the low rumble of men's voices on the other side of the blanket. A hand bearing a latex glove reaches around the blanket, holding a plastic evidence bag.

To help her focus on something other than being stripped out of her clothes, I talk to her. "My name is Miss Serena. Your name is Bethany, right?"

She nods, sniffling. Now that she's not squeezing my neck, I notice she's holding a black feather. "That's a pretty feather. Did you bring that from home?"

This time, she shakes her head in the negative. "It was on the car seat."

"Oh?"

She nods, putting a hand on my shoulder as I pull her shorts and panties off. I open the package of wet wipes and hand one to her. "Use this to wipe your thighs, then drop it into this bag, sweetheart."

The police will probably have a hissy fit, but there's no way I was going to have this baby sitting around in pee-soaked clothing after being terrorized by a deviant. I'm retaining everything in the evidence bag, so they're just going to have to be satisfied with that.

Once she drops the cloth into the bag, I pull out a pair of shorts and hold them up to her. She's a tiny little thing, and it looks like the things I bought for Sophie will fit best. We pull them up and they're a little snug but will do.

She's already pulling off her shirt and putting it into the bag, and I'm ready to hand her the new one. While she gets the shirt on, I seal the evidence bag.

"We're good, honey. You can lower the blanket."

When he does, I see a female officer standing there beside him. She takes the evidence bag from me and hands it to a man in uniform standing close by. I hitch my chin when she gives me a stern look. I will not apologize for doing what I did.

They have witnesses that saw him take Bethany and she should be able to testify. Any transfer evidence on her clothing would just be padding to the case.

"Bethany, one of these medical guys needs to take a look at you to see if you're hurt. I saw the bruises on your arm. Will you be okay to let them look at the bruises?"

She scoots closer to me. "This nice woman is Officer Simmons. She'll stay right here with you and probably has some questions to ask."

"Bethany!" a woman's screaming yell reaches us.

"Mama?" Bethany cries.

A frantic woman appears behind the ambulance in the open doors and Bethany bursts into tears, dive bombing into her mother's open arms. I move to step down from the ambulance, and Vance offers me his hand.

Officer Simmons follows us a few steps away from the ambulance. "Thank you for putting everything in the evidence bag, but you really shouldn't have changed her clothes."

"I was not going to let that traumatized child stay in those soiled clothes while the EMTs poked and prodded her and you all asked your questions."

Vance squeezes my hand and I take a breath, letting go of the righteous anger that was simmering.

"She got out of the car on her own and was so afraid she practically tackled me. If you want, I'll hand over my clothing, too, so you can check it for transference. However, if this case boils down to transfer evidence from clothing to get a conviction, y'all should get a new DA."

Vance chuckles and gently pulls me away. In my time in the ambulance, it seems as if the entirety of the Norman police department has arrived. When I survey the sea of officers, I see Ford and Carlos among them.

Ford spots us moving across the parking lot and lifts a chin in acknowledgement. I raise a hand in return, then fall in step at Vance's side.

"I think we're just in the way now," Vance says. "Jack, Jerald, and I have already given statements to Norman PD, so we're good to go."

Chapter 51

Vance

The next morning Ford and Carlos come over to interview both of us and Serena gives them a plastic zipper bag with her clothes in it. They take it, but agree with her that although they'll process the clothes, whatever they find or don't find is unlikely to make or break the case.

"This is not for public consumption, but I know I can trust you two," Ford says. "Graham is in the wind. Emptied out a bank account before we could get a freeze in place, so he's got a couple million dollars to get himself to wherever he's headed."

Carlos chimes in. "We've still got a be on the lookout in the system for him, but we're having a difficult time figuring out why he took the girl, only to leave her and his car behind."

"Maybe someone intervened," Serena says.

"Maybe," I agree.

"What did you make of the feather Bethany had?" Serena asks. "She said it was on the car seat when she woke up, but hadn't been there before."

Carlos shrugs. "It hasn't been thoroughly tested yet, but it was identified as a common raven feather. Nothing special other than the fact that in Oklahoma, ravens are usually only seen in the western part of the state. We've got tons of crows, but not a lot of ravens."

I look over at Serena to find her looking right back at me. Raven feather. The hacker's handle is Raven. Is it a coincidence or something more sinister?

My buddy who told me about the hacker had said that sometimes the subject of their searches would get dead or disappeared. Would he have come for Graham?

"What was that?" Ford asks.

"What was what?" I reply.

He points the pen he'd been taking notes with, swinging it between Serena and me. "That look you just shared. What aren't you saying?"

"I'm just perplexed as to why someone might put a feather on the seat of the car by her," Serena says. "It makes no sense."

"Imma call bullshit on that one, pardon my French, but I'll let it go. However, if the feather becomes relevant to something, we are going to revisit the topic."

Serena just shrugs and I keep my mouth shut. Yeah, as a former cop, it bothers me, but telling him about the Raven could taint the whole of the case regardless of them finding their own evidence to back up everything we told them.

With that, the conversation turns casual, and soon after, they take their leave. I'm not far behind them, heading into the office.

"How'd the questioning go?" Jack asks when he sees me come in.

"Fine. Told them the same thing I said yesterday, but get this, Serena asked them about the feather the girl found in the car with her. Carlos said it was identified as a common raven feather. Thing is, ravens aren't indigenous to this part of the state. They're only found in the far west of Oklahoma."

"No shit?"

I shrug. "That's what he said."

"Hmm... Maybe your hacker unalived him."

Based on what Ford and Carlos said, that's a possibility. Maybe Graham is in the ground instead of in the wind. I shrug. "Who knows?"

I'm working on installs for the rest of the day, so time goes by quickly. Although I'm not physically exhausted when I get home, my brain is fried. However, I go on full alert as soon as I see Serena get up from the kitchen island where a mostly empty glass of wine sits.

Her hands dash across her cheeks, and she plasters on a smile. "Hey honey," she says. "How was your day?"

"It was good. I was doing the install thing all day. What's wrong?"

She shakes her head. "Nothing. I'm fine."

Before she can turn away to put her empty glass in the sink, I pull her into my arms. "Baby," I croon. "Talk to me."

"Sophie's dad..." she starts, but leans into me, burying her face against my shoulder, and starts to cry.

I hold her, letting her get it all out. When she quiets, she pulls away and hands me a piece of paper from the island. There's also an envelope and I understand this was the letter the clerk told Serena about when she called.

It's surprising that it came so quickly. Sometimes it can take weeks for mail to make it out of the prison system. Maybe because he's deceased, they went ahead and sent it figuring anything inside couldn't do any harm anymore.

Then I read it. There's only one line, and it becomes clear that Sophie's father most likely committed suicide, whether by his own hand or someone else's.

Please give my girl a good life.

Realization dawns. This is Mrs. Jackson all over again, but this time, I'm here and I'll do everything I can to help her not internalize the unwarranted guilt. "You didn't cause this. He made a choice and based on what you told me, he was already killing himself, just more slowly."

"But thanks to me, he decided to do it quickly."

"No, baby. Because he saw a better future for his daughter, he took it upon himself to eliminate all the red tape."

She looks at me and blinks. I decide to enlighten her on some things Jerald found out from a contact he has in the prison system.

"He wasn't getting out," I tell her. "With good behavior, he could have been out two or three years ago, but he kept getting violated for contraband, which added time to his sentence. The drugs were eating him alive. You said yourself he looked like a walking skeleton. That's on him and whether you'd gone there or not, he was well on his way to dying."

She sighs, but she's lost the ghosts of grief that were shining in her eyes.

"I have an idea," I say. "Let's get out of this house and go get something for supper that's horrible for us, like greasy food truck tacos. You can have them with wine and we'll just chill and hang out."

She leans into me again. "That sounds wonderful."

Chapter 52

Serena

Vance takes me to a food truck, but it appears to be a permanent location because they have a few picnic tables in front. There are strings of fairy lights on metal poles over the picnic area and music plays on some speakers.

There's a bit of a crowd, but we join another couple and share a table. They're a sweet young couple who has recently moved to the metro. He's in the AWACS program at Tinker and she works from home as a graphic artist.

When I ask her what brought them out tonight, she pats her stomach and says, "Raphael had a craving for tacos."

That makes me laugh and her husband, Ramon, snorts in response, then says, "She blames everything on my son."

"I hate to tell you," Vance says with a chuckle, "but it probably is his fault. Pregnant women are slaves to the hormones in their body while the baby is in utero and for a good long while after."

"See. I told you!" Anna exclaims.

They had already been there for a while when we arrived, so they leave well before we do. Vance and I eat and talk, but he keeps the conversation light.

He got a beer to have with his tacos, but as promised, he brought wine from home for me. I laughed when he filled a travel mug with wine and put a straw in it for me. It turned out to be the perfect under the radar container and although I'd balked saying I wouldn't drink that much, by the time I'm finished eating, my wine is almost gone, too.

The crowd has thinned a lot and some people are still eating, but mostly they're sitting around chatting and drinking. Both the cooks come out and sit with their patrons, laughing and joking. A few times, a song will come on and a few couples will get up and dance.

The next time a slow song comes on, Vance says, "Come on. Let's go dance."

My initial thought is to refuse, but I'm just libated enough to set my natural inhibitions aside. With a smile, I take his offered hand and let him lead me to the small open area where two other couples are swaying to the music.

He pulls me into his arms, and we begin to sway, too. Gently, he tucks my head against his shoulder and I relax against him, following his lead. When the song fades and a more upbeat tune comes on, he kisses my temple.

"I love you, you know," I breathe into the air before I lose my nerve.

"Love you, too, baby."

"I think I'm ready to go home. It feels like I could sleep for days."

We're in the car and almost home when I say, "Tomorrow I want to start looking for a new house. We'll need to make sure it is in a district with excellent schools for the girls and in a neighborhood where there are kids to play with."

While we stopped at a red light, he leans across the console and kisses me. "What was that for?" I ask.

"You said we. Does that mean you're about ready to marry me?"

I duck my head and smile to myself. "Hmm. Seems like there's something you need to do before we start talking about marriage."

"I've got plans, baby. Just you wait and see."

"Plans?" I query with a laugh.

"Yep. Plans."

That's all he'll say about it. When I ask questions, he tells me again that I'm just going to have to wait and see.

"Mmm hmm...plans." I grumble after he keeps putting me off.

He laughs at me and pulls the car into the garage.

The next morning, I wake up alone in bed. When I check my phone and see it's after ten in the morning, I know why. Vance is usually up and about early. Hopefully, he left me some coffee.

I'm in the bathroom washing my face when Dale comes in dressed in shorts, using a t-shirt he must have just taken off to wipe the sweat off his face. "Hey baby."

"You must have gone for a run," I observe.

"Yep. It's hot out there today."

He leans into the shower and turns the water on. While he strips out of the rest of his clothes, I watch in the mirror unabashedly. This man has a truly beautiful body.

"You keep looking at me like that and I'm going to bend you over that counter."

I'd be just fine with that, but have something else in mind. He steps into the stall and is letting the water run over his face, so I pull off my robe and step inside with him. When I put my hands on his hips and kiss him between his shoulder blades, he says, "I was hoping you'd join me."

I step back so I don't get hit full on with the spray since I don't want to wash my hair. Vance steps forward and pulls me back against him, his hardening cock pressing into my soft flesh. He tries to kiss me, but I turn my head.

"I have morning breath because I wasn't going to brush my teeth until after I had coffee."

He nibbles my earlobe. "Baby, I don't care."

A strong hand cups my breast and he strokes the pad of his thumb over my nipple, bringing it to attention. I slide a hand between us and wrap my fingers around his shaft, discovering he's hard as a rock.

My core goes liquid and heat spreads between my thighs. "Vance," I breathe.

"Are you needy, baby?"

"Yes," I whimper.

I haven't had many partners, but none of them has aroused me the way Vance does. With them, I was satisfied having sex once a week, maybe twice. But with him, I need him, not just desire him, but need him all the time.

Because of my injuries and everything that's been going on, we haven't been intimate as often as I'd have liked, but that just means we have some lost time to make up for.

A finger slips into the valley at my center. "Very needy, I'd say."

He pushes me back against the tiled wall and kneels before me. I spread my legs, but it's not enough, so he instructs me to put one foot on the bench at the back of the shower. That opens me wide, and he dives in, putting his mouth over my sex.

With tongue and lips and even some gentle nips of his teeth, he drives me crazy. I put my hands on his head, urging him on, and I'm soon racing toward an orgasm. When I cry out in release, he stands and holds me because my legs are shaking so hard I almost lose my balance.

He sits on the bench and pulls me onto his lap, facing away from him, lowering me onto his cock. It's a little awkward at first, but once I get a rhythm going, it feels amazing. Then he reaches around to fondle my breasts and it's even better.

When he slips a hand between my legs and strokes my clit, it's phenomenal. It doesn't take long before another orgasm begins to build and this time, it hits quick and hard like the strike of a snake.

A besotted giggle burbles up my throat as I have the fanciful thought that I have, indeed, been struck by a snake. The snake that lives at the apex of his thighs. We shift positions again so that he's standing and I'm bent over, him still taking me from behind.

He's setting the tempo this time, pumping his hips, thrusting hard and fast. The last thrust is so hard I have to put a hand to the wall to steady myself. He groans and I feel his cock jerk deep inside me as he spills his seed.

We clean off quickly and finish getting ready to get our day started. Well, my day, anyway. His day started a few hours ago.

We take lunch to his mom and aunt and stay to visit for a few hours. Afterward, we go to the shop by my dry cleaner to replace the clothes I'd gotten for Sophie and given to Bethany in her time of need.

As I get the same outfit, I wonder how Bethany is doing. Hopefully, her mother isn't following the same path as the girls' mom did.

Perhaps I'll pay her a visit in the name of checking on Bethany in a few days once the media frenzy dies down a bit. I'm sure she has enough to deal with at the moment.

However, if there is any way I can offer support as we both walk through the aftermath of our children's trauma, I'll do it. The women that Graham and his ilk target often don't have others to turn to for help, but perhaps together, we can figure out how to best help our girls.

Chapter 53

Vance

We went down for the usual Sunday lunch and, since it appeared the danger had passed, we brought Isabel home with us. Sophie wanted to stay at the ranch with Maggie, who is doing a bang-up job getting the ranch's office operations organized.

Serena and Isabel spend their days together cooking and baking and talking about a new house. They also go see Mom and Auntie Dot a couple of times during the week while I'm at work.

Mom adores both of them and while Serena has fallen right in with the older women, Isabel is slowly warming up to them. I don't blame her. Between Dot's direct approach to everything and Mom's need to hug and love on everyone, they can be a bit overwhelming.

It's Friday and we're headed down to Ada to pick up Sophie and have dinner with Dale and Felisha. Serena has four houses that she and Isabel have picked out for us to go look at tomorrow, so it's a full family affair.

I have to say that I'm kind of digging the idea of being a dad again, but there's one more thing we need to get taken care of first. Serena is talking with Roni and Maggie while I go with Sophie out to the small house where she's staying with her cousin for the summer.

Isabel goes with me as we pre-arranged. Sophie grabs her backpack with her things for the weekend with us. Before we leave, I have something I need to talk to the girls about.

When we get back to the big house, Sophie is all giggly and bouncy. Thankfully, she's like that most of the time, so I don't think she's going to give anything away.

After supper with Dale and Felisha, we're sitting in the living room talking. Sophie's on my lap and pokes me in the chest. "What is it, baby girl?" I ask.

She leans up and whispers in my ear, but it's more of a stage whisper so everyone hears. "When are you gonna do it?"

Isabel groans. Serena frowns, and I chuckle.

"Well, with that introduction, I do have something I need to take care of." I stand and set Sophie down next to Serena so she's got our girls on each side of her. Taking a small black box out of my pocket, I kneel in front of Serena, my knees sounding like rice cereal when you pour milk over it while Sophie giggles her head off.

I open the box to reveal a simple solitaire engagement ring and present it to her. "Serena Chilton, I believe God brought us together years ago, but the timing wasn't right. He must've known we needed that initial hook to make the second time around so much stronger and more meaningful. I've talked to the girls and to your brother and they've given me the green light, so now it's up to you. Will you be my wife and forever partner for the rest of our days?"

Her hand goes to her mouth, but she doesn't answer right away. I start to feel a little concerned when Isabel elbows Serena in the side and says, "Go on, Mom. You know you want to."

The tears making her eyes shine start to fall with Isabel's words. She nods. "Yes. Of course I'll marry you."

I take the ring out of the box and slide it on her finger, hoping I got the size right. It seems to fit all right, but I'll let her be the judge. She extends her hand and stares at the ring on her finger for long moments and I start to feel nervous again.

"If you don't like it, we can exchange it for something..."

She leans over and cups my face in her hands, kissing me to quiet my words and declares, "It's perfect."

The next morning, we're up early because Serena wants to go to the farmer's market before we meet the realtor for the marathon of house showings we have set up. Sophie grumbles to be awakened so early, and promptly falls back to sleep in the car on the way to the market.

She's still asleep when we arrive, so I get her out of the back seat and carry her. However, once she sees all the people and things to look at, she's wide awake and ready to move under her own power.

Sophie wants to look at, touch, and taste everything. Isabel mostly stays by Serena's side, holding her hand as we make our way through the market.

I'd forgotten what it's like to try to keep up with an energetic child in a crowd. Getting some kind of kid's leash for Sophie might be a good idea because she's never where I expect her to be.

However, it's Isabel we lose track of. She was holding Serena's hand one moment and the next, she's gone. Serena is on the verge of panicking when she realizes the girl is gone.

"Calm down," Sophie says matter-of-factly and points. "She's just over there."

Isabel is standing at a booth where a woman is selling watercolor paintings. We don't go over right away, but monitor her as we continue to meander through the market, eventually catching up with her.

Surprisingly, Isabel is talking quietly with the woman. She's usually reluctant to engage with strangers, but maybe a fellow artist is the exception.

"I see you found a fellow artist," Serena says to her.

"Yeah, she says they're watercolor, but I told her I paint with acrylic."

"They're beautiful," Serena says to the artist, who thanks her. Then she asks Isabel, "Do you see one you like?"

It's impossible not to notice that Isabel seems particularly interested in a small painting of a flying blackbird. "I like this one," she says. "It matches the hair clip the lady gave me."

When she turns to show us, I see two strands of leather attached to a clip on one end, hanging down to small black wispy feathers and beading on the other end. To me, it looks very Native American.

"Did one of the vendors give you that?" I ask.

Isabel shrugs. "She wasn't at a booth. Just walking around like everyone else."

Serena frowns. "Did she say why she gave it to you?"

The girl just shrugs again.

I look at Serena and she's looking right back at me. With a lift of her eyebrows and a slight roll of her shoulder, she seems to agree with me that if someone gave it to her, there's no reason not to let her keep it.

We purchase the painting of the bird and Sophie declares she will positively be heartbroken if she doesn't get a painting of a sunflower. She is so dramatic that Serena chuckles and purchases it, too.

I don't know what happened, but as we go through house after house, Isabel seems lighter, less clingy to Serena. We've agreed to keep an open mind as we go through each house and not make any decisions until we sit down for dinner tonight when we can talk about all of them.

Serena gives each of the girls a notepad and colorful pen so they can make notes if they like. It cracks me up that she has her own notepad with things listed she needs to be sure to look at.

My logical lady is nothing if not organized. I don't take a notepad, but I also have my list of things to check out.

They're all very similar, with enough bedrooms that the girls won't have to share. The neighborhoods are gated with playgrounds and a swimming pool. And they're all in one of the best school district in the metro.

The ones we're looking at are way out of my price range, but Serena says that she made a lot of money when she sold her house in Atlanta. She apparently bought it when the market was in a downturn and sold when it was up.

That enabled her to pay cash for her house here with a decent amount left over that she hasn't had to touch. She wants to use that as a down payment so we can move in as soon as we can close. Then once her house sells, use that money to pay down the principle on the mortgage.

When we sit down to dinner that night, Serena has everyone put their first choice on a piece of paper and the number one reason why they like it. She then gathers the four pieces of paper and as she goes through each one, a smile begins to spread across her face.

"Well, the good news is that we all chose the same house. Vance says he likes it because it's the closest one to his mother. I liked it because that kitchen was gorgeous. Sophie liked it because of the water fountain kids could play in by the playground. And the most interesting reason of them all, Isabel liked it because there was a raven perched on the back fence."

I tilt my head and look at Isabel, but she's focused on her plate. This fascination with blackbirds seems to have come on all at once this morning and I'm unsure why. It's also interesting that she called the bird on the fence a raven and not a crow.

She wouldn't know the difference, but then, neither would I, except that, after our conversation with Carlos, I know ravens aren't really found in this area. My eyes catch on the hair clip with its black feathers, and I wonder exactly who it was that gave it to her.

The cop in me wants to find out, but the man and the father in me sets it aside and joins in the excited conversation with my family about our new home.

Epilogue

Serena

Six months later

"Come on, Mom," Isabel tells me. "You're going to be late."

"Baby, I can't be late," I chuckle. "They can't start without me, but you'll be happy to know I'm ready to go. Do you and Sophie have your things?"

"Yes. My bag was put into the car hours ago and Sissy took hers with her to Nana's house."

Today is our wedding day and Sophie couldn't bear that Vance was exiled to his mom's house lest we unleash bad luck upon us. Not that I believe in luck.

But rather than tempt fate, he spent the night at his mom's so we wouldn't see each other. I hope he slept better than I did. Without him next to me, I tossed and turned all night.

So that he wouldn't be lonely, Sophie begged to go spend the night with Vance at his mom's house. Having a grandmother is a novel experience for the girls and they are loving it. They call his mom Nana just like his other kids do and she adores having new grandbabies to dote on.

Isabel was placed with her grandmother for a time when she was a toddler, but has no memories of her. The woman died soon after Iz was returned to her mother. It took her a while to warm up to Vance's mother, but once the ice melted, she was all in.

I have a feeling that Isabel will always be leery of new people until she knows they can be trusted.

Tamara and Tyrone, Vance's children, have visited a few times and we've all gotten along famously. They simply love their soon-to-be new baby sisters. It might have been a different story if the kids had been closer in age, but his children are in college and well on their way to being adults.

I officially became the girl's foster mother soon after Sophie's father committed suicide. We told Sophie a couple of weeks after he passed, once I received his belongings. There was nothing in there of value to Sophie since it was, indeed, almost all his personal grooming items.

Soon after, she followed her sister's lead and started calling me mom, but she also started calling Vance daddy and became attached at the hip to him. She is still very much a daddy's girl.

Although it didn't take long for me to become their foster parent, adoption has taken six months so far. Any day we're expecting to be notified of the court date to be set for the final adoption. Now that we're getting married, Vance wants to adopt the girls as well.

I laugh. "I think your dramatic little sister is rubbing off on you."

She puts her hands on her hips, arms akimbo, and stares at me deadpan.

Gathering up my bag, I walk past her out the bedroom door, heading for the garage. "Come on, slowpoke. You're going to make me late."

She huffs like a true teenager and races past me to the garage door. Since she's a teenager now, it's fitting. Both girls have had birthdays in the past few months.

We've also moved into our new house, Vance moved right along with us. He and I talked about it and he had already been staying with me and this was going to be a home for all of us, so he never went back to his Mom's house.

The girls have started school and are doing well. Unsurprisingly, their placement scores were on the low side, and the school wanted to have them both repeat their current grade.

It wouldn't have been so bad for Sophie because she was near the age cut-off. She would simply go from being the youngest in her class to the oldest, but would still be close to her peers in age.

However, Isabel had already been held back a grade because she missed so much school after her mom handed her over to the attorneys. She would be significantly older than the other kids in her class.

Knowing Isabel was a pretty smart cookie, I made an agreement with the school that I'd hire tutors to help her get caught up and at the end of the year, we'd revisit the topic. It was an excellent decision because she has already surpassed expectations.

Between having a stable home life and therapy, she's almost a happy-go-lucky little girl again. Most days she seems completely carefree, but sometimes I'll catch her lost in thought, staring into the middle distance with a furrowed brow.

I've asked her what she's thinking about, but she brushes me off. Perhaps she's thinking about her tormenter who is still out there.

George Graham hasn't been heard from again. The officials tried to follow the money he cleared out of one of his accounts, but it was a dead end. I don't know how it's possible in this day and age that he'd be able to just vanish, but somehow, he did.

Graham's partner in the law firm has been to court and bore the brunt of the jury's outrage. Several of them were crying after hearing Isabel's testimony in the closed courtroom.

We didn't force her to tell her story. She said she wanted to and her therapist said she felt it would help Isabel take her power back.

Graham's partner was only tried for abusing Isabel. Although there were disgusting videos of several children, he's not seen in any of them and there were no other living witnesses who could testify against him.

Because of Isabel's age, he was given the maximum sentence of twenty-five years. If there had been even one more victim who had been able to tie him to the two decades of abuse, the sentence could have been upped to life without parole.

Prison isn't ever easy, but child molesters typically don't fare well in prison. Once he's out, if he makes it through his sentence, he'll be forced to register as a sex offender. His bar license has been revoked and he'll never be able to practice law again.

Draper couldn't make bail after he was arrested, so was held in county jail while awaiting trial. He made it two weeks before he was found with a shiv in his throat. I can't say I'm sad about it. His deeds set his path for eternity, and that's between him and his maker.

We make the short drive to the chapel and thankfully, most of my things are already here. All I need to do is get dressed and touch up my make-up. Maggie and Tamara help the girls get ready, so that's one thing I don't have to worry about.

I slip into my wedding dress, a simple cream-colored lace dress with long sleeves and a slightly flared tea length skirt. "Here, let me help," Tamara says when I can't quite get the zipper all the way up.

She's a lovely young woman, quick with a smile, just like her father, and seems to have also inherited his easy-going demeanor. Being able to roll with anything thrown at her will probably serve her well in the medical field.

She's undecided about whether she wants a nursing degree or something else. Personally, I think she is smart and talented and can do anything she wants.

"Thank you," I tell her. "I'm so happy you and your brother are here today."

She pats my shoulder. "We wouldn't have missed it for the world. It's been a long time since we've seen Dad this happy."

"Sissy!" Sophie says as she races into the room with Maggie close behind. She practically tackles Tamara, wrapping her arms around her legs.

"Hey squirt!" Tamara squats down, holding Sophie's hands and pushing her to arm's length. "Let me get a look at you."

Sophie preens under the attention.

"Come here, Iz," Tamara says. "Let's take a picture."

The three girls huddle together, smiling as Tamara snaps a photo on her cell. When she drops her phone into her pocket, yes, we had dresses made with pockets, she pulls out a piece of cloth.

"Oh, I almost forgot. This is from Nana. She said it should cover you for old, borrowed, and blue."

When I unfold it, I see it is an embroidered handkerchief edged with crocheted blue lace.

"She says it was her mother's who gave it to her when she got married and now she wants you to have it."

Tears prickle, so I take a deep breath and settle my emotions. I know I'll probably shed a few tears today, but I don't want to get started so early. "Thank you," I reply and tuck it into my pocket.

There's a quiet knock on the door and Isabel goes to open it. "Mom, it's Uncle Dale."

My brother sticks his head in the door and says, "Sister mine, you about ready?"

Turning back to the mirror, I give myself one more look. Smoothing down my skirt, I reply, "Yes, I believe I am."

At first, I wasn't sure if I wanted to have a wedding. I thought I'd be perfectly content to go down to the courthouse and have a purely legal ceremony. But it was Vance who convinced me it could be a ceremony for the girls just as much as it would be for me.

He knows me well and if he says something might be beneficial for the girls, I'm likely to agree to it. However, once he changed my mind, I got excited about planning a wedding.

We didn't want anything too fancy, just a gathering of family and friends to share in our day. Although with my brother's extended family by marriage now claiming me and the girls as relations, the crowd is sizeable.

Our ceremony is a little unique to us. Instead of bridesmaids and groomsmen, it will be a joining of our family. Vance and I will stand together surrounded by our children and Maggie because she is certainly family now, too.

There is no set color scheme other than my bouquet that matches my ivory dress. The girls got to pick out dresses they love. Sophie's is orange and Isabel's is black to match her dad's black suit. Dale is in navy and Tyrone in charcoal.

This fits our blended family. We all have varied starts in life, but somehow it works when we all come together. Isabel goes first, followed by Maggie, then Tamara. Sophie follows, dropping ivory rose petals down the aisle.

I wait in the back of the quaint little chapel in the woods, arm in arm with my brother. "You look beautiful, Serena," he says.

"Thank you, brother mine."

When Sophie steps up next to her dad, everything quiets as the music changes. Vance is smiling down at Sophie, but when the new song begins to play, he looks up at me. His smile turns tender, and he swallows.

Then he beams at me and I'm the one swallowing. I never, ever thought I'd be lucky enough to find someone like him. He's not perfect, none of us are, but he's good and kind.

His heart is big enough to love me and the girls and he leads our family with self-assurance and patience. He keeps us safe without clipping our wings, encouraging us to spread them and fly and be who we are meant to be.

I couldn't have asked for a better man.

When I talked to him about starting to practice law again, he was a fantastic sounding board, allowing me to pour out my thoughts and talk my way through it all. Rather than going back into a full-time practice, I talked to Cait about working with the charity she sits on the board for.

Their focus is on helping women in untenable circumstances find a way to build a better life. That sounds like something I want to be part of.

We reach the dais and Dale hands me over to my husband-to-be. The service is brief, and simple, just the way we wanted it. When we kiss and the girls groan, everyone in the audience laughs along with us.

Our reception is filled with good food, family and friends. We laugh and eat and dance. I'm surprised when Vance takes me by the hand and leads me to the microphone at the front of the room that has been used for toasts.

"We want to thank all y'all for coming," he says, his voice booming through the room. "This is a special day for us and I wanted to add another layer of special on top."

He turns to face me. "Baby, when I opened the mail yesterday, there was a letter in there you've been waiting for." My hand goes to my mouth. "We have a court date in two weeks to make the girls officially yours in the eyes of the law. Next week, we'll work on getting me sorted out to be their dad officially."

I don't know whether to laugh or cry, so I do a little of both, hugging him. Everyone cheers and the girls come to us, Vance swinging Sophie up into his arms.

We hang out a little longer before Vance comes to me, cutting in on my dance with Dale. When I'm in his arms, he leans in and says, "I'm about ready to get out of here and head to the hotel so I can get you naked, wife."

When I look around, he says, "I already talked to Tam and Maggie. They've got the girls handled."

Vance and I are going to do a mini-honeymoon for the night because we have to be back at work on Monday and the girls at school. The girls are up in arms, not because we'll be gone, but because we won't return until tomorrow evening.

We could make it if we rushed back, because we're just going to Tulsa. But neither one of us wants to rush. It took Maggie to convince them that the world wouldn't end if we missed one family lunch down in Ada.

We'll do a family honeymoon in a few weeks over Christmas break. Other than their summer down at the ranch, the girls have never been out of the Oklahoma City metro, much less the state, so we're going to Hawaii to spend some time on the beach. Vance and I will take an official honeymoon this summer, but haven't decided where yet.

True to his word, he takes me to our home away from home for the night. I was too keyed up to eat much at the reception, but neither of us wants to go to a restaurant, so we plan to order room service once we get settled into the hotel.

He changes into comfortable clothes quickly while I unpack my things. I turn my back to him to unzip me. Once he has the back of my dress open, his hands roam over the skin of my back as his lips explore my freshly bared shoulders.

"You are so beautiful, baby," he says, his warm breath caressing my skin and making me shiver.

When I lower the dress, he holds it as I step out of it, then lays it over the back of an armchair. He takes me into his arms, his kisses heated and hungry, causing my core to turn liquid as I lean into him.

I pull away and, taking him by the hand, lead him to the bathroom. My intention was to take a shower, but he stops, pushes down my panties, and lifts me onto the vanity. With my legs spread, he moves between them, slipping two fingers inside my slick heat.

real people who have their own demons,

ges to overcome.

r on online at:

w.kitmckenna.com

@authorkitmckenna

@kitmckennaauthor

@kitmckennaauthor

His voice is husky when he says, "As soon as we said I do, all I've wanted was to get you out of this dress so I could have my way with you, wife."

Reaching between us and snaking my hand into his shorts, I find him hard for me. "I'm all yours, honey. Do with me what you will."

He sucks in a breath, shoves down his shorts, and pulls me to the edge of the counter. As if he can't wait a moment longer, he notches his head at my opening and enters me with one powerful thrust.

His need is great and his pace is rapid, as we are frantic to sate the desire that's been simmering all day. Although he needs release, he is intent on taking me with him. In these past months, he's become well acquainted with my body and knows exactly how to make me come.

I wrap my legs around him and balance back on my arms as he slips his thumb between us to worry my clit. His other hand goes to my breast, teasing and tweaking the nipple.

An orgasm builds quickly and I pant out his name, letting him know I'm close and in the next instant, I'm cast into a freefall of sensation. He wraps his arms around me, pulling me close.

With my head nestled in the crook of his neck, he whispers to me with words of lust and love as he thrusts hard and deep. With a jerk of his cock, he empties himself into me, then holds me for long moments.

He pulls two washcloths from under the vanity and turns the tap on to warm. Once we clean up from our lovemaking, he goes to call room service while I step into the shower.

A minute later, he joins me, saying, "They said it would be about forty-five minutes, so there's enough time for round two."

With a laugh, I take him into my arms. "Then you'd better get after it, husband."

The End

Get a **FREE** copy of a bonus scene that tells you what really happened to Isabel at the farmers market.
https://dl.bookfunnel.com/ksxzixevea

If you enjoyed A Devil's Snare, do me a solid and leave a review! It's not a book report; it's okay to keep it short. Have fun! Be honest!
https://mybook.to/ThreatKitMcKenna
Thank you loves!
XOXO
Kit

A

Her stories are abou
drama, and challer
You can find h
Website – wv
Facebook –
Instagram
TikTok

Kit McKenna writes romance
sometimes have a splash of darkr
backdrop of Oklahoma.

Kit is a born and raised Oklahoma ga
whole life except for a brief detour to hang o
for four years. She is an artist and free spirit wh
around in the woods and finds great joy in the u
sometimes darkly beautiful. Kit has worn a lot of hats i
a server, a factory worker, nightclub manager, office adi
trator, state drone, and business owner.

A bit of a dichotomy, she loves all things positivity and light, but still loves to play in the dark. Her favorite book offerings range from authors like Eckhart Tolle to Stephen King. Her favorite movies are horror and holiday is Samhain (Halloween) but she still loves a good romance. She's a huge sucker for a story where the underdog comes out on top.

If the bar doesn't have a good cider, she'll opt for a fine whisky.

She comes to writing later in life after tiring of reading books that seem to only focus on perfect, perky, barely legal heroines.